I0557449

Cold Feet

A Gwen Arthur Novel

Olivia R. Burton

© 2017 Olivia R. Burton. All Rights Reserved
www.OliviaRBurton.com

All rights reserved. This book or any portion thereof may not be
reproduced or used in any manner whatsoever without the express
written permission of the publisher except for the use of brief
quotations in a book review.

Edited by: Alexis Arendt
https://wordvagabond.com

ISBN: 978-0-9976333-5-1

Peacock Deceiving a Suitcase
www.PeacockDeceivingASuitcase.com

OTHER TITLES

Gwen Arthur Series
Mixed Feelings
Business With Pleasure
Cold Feet
Hollow Back Girl
Change of Heart
~
Bone to Pick
Flesh and Blood
The Writer's Overnighter
Gut Feeling
Suckered In
Split Second

The Preternatural PNW
Rattle
Metal
Knell
~
Throb
Murmur

COLLABORATIONS
Passage Through Moonlight
The Godfather's Naughty Daughter
Song of the Argyle Goddess
Belladonna Clasped
Cash Grab

OLIVIA R .BURTON

CONTENTS

Chapter One	1
Chapter Two	7
Chapter Three	17
Chapter Four	25
Chapter Five	41
Chapter Six	49
Chapter Seven	55
Chapter Eight	71
Chapter Nine	81
Chapter Ten	87
Chapter Eleven	95
Chapter Twelve	103
Chapter Thirteen	111
Chapter Fourteen	125
Chapter Fifteen	131
Chapter Sixteen	145
Chapter Seventeen	153
Chapter Eighteen	167
Chapter Nineteen	173
Chapter Twenty	179
Chapter Twenty-One	187
Chapter Twenty-Two	195
About the Author	203

One

"Gwen Arthur, will you marry me?"

I looked up from the bite-sized cupcake in front of me and into the brilliant blue eyes of the man presenting it. The cupcake smelled amazing, a good distraction from the lunacy that I wasn't entirely sure I had heard correctly. It was late afternoon in The Internets, a café that doubles as a popular hangout for geeks of all ages. Perhaps the din of the crowd had crazied up Mel's words.

"What are you talking about?" I asked, frowning at him. Mel pushed the cupcake box a bit closer to my face, his hands holding it open as any man holds open a tiny box while down on one knee. When he didn't answer, I picked the mini cupcake up between my thumb and forefinger and inspected it. It had no ring in the mound of chocolate frosting and I saw no gold poking out the side of the cake. Still, he remained mute and hopeful.

I didn't buy it. I took a second to steel myself, sucked in a desperate breath, and then pushed my empathic powers forth poke around in his psyche to see if I could detect deception. I'm not just a pretty face and Mel knows it; if he was trying to play some sort of prank on me, he was doing a very good job of it. His popping, crackling emotions, like the chocolate morsel I held, told me nothing helpful, so I walled myself up once again, already regretting forcing myself to read him. Him being close was bad enough, but actively groping around his mind with my empathy was usually akin to coating my hand in gasoline and shoving it straight into a bonfire.

Focusing on his face once again, I considered the cupcake, hoping I could eat it without actually accepting whatever it represented. I needed chocolate to soothe me, and so, without answering his absurd question, I

1

popped the cupcake whole into my mouth. The result was a sensation so incredible I nearly had a mouth orgasm.

That's a thing, I swear, and if you'd tasted this cupcake you wouldn't be looking at me like that.

"Oh, sweet chocolate," I moaned around a mouthful of toe-curling succulence. Barely able to function over the pleasure running along my tongue and into my brain, I leaned forward, grasping desperately for Mel's shoulder, ignoring the fact that I had frosting on my finger and thumb. Casually, he rolled his gaze to the chocolate stain, amused rather than irritated. He rarely takes issue with a woman touching him; I could have had the face of a soul-sucking Dementor and he wouldn't have turned me away. My square jaw, dark hair, and green eyes were incidental to Mel Somerset so long as I identified as a female.

I'm not proud of myself but I did consider leaning even closer and sucking the chocolate-smeared shirt into my mouth to make sure I got every ounce of available cupcake. I wasn't even sure if I'd eaten a wrapper or not; that's how good the rich, cocoa treat had been.

"Well?" he drawled, and I realized I'd gone mute with enjoyment and lost track of time as I continued to lick my teeth and suck the chocolate off my tongue. I'd meant to demand more, ask where he bought them, or just shake him until more cupcakes fell out of his pockets, but I always go a little brainless when it comes to really good cake.

"Well what? I don't know what you want," I said, leaning back so I wasn't touching him anymore. My skin was tingling where it had made contact his shirt, fading into numbness like I'd held it against a block of ice so long it was going dead in an attempt to avoid the pain. Mel stayed low, still on one knee, still watching me expectantly as if he hadn't proposed something so patently ludicrous.

"He's proposing, dear," Chloe Warren said from my left, her tone striped with sarcasm. She's my best friend, but with that comes the permission to mock me when she feels I'm being particularly dim. I snarled instantly, whipping around to glare her way. She's cute, tinier than me in every direction but with a much bigger personality. Winking, she gestured back to Mel, wiggling her dainty fingers as if she was so excited she couldn't keep any part of her still. "Go on, answer him! Don't keep us all in suspense."

"Did you set this up? Am I being punk'd?" I asked, hoping that was still a reference the kids were using. "Is that why he's been gone for six weeks? To set up some ridiculous stunt?" Turning back to Mel, I stuck a finger into the tiny box in front of me, aiming to snatch up a stray bit of frosting. Like Richard Gere, he snapped the box closed on my finger; unlike Julia Roberts, I did not shriek and laugh. I looked back up at Mel, finding his thick brows up, a smile still on his attractive mouth. He was enjoying himself, which I wanted to despise on principle.

Sure, Mel and I had gotten friendlier over the last year, and maybe that was why his emotions were not entirely as insufferable as they usually were. But he and I had history. Seriously annoying history, wherein he showed up randomly to get in my face and flirt and I told him off in various and entirely not work safe ways until he laughed and headed back up to his office a floor above mine. He's not inherently a bad guy, but I'm the victim here, and don't let Chloe tell you different because she'll certainly try.

Yanking my finger out of the box, I leaned back in my chair and inspected every bit of the digit that might have chocolate left on it.

"What do you want, really?" I asked, disappointed I was chocolate-free.

Getting to his feet, Mel moved around the table, taking the tiny box with him. Like a dog convinced its owner is hiding another tennis ball behind his back, I peered around as he pulled up a chair. I didn't spy any more tiny boxes of orgasmic delight and that only made me crankier.

"I need help on a case," Mel explained.

"A case? You were gone so long, I figured maybe you'd up and retired, gone off to live the good life somewhere far, far away. That's still an option, you know."

Mel glared and I felt the crackle of his emotions shift toward irritation. I rubbed a hand along my bare arm below my sleeve, trying to get rid of the sensation. I knew it wasn't going to work, that you can't rub away something that isn't physically there. That's never stopped me from trying, though. Human irritation can be bad enough, but werewolf emotions? Extra, super, definitely no thank you.

"That wasn't some sort of vacation," Mel said tersely, the burning in his psyche sparking hotly enough that I felt my cheek twitch with searing pain. Chloe's curiosity piqued next to me and I glanced over to find that she'd managed to get herself a drink at some point during the conversation. She hadn't let me order when we'd arrived, yet here she was, sipping on a hot beverage.

"How come you get a drink?" I demanded, considering stealing hers. She ignored me, probably knowing for sure she could take me if it came to some sort of wrestling match over her soy whatever. Giving up on telling her off, I scanned around behind her, hoping I could catch sight of a waitress, or even just a distracted nerd whose hot chocolate I could swipe. Desperate times, and all that.

"So where've you been for the last month?" Chloe asked Mel when I effectively abandoned the conversation to eyeball every drink in the place.

"Recuperating. It wasn't exactly a picnic coming down from Norma's death." Throwing a pointed glare at Chloe, Mel finished with, "no thanks to you."

"Hey, buddy, we did you a favor."

"Yeah, big favor," he grumbled, his irritation with me morphing into something less Psycho-style stabby and more like a spiked, lead vest being dropped down upon my shoulders. Uncomfortable with having his despair press against my upper half like a hedgehog trying to suffocate me to death, I whacked his arm.

"Don't go there," I said, tucking my hand against my chest trying to ease the immediate prickling numbness. "Neither one of us can handle that right now. Just tell me what you want and scram before I have some sort of aneurism."

"I've been hired to investigate something and I need your help," Mel sighed, his usual delight at my reaction to him missing completely. He seemed down overall, like something major had changed since the last time we'd seen each other. I wasn't really sure what the proper way to handle it was, but my default reaction reared its ugly head.

"I don't want to give it," I said. I had somehow forgotten, with him gone, how much his emotions hurt to sense and the pain was making me a little nutty already. I wanted to flee upstairs to my office and my stash of sweets to cool away the feeling of burnt skin. Truthfully, though, Mel and I had really gotten friendlier and I couldn't justify leaving him there when he needed help. Especially not after everything I'd seen him go through just a few months before.

Dammit, being an adult sucks sometimes.

"You don't even know what I need you to do," he said, exasperation starting to burble, making me panic. He had every right to be irritated with me, I knew, but that didn't make my empathy any less receptive to his unpleasant emotions.

"Yes, but it's going to be something I don't want to do," I said, quickly, trying to explain myself before things got worse. "I can tell. That's why you're bribing me with chocolate. Speaking of chocolate—" He cut me off before I could ask for another cupcake.

"You won't hate it, I promise. It's like a vacation. A week of vacation."

Mel's gaze dropped suddenly, his body language changing. Before I could ask what was wrong, I noticed Jenny bring a tray of three iced drinks and four slices of cake over to the table behind Mel. Jealousy filled me as I watched the girl hunched into the only occupied seat at the table, noting that I hadn't seen her around in awhile. The last time she'd been in The Internets Mel had been a little nutty himself. The last time I'd seen her in, he had scared her off.

Waiting until Jenny had set the treats down, I called her name and gave a warm smile when she looked over. Sure, my lips wanted to twitch and contort in response to Mel being so near, but I forced myself to look friendly and polite instead. Never scare off a person who can bring you cake. It was a lesson I'd learned young.

Jenny smiled back but as she stepped closer I felt a bump of disapproval at the exact second she realized Mel was with us. She didn't have the best history with him either.

He'd been in *really* bad shape before disappearing for a month and a half.

"Hey Gwen. Your mocha'll be out in just a sec," she said, her gaze glued to mine as if she was afraid to look Mel's way.

"My mocha?" I asked. Mel kept to himself, keeping watch of the table like it might try to scuttle away and take Chloe's drink with it. It'd serve her right, dammit.

"Yeah," she said, nerves arcing out toward me like little baby lightning strikes. "Chloe called down an order for you before you guys came in? And said to bring it to you at ten after three?" She sounded worried, like she was suddenly convinced she'd messed the whole thing up..

"Oh she did, did she?" I turned to glare at Chloe, who winked at me over a smile. She could have *told* me I had a sweet drink waiting, but instead she'd bullied me to the table, insisted I sit down, and refused to let me order anything. Now I was starting to get why: she and Mel had probably planned this whole thing ahead of time.

"I … think so. Is that wrong?" Jenny asked.

"It's fine—it's great," I corrected, smiling up at her again to assure her it wasn't her service or the order I was unhappy about. "Just bring it when you can."

"Oh, okay." Jenny's eyes darted to Mel and I felt a little bit of dread swim through her. I wondered if she was getting up the guts to ask him if he needed to order anything. Before she had to take the initiative, he held his hand out, his face softening.

"Hey, I wanted to say I'm really sorry about the last time I saw you. I was going through some things and I got really inappropriate. I shouldn't have gotten in your face like that, and it was totally out of line to—well, everything I did was a problem, and I'm really sorry. It won't happen again, I swear."

Jenny gave a half-smile, confusion puffing around her, trying to consume the dread but not quite succeeding. Figuring I'd help both her and Mel out, I patted her arm, feeling her nerves jump from her to me as if they were alive and I'd whistled and called, "here boys!" The tension in her ebbed, and I smiled up at her, hoping the residual bit I'd sensed from her would disappear from my guts as quickly as it seemed to for her.

"He's really not a bad guy," I assured her. "I mean, I don't like him much, but that's my own issue. He really was having a bad week. You don't have to worry about him, I promise."

Jenny's smile was small and crooked but she seemed over the anxiety she'd initially conjured at the sight of Mel. "Okay, yeah. No hard feelings.

Did you want anything?"

"Just black coffee for me," Mel said, keeping his voice mellow, as if he might still spook her. Jenny nodded and headed back toward the counter, hopefully to bring me my hot chocolate-laden, whipped cream-topped sugar-bomb. As soon as she was gone, Mel looked back to me.

"I gotta go in another ten or fifteen, so I'm going to resort to bribery: if you help me, I'll tell you where I got the cupcake. In fact, I'll get you a dozen more."

"Two dozen," I said before I could stop myself. Mel leaned back, grinning at my frenzied and childish reaction. After a moment, his gaze moved to Chloe and his smile faltered a little. She was in on this and she was going to sabotage me, I knew it. If I let her get in the way, I'd end up legally married to Mel but without a single cupcake in sight.

"One dozen," Mel said after some unheard threat seemed to pass from her to him. "But I'll make them full-sized." Chloe's disappointment jabbed me in the ribs but I ignored it. This was a possibility? *Full-sized chocolate mouth orgasms?*

I needed them in my life. "Three dozen, all full-sized!"

"That's not how you haggle," Mel countered, trying not to chuckle. I could feel him waffling between finding me funny and being anxious over whatever Chloe had probably threatened him with should he give in to my deranged sugar addiction. He was unstable and off his game, the perfect time to strike.

"Four dozen and a sheet cake! Final offer!" I snapped, slapping my hand down on the table.

"Oh *god*," Chloe groaned, while Mel rolled his eyes good-naturedly. Shaking his head, he caught Chloe's attention once more. I saw her shrug out of the corner of my eye and knew I had won.

"Fine. If you promise to help me, I'll get you *forty-eight cupcakes* and a sheet cake."

"I'm not having sex with you."

"No—what? Of course not," he said, insulted at the idea. Something was up, he never reacted so properly to me refusing to bed him. Maybe I should have gone for five dozen. "I know that. So, do we have a deal?"

"Yeah," I said, giving Chloe one last look to make sure I wasn't stepping in something I wouldn't be able to get off my figurative shoe. She offered no guidance, so I just thought fondly on the cupcakes and agreed. "Deal."

"Excellent!" His entire mood changed with his exclamation, but happy werewolf wasn't much better than irritated werewolf as far as my empathy was concerned. "So, will you be wearing white for the wedding?"

Glowering at him as I realized I still actually had no idea the extent of what I'd agreed to, I grumbled, "I need cake for this."

Two

Mocha finished, half a slice of pastry in my belly (only half because Chloe is a tart tightwad, a morsel miser, *and* a pastry pinchfist), I leaned back in my seat and kicked at Mel's ankle. He finished his sentence about a band he and Chloe were really into and I tried to pretend I'd heard none of it. I had history with that band from before they'd been a band and wasn't about to let Chloe grill me about it. She might find a way to go back in time and prevent me from having eaten the pastry just out of spite.

"Now that I've been less than adequately filled with sweets, tell me what you want from me," I demanded.

"I've already explained what I need," Mel claimed, though I could tell he was just being difficult.

"Have not," I countered maturely. Maybe Mel had explained everything, but the amount of emotions zinging around The Internets—several of them not human, though I was sure the humans playing games with the people-shaped creatures had no idea—had just made me stupid. I didn't recall any specifics, but somehow I didn't think what he wanted from me would be as simple as me just saying yes for a week or two if someone asked if he and I were joined in holy matrimony. If he'd explained the whole plan in detail and I'd managed to wipe it from my memory, I was going to feel pretty stupid.

I did my best to concentrate, despite my meager mental abilities, and managed to get the emotional din around me down to a tolerable buzz. Having shields up isn't really like putting on a coat and forgetting about it. Sometimes, especially if I'm tired, hungry, or distracted, it's like having to hold an umbrella with a lead handle up above my head. Inevitably it's gonna slip and I'm gonna get drenched.

"I wasn't messing with you," Mel said, setting down his coffee and turning back to me. "I really do need you act like my wife."

"Don't I already? We don't have sex, I don't cook for you, and I'm always nagging you to go bother someone else. Sounds like the perfect sitcom marriage to me."

Mel ignored my comments, forging ahead as if I'm not a comedic genius. "I'm investigating a shady marriage counselor."

"And you need me to tell you if he's on the level?"

"Sort of. Everyone at the center has all the necessary credentials but the families who hired me said that this couple went in just to work on their communication and then called home to say, 'You can keep our worldly possessions, we're moving in with the doc!' It's hinky, and—"

"Called home?"

"Yeah. They're—"

"No, I mean, what do you mean they called home? Like, from his— wait, is this a person or a company?"

"Oh, it's like a … it's sort of a sleepaway camp for couples. Some people go in just for counseling here and there, but they also have a two-week-long course that really goes into the nitty gritty of a relationship. It's very involved."

"And just like that, they're supposed to be fixed and happy?"

"No, it doesn't promise anything that miraculous. It's—look, I skimmed the brochure and looked mainly at the background—financials, criminal history of the employees, that sort of important stuff."

"If it's a joint that's claiming to save a marriage, I'd say it's pretty damned important whether or not it can deliver."

"Not to us, not now. Now it's important whether or not this place is killing people or brainwashing them and shipping them off to some ranch in the middle of nowhere Montana or something."

"Hey," I said, prickling with insult now, as well as Mel's irritation with me. "Montana's nice."

"You're just missing my point."

"And you're ignoring my question! Are they promising to fix everything with campfires and a trust fall here and there, or what?"

"I'll give you the brochure and you can read it later, got it?"

I rolled my eyes, wanting to fight with Mel some more just out of habit. The two-week course wasn't a bad idea, exactly: force bickering couples to spend a lot of time together and make sure they have constant access to a therapist to tell all their problems to. It could help, I knew, though like all therapy it had to be something the couples were actually interested in working through.

As a therapist myself, I'd had no shortage of clients who really just wanted to pay me to tell them they were right and everyone around them was wrong. I had a particularly difficult older woman in once a week doing exactly that.

Presumably, anyone willing to pack some luggage and go sleep in a strange bed really did want to work on life problems, though. I still would have bet some of the couples came out of the two weeks just as angry at each other but with much depleted bank accounts, but I could see it helping more than its fair share of people at least seek further help or realize they were headed for divorce in the end.

"Is that good enough?" Chloe asked, though her focus was on the girl at the table behind Mel. I wondered if Chloe had picked out that she wasn't human, or if she just thought she was cute and was considering chatting her up.

"It's … fine. I was just thinking about the whole idea is all," I said. "It's not unprecedented. I just can't imagine spending twenty-four-seven with any of my patients."

"I don't think there are many people who could spend twenty-four-seven with you, either," Chloe said, patting my thigh. I glowered her way, but Mel jumped in before I could bitch.

"The families who hired me, they're thinking this might be some sort of cult. This isn't the first time something like this has happened, though the place isn't on any sort of watch lists or anything. People who check in check out, it's just that some of them happen to abandon their home lives before disappearing into the ether."

"Just like that? One phone call and Goodbye Blue Sky?"

"Well, legal documents have changed hands and property has been gifted—so on and so forth—but it's all done through intermediaries. Since the phone call, no one can get ahold of the missing couple. Let me repeat: this isn't the first time it's happened, either. It's a bad situation and I want to help if something's truly wrong."

"Why do we need to pretend to be married? Let's just head over there now and I can tell you if anything's up."

"It's not really an afternoon drive sort of thing. It's a retreat over on Harstine Island."

I blinked, trying to figure out if I'd heard of the place. Mel let me have a few seconds of silent staring before he answered my unasked question.

"It's not too far. I can drive us, we can leave Monday. We'll have to convince them we even need the help, too. They won't let me snoop just for the hell of it, which is why I need you."

"That's in two days. I can't call every one of my clients and—"

"I already rescheduled everyone. All you need to do is pack," Chloe said.

"You knew about this!" I accused, poking her in the arm. She shrugged, jerked her thumb back toward Jenny behind the counter.

"Of course, why do you think I set up your mocha and cake to get here right at the moment it would put you in the best mood to agree to go out of town with Mel for a week and pretend to be his wife?"

Mel let out a bark of a laugh at her admission and I felt the glee hissing out of him like a busted steam pipe full of radioactive bees. Not only had she dragged me here under the pretense of just grabbing a drink, but she'd known what Mel was asking and how to make sure I'd say yes. I bet she'd know about the cupcake orgasms before too and just refused to share the knowledge or chocolate with me.

"You bitch," I whispered, my offense making Chloe laugh. Leaving us to fight it out, Mel got to his feet, arms akimbo.

"I'm off, but I'll give you a call Sunday night to make plans."

"You're paying for my hotel while we're out there. Separate rooms!"

"Lodging is already handled, don't worry. I'll get your food, too."

"And cupcakes."

"Yes," he sighed, shaking his head. His hands dropped off his hips as if he was beaten down by my dogged pursuit of sweets. "And cupcakes. Jeez, don't you trust me to keep my word?"

"Not as far as I can throw you. Now get out, I've got a headache."

"You know what's a great cure for a—"

"Shut up I hate you," I spat out in one quick breath. Mel shook his head at my behavior, deciding not to take our squabbling for another go-round. It wasn't really his style, but maybe he was starting to think of us as friends as well.

What the hell is the world coming to?

"Talk to you later. Thanks, Chloe," Mel said, reaching into his back pocket. He pulled out his wallet, peeled a fifty off the fan of bills clipped in the center and tossed it down on the table. I considered pocketing it and calling it payment for emotional distress, but figured it was probably best to leave it for Jenny.

Once Chloe and I were outside and I was sure Mel was gone, I gave her arm a little slap.

"What are you getting out of all this?"

"Other than a week off? Not much."

I squinted at her, not entirely trusting her words, despite the fact that I could read honesty off of her. Chloe seems overly fond of shoving Mel and me together at every opportunity and, while I was sure it was mostly friendly ribbing, sometimes I wondered if it was more. Before I got the chance to demand once again to know if he was paying her or blackmailing her, I felt a bubble of surprise burst inside her, like she'd just thought of something important and couldn't believe she hadn't realized it earlier.

"I almost forgot! I'll bring Sonny to my place while you're gone, so get me care instructions, okay?"

"Oh yeah," I said, the thought of my happy pet sun Conure softening my anger a bit. "Will he be safe there with the cat?"

"Trust me, Poopy has no interest in hurting your bird. They'll probably be good friends. She's a cat, but she's the least cat-like cat I've ever met."

"That's true," I said, thinking of how Poopy didn't fill me with mortal terror like most felines. "Though, I'd rather not risk a face to face encounter, if you don't mind. Sonny's cage is pretty big, are you sure you can get it over there?"

"You don't have a travel cage?"

"I don't go anywhere, what would I need with that?"

"Of course. If it's trouble, we can get a smaller one for the week. I'm sure someone on Craigslist or something has one they don't want. I'll check it out tonight. Barring that, we'll make Mel carry it. He can take his shirt off and you can oil him down and then we can ogle while—"

"Shut up," I said, shaking my head as if I could get the image she'd created in my mind to erase like an Etch-a-Sketch.

"Don't pretend you won't be coming back to that thought later," she teased. As I stared at the ground trying to relax my scrunched up expression, she reached out and poked me in the shoulder. "You should go pack!"

"I have two days. I don't need to pack yet." Chloe just sighed.

"Well, don't leave it to the last minute. You might forget the necklace."

I stared at her blankly, not realizing what she meant. When she remembered I tend to miss the obvious, she snorted.

"You know, Merrin's necklace? No way you'll stay sane around Mel for a week without it."

"Oh god," I groaned. "He's just going to use it as an excuse to never stop hitting on me."

"Hey, maybe you'll get lucky!"

"Stop," I warned. Chloe laughed and shook her head.

"No, I was gonna say, maybe some of the other women will be there because they can't stop cheating on their husbands with guys just like Mel!"

"Your mouth to God's ear."

The weekend went by way too fast, making me think the universe was out to get me. All I want in life is to sit in comfortable clothes, surf the internet, and eat junk food. I know I'm not alone in this, so why hasn't science made this profitable yet?

Stupid science.

I stood over my bed, staring down at the empty duffle bag I'd pulled out for packing. I was at a total loss as to what to put in the damn thing. What does one wear to pretend to be married to a person one mildly loathes? Sweat pants and a stained shirt? Had them, loved the idea, couldn't bring myself to actually pull it off. Jeans and t-shirts seemed a good bet, but did it send the message to this marriage counselor that I didn't care about my appearance? Somehow, despite the fact that we were only pretending to be married to find out if there were dastardly deeds afoot, I still found myself worried I would be blamed for any marital troubles Mel cooked up to get us in the front door.

Assuming we even got in the front door. Mel had said something about having to convince these possible lunatics they wanted us to join their weird cult in the first place. How the hell was I supposed to prepare for that?

Mel is a charming, good-looking, smooth-talking, snappy dresser who gets along with everyone (even empaths who can barely stand to be in his presence, apparently). I like to stay home in a stained shirt and eat cake alone. Anyone looking us over would probably wonder if the marriage had been arranged.

Somehow this thought made planning easier.

"Jeans and Ts it is," I said to no one as I spun on my heel and padded toward the closet. I yanked out four pairs of jeans, a pair of fancier pants for good measure, and six shirts chosen at random. I looked over my nicer shirts for a moment before plucking a mustard yellow blouse with some beading along the collar that Chloe had gotten me. It would go with all the pants, and that was about all I was concerned about.

I hummed and danced back to the bed, plopped the clothes down and paused with my hand on a hanger as my phone rang. Was that Mel already? I didn't want to talk to him, but I answered without looking at the number. It was just as well; I wouldn't have recognized it anyway.

"Hey," I said, tucking the phone against my shoulder as I slid a pair of pants off the hanger.

"Hey Chipmunk," my baby brother said. I froze, unsure if I was irritated at the nickname or overjoyed to hear from him.

"Thom!" I exclaimed, settling on joy. "Where are you?"

"Back home, actually."

I went silent, panic firing through me. When I didn't say anything immediately, Thomas started chuckling. It was low and teasing, making me sigh when I realized he was trying to get a rise out of me. As his laughter died off, I dropped the pants I'd just folded on top of the duffle bag and turned to head down the hall to my office.

"Don't worry, dad's not here."

"I didn't ask," I said.

"Yeah, because you know better."

I ignored his comment, true as it was. "They're doing well?"

"Yeah, they're great. Mom dragged him out grocery shopping so I could sleep, but I thought I'd call you while they were gone."

"Smart kid," I said as I dug through the top drawer of my desk for my Bluetooth headset. I finally found it under a candy bar wrapper that had maybe half a bite of chocolate-caramel goodness left. I didn't remember leaving it there, but the only other candy-eater in my house never left anything partially eaten, so it must have been me. Thomas didn't even seem to notice when I went, "ooh," and stuck the old candy in my mouth.

Dusty but decent.

"How long are you in Montana?" I asked with my mouth full of caramel.

"Probably for awhile this time. I was in Poland and I just suddenly decided I wanted to come home."

"Well that's sweet," I said, tucking my phone into my pocket. Thomas started talking about the places he'd been since the last time we'd spoken and I got to finishing my packing, forcing myself to check the list Chloe had made up for me so I wouldn't forget underwear or deodorant. While I wasn't trying to impress Mel on this trip, it still seemed like a good idea to be presentable instead of stinky.

"Mom, of course, freaked out as soon as I got home. She's convinced I have the plague or some form of Polish leprosy—which I don't think is a thing, but mom wouldn't listen. She made me go straight to the doctor and get tested for everything from Ebola to vitamin D deficiency."

I laughed but it did all make me miss my mother and feel like a terrible daughter.

"Well, let me know if you've caught Polish Ebola or German leprosy, okay?"

"Oh, of course. You'll be the first."

"What are you plans now that you've been poked and prodded?"

"I'm just staying here in my old room for a bit until I find an apartment."

"Who's gonna give you a place?" I sneered. "You haven't had a job in three years."

"It'll be fine, I think."

For Thom, it probably would. I'd long been convinced that he got a power like I got mine, but that his was much better. He is incredibly lucky. Almost everything goes his way, up to and including winning the lottery the first time he'd played at the ripe, old age of eighteen. He'd spent the next two years seeing the world, never staying in one place for too long. I couldn't really be too jealous; he'd been very generous with his winnings.

"How's the business?" he asked.

"Pretty good. If I still had student loans, I'd probably be close to paying them off," I said as I zipped up my bag and crossed the last of my things off my packing list.

"That's pretty cool. Sonny's good?"

"Yeah. He knows Morse code, now," I said off-handedly. It was another thing the candy thief that had been invading my space for the better part of a year had left as a surprise for me.

"Why'd you teach him that?"

I sighed, shaking my head. "I didn't, but it's a really long story."

Making my way to the kitchen, I considered my options, staring at leftovers in the fridge, boxed pasta in the cabinets, and frozen food that was easily microwavable. Taking the lazy way out, I grabbed the leftover box taking up the entire middle shelf of the fridge and wondered if people actually like cold pizza or if they just tell themselves they do because it's easier than trying to warm it up. Dropping it on my dining table, I slid into one chair and propped my legs up on another.

Thomas didn't comment when I chomped into a slice and spoke with my mouth full. "What're mom and dad up to?"

"The same. Mom's taking all sorts of classes to cook better—"

"Impossible," I said, thinking about the fact that even vegetables were palatable when my mother had made them. Thomas let out a soft laugh, continued.

"Knitting, gardening, aerobics. She keeps pretty busy."

"And dad?"

"Well, what do you do? That's probably what dad does. You two are the same person."

"That's not—" I cut off as my phone vibrated. I dug it out of my pocket, frowning when I saw Mel was calling. I let it go to voicemail and tucked the phone back in my jeans. Almost as soon as I did, the phone started ringing again. Unsurprised by my half-argument and confused silence, Thom pushed on.

"If I'm not flying everyone out until the holidays, I should come out there before then. Maybe I'll hold off getting an apartment and come soon," Thomas mused as I ordered my phone to ignore Mel. If only doing so in real life was as easy.

"That would be fun. I'm taking time off this week to help a friend, so it'll have to be a few weeks out, but I'm definitely game. I'll show you around, you can stay in the guest room."

"What are you doing this week?"

"It's uh …" Mel called again and I decided to let it be my out. "Actually, said friend is calling now and it might be important. I'll call you next week after I'm done. That okay?"

"Yeah, that works. Good luck, whatever it is you're doing."

"Thanks, Thom. See ya." I hung up and switched calls.

"What is it, Mel?"

"Another couple went missing."

"What?" I asked reflexively as I noticed I'd forgotten all about the cold pizza. Taking a bite and not bothering to chew quietly, I adjusted my position to stop my butt from falling asleep.

"The families who hired me said that another couple's gone to the dark side."

"I didn't peg you as a Star Wars fan," I said. Mel ignored me and continued.

"Same thing as before. They called home and told their families to give away all their things and sell the house. No one can get ahold of them now, though."

"Well that's weird," I said through a mouthful of rubbery vegetables that were only edible because I'd ordered extra, extra cheese.

"I'll pick you up tomorrow at five."

"Five at night, right? In the evening?"

Mel said nothing, but I was betting he was either rolling his eyes or silently cackling.

"Five in the *morning*?" I demanded after a few seconds.

"Be ready. We've got to drop our things off before we head to the center."

"Chloe reminded me, you're wearing Merrin's necklace this whole week."

"Oh, come on."

"Bet's off if you don't. I can barely stand you for five minutes without that thing, let alone five days."

"Rude," Mel said offhandedly. "Be ready tomorrow morning. You can nap in the car on the way if you really need to."

"Damn straight I will. And you're buying me breakfast."

"You are incredibly high maintenance."

"That's why you married me," I said and hung up.

Three

True to my word, I'd dozed off shortly after climbing into Mel's car and forcing him to put on the enchanted necklace that a witch friend had made for me the year before. It was a only a small blue-black square on a short leather cord, but it made him tolerable by blocking me from reading his emotions. Mel wasn't too forthcoming about where exactly we were staying so I'd taken his smug smile as a suggestion to spend time being too unconscious to think about what horrors awaited me.

When I came to, my brain had taken a few minutes to process the soft music playing and the trees outside my window. The road was narrow and bumpy, penned in on both sides by wilderness that I felt would have been too close even if I'd been outside, standing still. Another section of my brain woke up then, shouting a panicked warning that Mel was driving incredibly fast.

"What if another car is barreling straight for us?"

"There isn't one," Mel said, his thumb bobbing on the steering wheel in time with the music.

"But what if there is?"

"Trust me, there isn't. This is a private road."

"Private to whom?"

Mel only smiled, refusing to even give me a comforting glance or kind word. Glowering, I felt around for the button that would adjust the back of my seat into an upright position. It took an eternity and made me wish for the archaic days of my youth, when there had been just a lever that sprang the seat forward so fast it risked tossing small children through the windshield.

I did my best to stretch in the tiny car, wondering if Mel had spring for a rental because it fit between the narrow trees and his massive SUV didn't. The car looked lived in, though, so I reconsidered it being a rental and figured he'd borrowed it from a friend.

Mel, who has a supernatural awareness of when breasts are pressed up against cloth (or metal, or glass, or—well you get the point) glanced over to take a gander at my girls as I grunted like an old man trying to get off a couch. I rolled my eyes but didn't put up much of a fuss. Without the burn of his werewolf emotions to back up the leering, it wasn't so bad.

"How much farther is this hotel?"

"No hotel," he said. His smile was back and it was a touch more irritating in its smugness. I narrowed my eyes.

"I am not camping out in the woods in a tent and a sleeping bag. Best-case scenario, you get fleas. Worst-case, I whittle an axe and chop you up out of irritation at how stupid you are for getting fleas."

"Whittle?"

"Yeah, I got skills," I lied.

"Why not just chop me up with whatever blade you're using to whittle? What's to keep me from running off while you're furiously slicing at a dangerous weapon with another dangerous weapon."

"I'll do it in stages while you're asleep. You'll have no idea."

"What're you, gonna smuggle the shavings off into the woods and dump them out your pant-leg where I won't notice?"

"I told you, I got skills."

Mel snorted out a laugh and I tried to figure out why he was so jolly. The car slowed and we rounded a final corner into a clearing that held a well worn, dirt driveway and a very large house that looked like someone had built a mansion out of angled glass and Lincoln Logs. My eyebrows shot up and I caught the giddy look he threw me as he slowed to a stop.

"Is this a B&B?" I asked. Mel ignored my question and pushed open the car door, pulling the keys out of the ignition and then unbuckling his seat belt in two quick motions. The door to the house opened and two stunning people stepped out. The woman looked tiny and I wasn't sure if it was the distance or the height of the man with her that made her appear so. As she got closer I realized it was actually both. The top of her blond head came only to my chin, but I was betting people would've just noticed her sturdy frame and confident smile and assumed she was taller.

The man with her was rangy, half a head taller than Mel with lanky arms and dark hair. His brown eyes and square jaw complemented good bone structure and great lips. He moved casually, like a satiated leopard with nowhere to be, and covered the distance between us in the same time as the woman, even though her muscular legs were moving quickly. Mel moved around the car and embraced the taller man, peering behind him when the front door slammed.

The woman came straight to me, pulled me into a hug that made me grunt in surprise and pain. When she pulled away, her expression was happily apologetic.

"Oops, sorry. Been awhile since we had a human around."

Rather than answer, I stared down at her, considering her words. She definitely wasn't human, but her emotions didn't match anything I'd felt before. The buzz of having her near was familiar, but I couldn't place it, couldn't label it. I recognized the emotions I could feel—eagerness, happiness, affection—but couldn't have told you why.

Usually it takes me some time to really match everything I'm feeling up with the right emotions. Often it's like those kids diagram games where you have to draw a line from one column to the thing that matches it in another. Even the dumb kids can get that cow connects to barn and person connects to house, but then there are other options that take some time to figure out.

Unable to speak, I tried to figure out exactly why they felt so familiar as she turned to face the men. The taller man came around to my side, pulling me into a hug that folded his upper body around me like a blanket. His hug was gentle before he pulled back and took a second to admire my face before he turned to speak to Mel.

"She's the one, eh?"

"The one?" Mel asked, a frown creasing his forehead. The woman moved closer, crossed her arms over her chest and smiled at him. The expression on her tan face matched the mischievous intent I caught bubbling out of her psyche.

"Your mate."

"His what?" I demanded. The last time a woman had been Mel's mate it hadn't ended so well for her. Granted, she'd been a murderous succubus who'd tried to kill him and eat my ex-husband, but I didn't want to be lumped in with her no matter what.

The taller man started laughing, nearly drowning me in amusement. A bubble of laughter escaped my throat before I realized what was happening, and before I knew it, I was grinning at Mel, caught up in the burbling feeling of teasing a loved one. Mel took a rough breath, his expression screwing up into blatant disgust

"She is not. My. Mate," he hissed, biting off each word. My own insult seeped in, pushing away the humor and glee. I didn't want to be his mate and it shouldn't have bothered me that he wasn't into it, but he didn't have to be so bitchy about it. I'm a catch, dammit.

"Whatever you say," the woman said. The man next to me glanced down and I felt a burst of surprise crackle out.

"I'm so sorry, we haven't introduced ourselves and I'm betting Mel didn't fill you in, either. You've got that look women get when they're not really sure how they ended up alone with this oaf and they've just realized they want to run away screaming."

"Hey!" Mel snapped.

"I'm Julian and this is my wife Sarah," the man said, ignoring Mel completely. "I'm his brother."

"Oh. Okay," I said, feeling even more lost than before. Was Mel adopted? Were these two part of some family of other creatures who'd raised him? It would explain why they seemed so decent and he could be such a jackass. "Brother?"

"In the flesh," Julian said, his lips tugging up in a perfectly proud big brother grin.

"We've got your room all set up," Sarah explained. "Mel told us you're an empath, so I set you up in a room away from where the kids sleep."

"Kids?" I like kids, but I hadn't been expecting them. Did Mel and I have to bring them with us to the retreat? Did I have to learn names of tiny children and pretend to not mind their quirks and sticky hands?

"You look completely lost," Sarah said, her eyes narrowing, before she turned to aim the mother of all Mom Glares Mel's way. Insult at the idea of wedding me gone in an instant, Mel smiled his most puckish grin, his entire demeanor changing.

"Mel!" Sarah snapped, lifting her fist as if she'd slug him. Julian got there first, his speed incredible. Before I could detect the exact motion leading up to it, he had Mel in a headlock and he was dragging him toward the house. Mel was growling, shoving at Julian's arm but Julian was just laughing, unbothered. There was a growl edging his voice as well, though both reminded me of a dog playing tug of war, rather than one threatening to rip an intruder's face off.

Sarah turned toward me, gave me a mild smile. "Boys."

"Yeah," I said, still unsure of what I was supposed to be doing. Sarah watched me and I felt something fizz against my skin as she tipped her head. It took me another second to realize she was pitying me. That one I should have recognized right away with the amount of times I've felt it in my life.

"He didn't tell you about us?"

"No. He didn't tell me anything, really. Well, he said we were here to investigate a shady marriage dealy, but now, instead, I'm standing in the middle of nowhere with … You. I don't know … what …" I trailed off, still distracted by my brain grasping desperately for some sort of recognition or knowledge of what I was feeling.

"Me? Mel's sister-in-law? Or me in the more general sense, a woman?" When I still didn't have an answer to what I wasn't even sure I was asking, she elaborated further. "Me a werewolf?"

"Ahh!" I said before I could control myself. "Yes! That's what you are?"

"Indeed," she said, chuckling but still not sure what to make of me. "You didn't know?"

"I don't know anything. I mean, I didn't know—I've only ever been around werewolves like Mel. Feeling you is a whole new experience."

"Ah. Well." Her emotions bubbled against me like a roughly shaken can of soda, and then she quirked her lip slyly and said, "Hopefully feeling me is a nice experience."

"Oh, it is. Uh, I mean—"

"Let's go meet the family, shall we?" Winking, she stepped around me to open the driver's side door, pop the trunk, and then grab the bags Mel had stashed there. Despite being half my size, she slung my duffle, Mel's duffle and a suitcase I hadn't realized was in there over her body like they were nothing. Slamming the trunk, she gestured to the house.

"I promise we're not going to eat you. Come on."

Lost, I stayed behind trying to get a handle on what she was feeling, though ultimately I gave up once she hit the front door. She'd slipped just barely out of my range and I wasn't sure if I was disappointed or grateful. Her emotions weren't painful like Mel's but they were damned distracting, like having a pebble in your securely zipped up, knee-high boots.

Before I'd even started moving, I heard a chorus of tiny howls break out across the yard. When a longer, louder howl joined them, most of the smaller howls cracked and trailed off, though one picked up again, louder than others, like it had something to prove. Sarah laughed loudly and it sparked off of her, hitting me even from my place near the car.

I thought again of the cupcake Mel had given me and considered that this would all be worth it once I was rolling around in orgasmic, chocolate glee.

I stepped in through the front door and paused. The ceiling was nearly level with the sky, the décor mixed rustic with luxury, and there were naked children playing with puppies throughout my field of view.

Mel had one of the puppies draped over his shoulder, its tail wagging spastically and slapping him in the face. Julian was chasing one small, naked girl around with a purple, shapeless piece of fabric. She was shrieking and laughing in equal measure. When Sarah appeared to my right, the little girl made a quick course change and took off toward her mother. Julian paused, stood tall with a bemused frown on his face and watched as Sarah scooped the girl up, tucked her under one arm like a football and made her way toward her husband.

One of the clothed boys noticed me then, pausing in his attempts to climb Mel's legs to stare at me in awe. Something about his stillness caught the attention of the other little ones and they all quieted, shifted, and turned to watch me. It was a sea of dark hair and dark eyes, among both the kids and the puppies. All the kids looked about the same age and I wondered if they were all siblings or if some were visiting from some other homey cabin in the woods.

Even the shrieking girl under Sarah's arm strained to peer around her mother's hips to look at me. Unsure of what else to do, I gave a small wave.

"Hey."

Several of the kids and one puppy bounded toward me and I considered backing up, running to the car, and driving home. I had my cell phone in my bag back there; I could probably navigate my way off whatever island Mel had dragged my sleeping self to. When the kids were just out of arm's reach, Sarah let out a loud whistle, handing the naked girl to Julian. The puppy slid on the smooth wood floor, attempting to stop itself. I felt a fuzzy face smash against my leg before a paw hit my shoe. One of the boys who'd run over abruptly stopped dead, his eyes rolling in their sockets to look toward his mother, even though he was facing away and couldn't possibly see her.

As Julian tried to wrestle the little girl into the purple dress, Sarah stepped toward us.

"This is Gwen. Kids, say hi."

The puppy at my feet struggled to right itself and then sat back on its black and gray spotted butt, looking up at me. After a second, the pup's jaw dropped open and a little pink tongue lolled out, eyes squinting in a happy, doggy grin. One little boy who'd run over leaned forward in what he thought was a stealthy way and sniffed my thigh. I watched him but said nothing. I like kids and dogs but don't have extensive experience with either so I wasn't sure what was protocol. My sister and her three children live far enough away that I mainly see them through a computer screen and the internet, but I was certain that didn't qualify me to deal with werewolf puppies in the least.

"Don't be rude," Sarah ordered, her voice mild. The boy jerked back, his cheeks going red. I looked down at the children and tried to discern how many of them there were. On a cursory count, I figured roughly eighty-seven. In reality there were six, but I was still adjusting to the chaos and couldn't quite see that clearly through the fizzy haze of emotions. There was no way I was picking out who was feeling what, at least not so soon after being exposed to the tiny pack.

Once Sarah got closer, she turned fully so she could look out over the group and see Mel, who was still getting whacked in the face by a tail.

"Come on over, Jeremy, Lorelai. Be polite."

Mel tipped to plop the puppy onto the floor, reaching to grab another purple piece of clothing. I watched as the puppy on the floor plummeted awkwardly onto his side to lie down, tucked his head against its front leg and instantly went completely bald. I resisted the urge to ask what had happened or point and yell, "Witch! Tiny witch!" For all I knew, spontaneously balding puppies were completely normal in the werewolf world.

Mel stood over the naked dog as it contorted a bit on the pile of fur its body had rejected. He looked utterly unbothered by the writhing skin and tiny grunts, though I was experiencing the clamorous feelings of discomfort and strain and couldn't keep his level of calm. Jeremy—I was assuming, since the little girl was still struggling against her father's attempts to get her into the purple dress—was running through the spectrum of kid emotions all at once, making me squint and lean closer as if I could figure out how to help him.

As his puppy-shape turned into a little boy shape, his wild emotions calmed to relief and pride, though it quickly got overtaken in my brain by the interest pumping off the others as they stared up at me from near my feet. I wasn't even doing anything, but maybe I smelled amazing. I had eaten my (and Mel's) share of croissant-egg sandwiches on the way; maybe the kids could smell my food breath.

Finally, when a completely hairless little boy sat up in place of the bald puppy, Mel leaned down to shove a giant, purple shirt over his head. The boy struggled to push his arms through the holes and Mel helped him to his feet. When they approached me, Mel tapped the top of his bald head. The boy looked up at him and grinned but said nothing.

It took a bit more maneuvering but soon four boys, one girl and a black puppy stood more or less lined up in front of me. Mel stayed slightly behind the kids, a wide, goofy grin covering his mouth. Sarah gestured to each kid (and puppy) as she spoke.

"Jeremy, Lorelai, Oliver, Christian, Walter, and Clara," Sarah explained, stepping forward to rub a hand over Christian's bald head. He squinted slightly and I saw the hair on his arms darken and get longer. Lorelai stifled a laugh when she noticed but Walter frowned at his brother and I felt some another emotion bubble like tonic water.

I stood in a room surrounded by werewolves and wondered silently why I hadn't cracked up or fallen to the floor mumbling nonsense. Mel's emotions were dammed in by the necklace, but even Sarah and Julian were tolerable. I had only met two werewolves up until this point, but both had possessed an emotional pattern akin to being tied down on a bed of hot coals and poked with pitchforks. This was definitely different and I was going to have to figure out why. Maybe something had happened to me while I'd slept and I no longer had to worry about werewolf emotions that I had before.

I wasn't jumping at the chance to have Mel pull of the necklace to see for sure, but I remained cautiously optimistic.

I realized then that everyone was staring at me expectantly. I was being rude and stupid and I instantly felt bad. I smiled, though it was forced, and crouched down to look the kids in their adorable little faces. The puppy next to me, Clara, took a half-step forward before freezing and looking to her mother. Sarah just watched us with a smile.

"Hi guys, I'm Gwen. I'll be staying here for a little while. I guess." Looking around at the kids, I bit my lip, unsure how to interact with baby werewolves. Deciding it was probably quite a bit like dealing with my nieces and nephew, I figured I'd let them feel important. "Can anyone show me to my room?"

"I can!" Lorelai of the hard-fought purple dress announced, reaching out to grab my hand. She gave a tug and turned, shoving aside her brothers. They let her assault them without incident (though Christian couldn't quite catch himself and toppled) and I got to my feet, following her lead. Apparently Lorelai had signaled the end of polite time; Walter tackled Clara to the ground and bit her ear, the hair on his arms going dark. I was able to keep my eyes on him long enough to see him struggle to pull his baggy shirt off while still holding Clara on the ground, before I was yanked around the corner.

Sarah followed us, not bothering to look back when a bark and a laugh screeched our way from the living room.

We passed a large kitchen and dining room on the left, a doorway and staircase leading downward on the right, and finally came to a pair of bedrooms. Little Lorelai dragged me all the way into the room, stopping only when we were near my bag, which Sarah had set on the bed. Staring up at me as if expecting a tip, Lorelai stood close, dark eyes intense. Her face was round, her hair messy and stopping just above her shoulders. One eyebrow was slightly thicker than the other, but her arms were completely hairless. She didn't seem to mind my inspection of her and I wondered if it was a werewolf thing or just the fact that she looked about five years old and was too young to notice.

"Um. Thanks," I said, finally. She nodded, looked past me to her mother.

"Momma?" she asked. I didn't hear Sarah say anything but by the time I turned to face her, Lorelai had taken off through the bedroom door.

"This is …" I paused, unsure what I could say that wouldn't be confusing or insulting. Sarah laughed, gave a small nod.

"Don't worry about it. Mel said you guys have to get going pretty soon, but I'll leave you be until you do."

"You don't have—"

"I should, anyway. Julian's definitely the good cop."

With a wink, she grabbed the door, yanked it shut and left.

Four

I didn't think I'd fallen asleep but I felt the bed sag next to me and the surprise jerked me upright with a cry. Disoriented, I whipped my head around, scanning a room I didn't recognize, until I spotted Mel. Despite my usual reaction of irritation at the sight of him, I felt instantly comforted finding someone I recognized. When my brain caught up and realized he was giving me a pompous smile, I let out a wordless grumble. He ignored my disapproval of his general state of being and nudged me gently with his elbow.

"You think we should consummate this fake marriage before we head out?"

I decided I could probably blame the relief on being stupid from sleep and not on actually liking him as a person or anything. Surely there was no legitimate reason for me to not be disgusted and outraged at finding myself alone in a bedroom with *Mel*.

"There are six children out there," I protested, shaking my head wearily.

"They won't hear us. They don't get the super senses—" he gestured vaguely to his own ear, "—until puberty. Right now they're just occasionally puppy-shaped."

"It's not—the answer is no. Regardless of children, the answer is always no."

"Well then, we should go." Getting to his feet, Mel twisted to hold a hand out to me, catching my eye as he did. The smug smile was back, though I wasn't sure why. He always looked so full of himself, even after having just been rebuked. Then again, maybe my refusal to submit to his charms had become so routine that he barely noticed anymore. It was as normal as both of us needing to breathe or eat. It was our thing, like our version of friendship necklaces. His charm said, "Sex?" and mine, "NO!"

I chuckled at the mental image I'd given myself of Mel decked out in bedazzled children's charms and dropped my head forward, stretching my neck. My body was still not ready to get up, to leave the cozy mattress and the homey house and let Mel take it somewhere that might have been dangerous.

Duty calls, however, and this time it had left a message promising sugar, so I put my hand in his and let him pull me to his feet. Surprisingly, he didn't yank me close and try to cop a feel. He just tugged me upward, let my hand go, and turned to look around the room.

"Do you need anything else before we leave?" he asked.

"Is there something I can take that makes you less annoying?"

"There is, but it's my penis."

"Then no."

Mel, forever undeterred by my disgust, just made his way toward the front room of the massive house. I followed, trying my best to prepare myself for the onslaught of emotions. Eight people is a lot for me when those people are pure people. These people were all partly wolf, which made being around them hit me at least twice as intense. It reminded me of feeling my cell phone buzz in my hand, only it was all over and non-stop.

As we got to the living area, where half the kids were puppy-shaped and the rest were naked, I found myself reaching to rub at my scalp. My skin felt like I'd rubbed it against a dozen helium-filled balloons and I'd almost convinced myself my hair was standing on end.

We made it to the car without being noticed by the kids and, once I was buckled safely inside, I dug into my bag, looking for my phone. After a few minutes, as I realized I'd gotten distracted from my original purpose by social media and pictures of babies, I frowned, peering out the front window as if I could see the internet in waves across the sky.

"I can't believe I get signal out here."

"You won't, once we get to the Tough Love center."

"Is that the name of it?"

"Yeah, why?"

"It sounds ridiculous."

"Hey, I didn't name it."

"No, but I bet you've named your penis," I groused, remembering instantly what I had been meaning to do. Sending off a text threatening Chloe with bodily harm, I continued under my breath. "Something stupid, too."

"I have, but it's not stupid, and I can properly introduce you two if you'd like."

"I would not like, even a little."

Still taking the path of no resistance to my dislike, Mel sped up, cornering the turns even faster than he had on the way up to the house. I clenched my whole body, leaning toward the center console as if that alone would save me if Mel got us into some bone-crunching, flesh-rending wreck. I needed a distraction or I was gonna crack my jaw grinding my teeth.

"So, what exactly did you tell them our marriage troubles are?" I asked, trying not to notice the trees around us blurring into one green and brown mess.

"I played the man, claiming I wasn't sure why you'd wanted me to call them, but that you'd heard from a friend they did good work."

"You played the man?" I asked, turning to him. My phone buzzed and I glanced at it; Chloe had just sent a mocking emoticon sticking its tongue out at me.

"Yeah, you know, I said you'd been nagging me, harping about how you were unhappy, that I didn't see any damn problem, but I've gotta keep the old ball and chain happy. That sort of thing."

"That's not playing the 'man' that's playing the 'asshole.' Which you do quite well, most days."

"Hey, who made you pizza and let you sober up on his couch?"

"Who then knocked me out by not being smart enough to keep his necklace on?"

"I thought we'd established you passed out because you couldn't handle my hot body."

"I could handle it, I just really, really don't want to."

"Liar," Mel spat.

Deciding a change of subject was in order I got back to business. "What do I need to know for this whole sham?"

"What do you mean?"

"Well. We're pretending to be married, right? How long have we been together? How did we meet? Do we have any humiliating nicknames for each other?"

"I'll call you Sugar Tits."

"Not in this lifetime."

"Sweet Ass?"

"No! Look—"

"Honey Legs?"

"Stop! We need to be serious here!"

"What about—"

"I swear to god if you don't stop, I will only refer to you as Floppy Dick for the rest of this stupid job."

"Floppy Dick has a job for you."

I took a deep breath, aiming to calm myself away from the homicidal urges bubbling up inside me. His joke barely even made sense but that didn't stop me from being irritated. His casual disinterest in talking about our relationship, be it fake or not, made me consider how awful it would be were we actually shackled together in holy matrimony.

"Will you please be serious? This is your thing, not mine. I should not be taking it more seriously than you are."

"I'm taking it plenty seriously. I'm just not worried about the small details."

"Small details? Is that what you think of our marriage, Somerset?"

"Why do you think we're going to a marriage counselor?"

I fought the urge to grab the steering wheel and careen us into a tree. It would be better than having this conversation. Several minutes passed as I considered my horrible life choices and my desperate stupidity where chocolate was concerned. Damn those delicious cupcakes and the asinine things they made me agree to. Mel broke the silence casually, as if our previous spat hadn't happened.

"So, what do you think our problems should be?" Mel asked, tapping his finger on the wheel as if to a song only he could hear. "We're going to need some in order to get in there for more than a consultation."

"Are you kidding me?" I demanded. "*Now* you want to come up with a plan?"

Mel chuckled and I got the feeling he'd been deliberately obtuse just to aggravate me. I realized I couldn't really tell his motivation without the aid of his emotions. Painful as they were, I'd apparently relied on them without realizing it in the past. Suddenly frustrated by my impotence, I decided I wanted to hit him.

Instead, I carefully considered my options and made a very sensible suggestion. "We can say you're bad in bed."

"They'd never believe it. We'll say *you're* bad in bed."

"They'd believe it. I know I believe it."

"You don't know what you're talking about. Just look at me. I'm amazing. Everyone can see it."

"That's our problem, then: you're completely disconnected from reality."

Mel threw his head back and laughed and I wondered if he found me clever or if the thought of him being bad at sex was so ridiculous he found it hilarious. We rode in silence for another few minutes before I noticed a giant blue sign coming up fast on the right. The words 'Tough Love' were spelled out in curvy letters next to a dove holding an olive branch in its beak.

We took the drive through a pathway of well-groomed trees onto a wide roundabout in front of a giant house. The building was massive, painted a pale yellow and decorated with cutesy items like wooden cows and wire chickens.

The style looked like country chic had gotten drunk and thrown up all over some perfectly respectable luxury home. I already didn't trust the place, thanks to why we were there in the first place, but the décor compounded my suspicion. I could see other, more modern buildings decorating the landscape behind it, like guesthouses that had been built more recently.

"This is it?" I asked as Mel came around the car to stand next to me. I was gawking still, wondering if they'd hired a decorator for this mess or just let someone's great aunt Ida go ballistic with an outlandish flea market budget.

"Yep. Here." As I stared at a metal frog tacked to the open front door, I felt Mel grab my left hand. Turning just in time to see him slip a gold wedding band over my ring finger, I jerked as if I could pull my hand back and rewind time to where that hadn't just happened. Mel held fast, making me think I should be more careful about such actions in the future lest I accidentally pull my own arm out of its socket.

"What the hell?"

"We're married, remember?" he smiled sweetly and brought my hand to his lips. "Honey-butt."

I snarled at him, but he was already leaving me behind to stride confidently up the front walk. I hustled to catch up, rubbing at the ring uncomfortably. It had been a long time since I'd worn a wedding ring and just the feel of the metal on that particular finger sent jitters through my nervous system.

"So where did we land on this whole fake marriage thing?" I asked quietly as we moved up the walk. "Do I have amnesia and that's why we can't answer any of their questions? Oh! Are we going soap opera? Can I pretend to be my own transsexual twin brother and you're forcing me into this outdated and unfair gender role and so I hate you but also I might be pregnant with—"

"If they ask anything you can't answer," Mel interrupted. "Just scowl angrily and let me handle it." Mel looked down at me, pointed to my sour expression. "Yes! Just like that."

I did my best to blank my face as we stepped into the building, despite the fact that I was still boiling inside with frustration. Who knows where I could have taken that soap opera thing? I could have had the next All My Children come tumbling out of my mouth and now we'd never know thanks to Mel's refusal to play along.

He was acting outwardly as if he was perfectly fine but something was off. At least, I thought something was off. I had to admit to myself that I wasn't a hundred percent sure what was going through his head without his emotions to back it up. The only other time we'd spent awhile together with the necklace between us there had been wine and pizza to distract me.

This time, he had managed to get me to agree to spend a week with a house full of werewolves. This time I had to pretend to be his wife, a role I hadn't been any good at even when I'd liked the person in the role of husband. *This time*, there didn't seem to be any pizza at all, dammit.

In that instant, I remembered I wasn't terribly happy with him or the situation and it wasn't just because I'd lost my one shot at producing a cheesy daytime TV show. Luckily for both of us, I was supposed to be unhappy with him. It would help make our fake marital troubles more convincing to the outside world. I could be snotty and insulting and no one would think twice about it. So, I decided to go with that feeling.

To Tough Love's credit, their center was much less kitschy inside. The walls were a tamer yellow and I only spotted two cow decorations on the walls; the mooing clock was actually pretty cute, I had to admit.

It was clear the place had been a house once upon a time. We stood in an open floor plan, with a freestanding reception desk to our left and a few couples milling about here and there. A woman with short red hair cut similar to mine stepped up to us, a warm smile on her face. She held out a hand to me and then to Mel after we shook.

"Welcome to Tough Love, do you have a consultation or have you come to learn about how we can help?"

"Appointment, Mel Somerset and Gwen Arthur," Mel answered, shifting into the skin of a man who wanted to appear polite but couldn't quite master it. He wouldn't meet the lady's eyes, and kept a faint snarl of annoyance on his face as he scanned the room. The receptionist wasn't bothered.

"Yes, I see your names right here." She pointed to the tablet computer she held, but didn't show us. "Would you like some refreshment? Tea? Lemonade? We have coffee, too, if the heat doesn't bother you."

"I'll take some lemonade," I said, hoping it was sixty-percent sugar water and not some tart, fresh-squeezed junk.

"Of course, have a seat right over there and I'll call you when Dr. Coontz is ready for you. We'll have fresh juice for you in the room, how's that?"

I nodded politely, even though I wanted to spit, "Damn." She gave us a little head bow and turned to make her way to the back corner, where a small kitchen folded around an empty island. I wrinkled my nose at the idea of sour citrus, leaning close to Mel to make sure no one heard us.

"I'm already sure this guy's a creep. You can't have that last name and not be a creep."

Mel's lip quirked but he was scanning the room intently. After another minute of looking around, he made his way toward the couches set in a square off to our right.

"Consultation?" I whispered, tugging on his arm to slow him down.

"Yeah," he whispered back. "Be convincing. We want them to want us here so we can get all up in their business."

"Speaking of, why didn't you just seduce one of the receptionists and steal her keys or something?"

Mel was quiet and I wasn't sure for a moment if he was ignoring my question or if he just didn't have a good answer. Finally, he glanced at me so quick it was like he didn't want to, and swallowed.

"It wasn't really … it wouldn't have worked."

Without giving me a chance to ask why, he took a seat next to an older couple, giving them both a quick smile. I followed him over, dropped down next to Mel, and looked around. There was one other pair sitting on the couch to our right and they were chatting quietly, their emotions mild. I wasn't sure why they were there; they seemed to be getting along just fine. No subtle resentment, frustration, disappointment, or even a trace of silent loathing. It was nothing like how I imagined it would be to step outside myself and read me with Mel.

"Are you here for the retreat?" Mel asked the older couple. The wife smiled at him, her body language indicating she was all too happy to make conversation with the attractive, muscular young man. The husband gave Mel a look of mild disapproval but there wasn't any hostility behind it.

"Oh no, just for therapy. We've been here once a week for a few months. We've been married longer than you've been alive and you can't go wrong with a tune-up now and then," the woman said, delight lighting her up. She was just so happy to have someone interested, she pushed on, spilling more information than Mel had asked for, while he smiled politely at her. "I thought we'd better see what we could do to make our lives more content. We've tried changing our diet and taking supplements, different sorts of activities, and now we're trying this."

"And how's it working for you?"

"Very well, I think." She reminded me of everyone's favorite grandma, at ease and soft, nice to have around. It was like sitting two people away from the personification of a fuzzy blanket.

"That's fantastic," Mel said, and it seemed genuine. "I hope the wife and I have as much success as you two."

The man leaned forward, pointedly ignoring Mel so he could catch my eye and wag his brows suggestively.

"Let me save you a lot of money, darling, and tell you what the doctor told us: Have more sex."

"Cornelius!" His wife's cheeks went red, embarrassment spewing out of her like a broken fire hydrant. He gave a nod before turning to give Mel a challenging grin. Mel just nodded and looked to me.

"You hear that, *sweetie?* More sex."

"Bite me," I said without thinking.

"Well *that* wasn't prescribed," Cornelius said. "But I'm sure your husband here wouldn't mind."

Mrs. Cornelius slapped his arm three times in rapid succession and I gave in, laughing along with the feelings rumbling out of him. Satisfied, Cornelius leaned back in his seat, laying a hand over his wife's pleated khakis. She wiggled a bit like the embarrassment of the intimate touch was almost too much to bear, but she didn't stop him.

Soon after, a woman in her mid-fifties came out to stand in the gap between the two couches.

"Cornelius, Mira, are you ready?"

"We are," Mira said. Cornelius turned to give me one last lascivious grin before heaving himself up and following the women toward a hall to the left. When they were out of sight, Mel shifted to throw his arm over the back of the couch, pulling me close to him.

"Well there you go, all our problems solved. We're just not having enough sex."

"You're having plenty of sex. Just not with me. Which I'm grateful for," I added before he could offer.

"Maybe that's our problem. You don't want to take advantage of all of this," he said, gesturing to his body, and then specifically to his crotch.

"I don't consider not wanting to have sex with you a problem," I sniffed, turning away. I only then realized that the couple to our right had stopped talking and were watching us. I blinked, tried to give a convincing smile. "He's kidding, of course. I have … s—" I didn't want to say it. I'd had to suggest it just a few weeks before and it had felt like swallowing a jar of worms. "—sex with him all the time. That's not my problem—*our* problem."

Realizing we had an audience, Mel pressed his arm around me even tighter, smashing me against his firm body and making my shoulder hurt.

"It's true. She can barely keep her hands off me. Especially in the mornings. It's like taming a lion trying to get out of bed each day." He winked at them, mimed cracking a whip and, then moved on to imitating some other action that I didn't recognize but could be sure wasn't work safe. They nodded silently, trying to hide the fact that they were both stifling nervous laughter—or maybe the urge get up and run away.

Luckily for all of us, the doctor showed then, calling our names. Mel let me go and I was able to push to my feet and step away from him. Immediately I regretted moving closer to the doctor. I did not like standing near this man.

Doctor Coontz was just as greasy as his name implied, though not terribly so physically. He had a smattering of stray wiry hairs on the sides, with what little he had left on top slicked back severely. His eyes were a little too wide, slightly buggy and too grey to be considered blue. I'd met men with attractive grey eyes, but these were from a different manufacturer. They looked like newspaper that'd been left in the rain, rather than the sky before a storm.

I felt myself squinting as I looked over his thin body and wondered why my nose could almost-but-not-quite detect a smell somewhere between good cheese and old socks. My lizard brain started hissing and spitting and I immediately wanted to turn to Mel, forfeit the cupcakes, and leave.

My fake husband got to his feet, stepped around the coffee table with its dozens of magazines, and held out a hand. The doctor shook his hand and then turned to me, his hand still out. I pretending to be fascinated by the cow clock on the wall and hoped he took my rudeness for distraction. He faltered a bit, dropping his arm before gesturing to a hallway off to our right.

"If you two are ready, just follow me."

"Lead the way," Mel said, glancing down at me. He seemed to notice my discomfort and put a hand to my shoulder, pushing slightly. "Let's go, Pumpkin."

The doctor turned toward the hall and I couldn't help but critique him as he walked. Even the pattern of his steps bothered me; his feet dragged on the wooden floors and his steps were too small. When I didn't start moving immediately, Mel shoved harder, leaning down to whisper in my ear.

"Get it together, Arthur."

"Shh," I hissed at him, moving to follow the doctor. The hallway was long, curving past several closed doors and a few open ones that revealed small rooms that all matched each other in décor: three comfortable chairs, one coffee table, and an end table. The art was all fields and forests, with the occasional lake thrown in for good measure. It felt kind of like a dentist's office, but without the scary warnings about gum disease and cavities.

"Right through here, have a seat." The doctor stopped at a room toward the back of the hallway, letting us enter first. I darted forward, squeezed between Mel and the doorjamb to keep Coontz from trying to shake my hand again. I took the seat that looked slightly farther away from what I guessed would be the doctor's seat and busied myself with pouring some lemonade from the carafe on the end table. Mel gave me a look that clearly disapproved of my nutty behavior as he moved toward me, but his expression was plain before he faced the doctor.

Instead of offering Mel any of the lemonade, I took a gulp of mine and looked around the room. I forced myself to be fascinated by the boring photographs on the walls so that I wouldn't have to make eye contact.

Doctor Coontz sat in the chair across from us, crossing his chicken legs in what I deemed an overly feminine fashion and looked at us both in turn. I likely wouldn't have noticed the action in any other man, but I just really couldn't get over how uncomfortable he made me feel. It was weird and I didn't know how to handle it. I couldn't leave, I couldn't really ask him why he creeped me out, and I couldn't tell Mel, so I had to just sit there and feel like my skin was crawling.

He'd grabbed a notepad and a pen from somewhere along the way and he perched the pad on his knee. I didn't speak and neither did Mel. Finally, the doctor gave a small chuckle, shook his head, his gaze falling on me and staying. I snuck a peak at him before turning my attention to Mel, as if I expected him to do all the talking.

"First time jitters, I see. Let's just talk about you two for a second. How long have you been married?"

I ignored the question and pretended he wasn't still watching me, looking to the lemonade as if I was trying to read a label, which of course it didn't have. Coontz's emotions seemed pretty normal, not overly inappropriate or outrageous. He was just a human man with unfortunate genetics, but good god did he make my stomach do flailing flip-flops.

Mel cleared his throat harshly and I jerked my head up to look at him. When I offered nothing helpful, Mel gave a slight roll of his eyes and turned to Coontz.

"We've been together three years, married one."

"How did you meet?"

"In a bar," Mel said. He gave a shrug of his shoulder. I was wondering if he'd thought of any of this beforehand or if he was just about to wing it. He'd distracted me from deciding on a fake history to back up our fake marriage, so now we were left in the position of possibly contradicting each other. Frustration welled, distracting me from my unease and I spoke up, desperate to contribute something, even if I was risking sounding snide or dishonest.

"Who could resist that face, right?" I said, setting down my lemonade. Mel glanced over, tension pulling his brows together ever so slightly. "He was quite a cad before me, bedding everything that moved. He's even slept with my best friend."

"Really?" the doctor asked, making a note on the pad. "So you had met before?"

"No, not really," I said before he could make up something I wouldn't be able to follow. "I'd seen him in passing, but it was nothing."

"It was love at first sight for me," Mel said, his tone a challenge. I threw him a glare. "I saw her across that crowded bar, sipping on her pink, fruity drink and thought, 'my od. That woman is incredible.' So, I went right up and asked her out. I wanted to propose that instant, but I didn't want to scare her off."

"Oh god," I groaned, before catching myself., "Um. I—he always tells it that way, but that's not … He's embellishing. It'd be pretty weird if he *actually* wanted to marry me before even knowing my name, right?"

Mel's lip quirked before he looked back to Coontz. "And now here we are."

"Yes, here you are," Coontz said, scribbling something else onto the pad. He wasn't particularly amused or unhappy with our responses. He was curious, but it was mild. I probably would have been picking up on the friction between the two of us, even if I wasn't an empath. Maybe he wasn't on the level and I could just explain that to Mel, he could call the cops, and we could be on our way. Good god, did I want to be on my way.

"So, why *are* you here?"

"We fight all the time," I said, knowing the easy answer to that question, and happy I wouldn't have to lie. "I can barely stand to be in the same room as him."

"What do you fight about?"

"Everything. He never listens to me. If I ask him to do something he just laughs. It's all his fault. Our marriage is falling apart and it's all his fault."

"Hey, you're part of this marriage, too," Mel argued, turning in the chair so he could almost face me completely. "You never do what I want, either."

"Now, now," Coontz said, leaning forward. "Let's take a second before we start to argue." I realized too late what he was about to do as he laid a hand on my knee. It felt like spiders were wriggling along my skin. Crossing my legs just to get my knee out from under his hand, I glared his way, giving him a look that clearly explained that touching had been going too far. He stayed folded forward, watching me mildly, his psyche completely guilt-free. I really didn't like this guy, but I had to consider that maybe the worst of his offenses was being a sociopath. Perhaps he'd done nothing wrong except choose a profession he had no business being a part of.

"Let's have a discussion instead of a fight. Can we do that?" Coontz asked, finally sitting up straight again. Mel crossed his arms over his chest, flicked his gaze to me, and then nodded.

"Sure," I said, keeping my crossed legs squeezed against the armrest of the chair, hoping it kept me out of touching range. I wanted to talk to some of the other couples under his care, I thought, hoping we could find a few before we left. Maybe we'd be allowed to tour the grounds and I could grill other women about whether or not Coontz made them want to crawl inside their own belly buttons and disappear.

Him being a creep wasn't exactly illegal, though, and we *were* there looking for cultish wrongdoing, not just some dude with bad hair making women uncomfortable. That was something you could find at any nightclub, not something worth prosecuting.

"Good, that's good. Now, why did you come here?"

"To work on our marriage," Mel answered, as if unsure if he was answering two plus two with four.

"And why do you want to do that?" Coontz asked. I watched Mel, at a loss. I'd been through a real crumbling marriage and hadn't known how to handle it then, either. What the hell was I supposed to say when asked why I wanted to work on a fake marriage to a slutty werewolf?

When neither one of us spoke, Coontz sat back and gestured like a teacher offering the answer to a student who should already know it.

"Because you love each other, or just because you feel you have to? Are you trying to save your marriage, or just save face?"

"Our marriage, of course," Mel said. He let his arms drop onto the rests and sighed dramatically. "We still love each other. I can tell, even when we're having issues that she still loves me, and I know I love her. Please say you'll help us out. Please say you'll have us for the retreat."

Coontz looked between us and I felt something new move around his psyche. I couldn't quite place what it was, but it reminded me of curiosity. It was dangerous, though, something altogether different than anything else in his head—or anyone else's head, really.

No, I realized, that wasn't exactly true. I'd felt something similar in Stan and in Mel when they'd been under the influence of a succubus. Maybe whatever was going on at Tough Love wasn't just some strange cult, after all. Maybe we had bigger problems on our hands.

Swallowing nervously, I found my mouth was dry as a bone, and I let out a small cough. When I grabbed for the lemonade and took a few sloppy gulps, Coontz turned back to Mel, regarded him silently for a moment.

"Let me ask you a few more questions," he said finally, as if he was still making up his mind." When Mel nodded, the doctor looked back to me. "Do you have any children?"

"No," I said. He gave a nod, made a mark on his paper.

"Are you planning on having any?"

I turned to Mel, my brows up. Yet another question I couldn't answer. In real therapy there isn't a right or wrong answer. Some couples want kids, some don't and I wasn't about to judge, unless it was a problem between them or unless it was a decision based on biology or trauma.

We were trying to get in good with this guy, though. We had to make him want us around so we could poke and prod to see if Tough Love was luring couples in and forcing them to worship at the feet of some long-haired loser with an acoustic guitar. Mel had been the one to do research on this place. Did we want kids? Would that make us more or less attractive to a possible cult? This had been exactly what I'd been afraid of happening. Mel caught my confusion and turned to the doctor.

"We've talked about it but we're still using birth control, so it's not something we're planning in the near future."

"All right. What about your families? Are they big families? Do you have a history of multiple births?"

"I do," Mel said, though I could hear a note of suspicion in his voice. I just shook my head.

"And your families? Lots of brothers and sisters, or just a few?"

"I have a big family," Mel answered. "Gwen, too."

"Yeah," I added lamely.

"Excellent." Coontz's emotions were keying up, excitement crackling through him alongside that strange extra grinding thread I couldn't place. "May I ask what you two do for a living?" Again, Mel took the initiative and answered for us both.

"Gwen owns her own consulting business and I'm a personal trainer."

"Good, good." Coontz looked over what he'd written as if considering, adding up facts and data. He made a show of it, but his emotions didn't fit. He'd gone giddy as soon as we'd talked about children, and I didn't like it. Finally, he looked up at us.

"I would be happy to help you both. There are a variety of exercises we go through and some might seem very invasive but I assure you they are only administered for the health of your marriage. Now, because this is only a consultation, we won't start quite yet. I have a few other appointments today, but I'd like to see you back here first thing in the morning."

"That's perfect, thank you so much, doctor." Mel stood up, reaching out a hand. Coontz stared a little too long at me before standing up as well. Taking Mel's hand, he let him pump it once.

"You can call me Gordon, please. Ms. Arthur?" He tried to take his hand back and reach toward me but Mel wouldn't let go. I watched them, getting to my feet but refusing to acknowledge that Coontz clearly wanted something from me. Mel resumed shaking his hand eagerly, like he couldn't control himself. It gave me the chance to move far enough away that Coontz couldn't reach out and touch me again without chasing me down and making it weird.

Finally, laying his other hand over Gordon's, Mel stopped the shaking and waited until the smaller man looked up at him.

"We hope to learn a lot from you, Gordon," Mel said. Coontz nodded and extracted his hand from Mel's with an awkward stiffness. Then, as if worried he might lose it again, he took a full step to the side.

"I hope so, too. Can I show you two out?" Circling wide around Mel, Coontz aimed himself squarely at me, but Mel slid himself between us like a dance move, keeping all attention on himself.

"It's okay, really. We'll find our way. Should we speak with the receptionist to get the ball rolling?" he asked. Coontz shifted to the left, but

Mel shifted as well, keeping himself between us. Irritation popped out of Coontz like sizzling embers, pricking at my skin, but it only made me want to laugh. I liked seeing him not get his way.

"Oh, yes. Rhonda will see to your intake and give you our welcome packet. Really, let me show you out." Gordon moved again to take a step around Mel's right, but Mel was quicker, anticipating the move. He mirrored the doctor, blocking his access, and then took a step back toward me. Still between us, he patted Coontz on the shoulder just this side of too hard and then turned to me as the doctor reacted to the blow.

"Come along cupcake, Gordon's very busy." Wrapping an arm around my shoulder, he kept his body folded like a shield between Coontz and me as he pulled open the door and shuffled me out. We moved through the hall quickly and Mel glanced back as we rounded the corner, throwing a wave and an excited smile back at the doctor after I was out of eyeshot.

"He was weird, right? No matter, we just need someone to get us in the door," Mel said as we passed the closed doors and empty rooms. I gave a small nod but, before I could respond in kind, the receptionist from earlier appeared in front of us at the end of the hall. I let out a yelp and stopped dead, causing Mel to smack into me and almost knock me over. Lightning quick, he wrapped an arm around my waist and held me upright. The receptionist smiled, taking a step backward.

"I didn't mean to startle you. Doctor Coontz said you were on your way out and that I should coordinate with you about tomorrow. Is nine okay?"

"Yeah," I said, noting that Mel had yet to let me go. "Nine's great."

"And don't forget to fast after midnight! Nothing but water!"

"What now?" I asked. Was this woman seriously asking me to go without breakfast? Without a one A.M. snack?

"Oh yes, we like to do some basic blood tests to make sure you're healthy."

"For marriage counseling?" I asked, my skepticism blatant. She just nodded, still pleasant.

"Oh yes. You'd be surprised what deficiencies will contribute to mood problems. We need to make sure you two are healthy as horses!"

"One of us is closer to a horse than the other," I mumbled, hoping after I'd said it that Mel didn't take offense.

Or assume I was making some reference to the size of his manhood.

"I'd really rather not," Mel said as if he hadn't heard me at all. Rhonda the receptionist turned to look at him, her expression faltering. She projected gentle disappointment but I could tell it was an act, a way to placate many others who'd tried to refuse the strange and, as far as I was concerned, wildly unnecessary blood tests.

"You do want the doctor to be able to help you, right?"

"It's just—" I started. Mel got there first.

"I'm terrified of needles."

"Oh," Rhonda said, her disappointed expression softening into pity. "Well—"

"But he just had a full physical recently," I offered. "I'm sure we can get his doctor to send the records over." Mel's grip on me loosened and he leaned around just enough to catch my eye. I wasn't sure what his expression said without his emotions to back it up, so I just smiled as if I was sure he was thanking me for saving the day.

"Well, then Mr. Somerset, you can eat breakfast. But just water for you, Ms. Arthur!" Rhonda announced, giving in suspiciously easily. "Now, before you leave we do have some forms we'll need to have you go over, if you don't mind."

I did mind, but I followed her to the reception desk and took the clipboard she handed me anyway. Mel led me back to the couches and we got to work. I was most of the way through mine when Mel elbowed me.

"That's your address."

"So?"

"So we're married," he said, expecting me to instantly understand. After a moment, he elaborated under his breath. "We don't have separate addresses."

"We have different last names, why can't we have different addresses?"

"I'll get you a new one," Mel said in lieu of answering my question.

I groaned under my breath as he got to his feet and went to schmooze Rhonda into giving him another form for me. I couldn't exactly hear what he said, but I think he called me a dolt. I mean, he said it with affection, but still.

Floppy Dick was getting on my nerves.

Mel filled out my form for me, I signed it, and we were done without further incident. Rhonda offered to toss the mistaken form for us, but Mel pretended he didn't see her grab for it. As he tucked it into his back pocket, I caught an odd spike of concern jerk out of Rhonda. She was outwardly pleasant, though, handing us a little card with the Tough Love dove on one side and our appointment written in blocky letters on the other.

"We're so glad to have you. Have a good evening and we'll see you in the morning!"

"Have a good one," Mel said, pushing me toward the door as if I needed encouragement to get the hell out of there.

OLIVIA R .BURTON

Five

"Where exactly am I going to get blood tests from?" Mel demanded once we were in the car and on our way. I frowned over at him.

"What do you mean? Don't you have any?"

"Why would I have blood test results for a human lying around?"

"Because you're a werewolf?" I hazarded. Mel turned away from the road long enough give me a look that I couldn't entirely discern but that I knew wasn't good.

"And werewolves of lore just keep blood tests around, do they? What books do you read and where can I find them all and burn them?"

"For things!" I snapped, flailing my hands. I couldn't figure out why he was so irritated with me, though maybe my inability to explain my own rationale was part of it.

"What things? I don't do things that require blood tests. Do you?"

"I—" Stopping, I realized he was right. I hadn't been to the doctor for anything other than my yearly lady parts appointment in years. On a sigh, I tossed out a guess. "Don't you need shots or something to leave the country?"

"That's *pets*!" Mel growled. "I am not a pet."

Unable to resist, I gurgled out, "I am not an animal!"

Mel growled, but his expression didn't match the depth of the anger in the sound. He was quiet for awhile, refusing to look at me, and I wondered if I'd seriously offended him. After a sigh, he snorted out a laugh and looked over at me, his expression mild. I gave a harmless smile but couldn't resist ribbing him some more.

"So you don't need rabies shots? You're not micro-chipped?"

"I'm not micro anything." Despite the limitations of his seatbelt, he gave a thrust of his hips. "Come on over, I'll show you."

"Down boy," I ordered, still grinning. Mel shook his head, relaxed his pelvis. We both went silent as we drove back toward his brother's private driveway. Finally, he spoke.

"So how do we get around this blood test thing?"

"I have no idea," I admitted. "Couldn't we just pretend we didn't hear her? And I could eat breakfast? And one of the chocolate bars I have stashed in my bag? Or *two* of the chocolate bars I have stashed in my bag?"

Mel shook his head. "I don't think that'll fly."

"I honestly thought you'd be able to pull something out of your ear. You know, like paying a baby to get pee for a drug test."

"I don't think you actually pay the baby."

"You pay the baby or it breaks your legs. Babies are bad-ass."

"You're thinking of gorillas," Mel corrected.

"Well, then where can we get gorilla blood tests?"

"I have no idea," Mel said, going with my bit like it wasn't absurd. "I don't generally have this problem."

My phone buzzed in my pocket and I lifted my hips to slide it out of my jeans. Mel gave an appreciative nod at the arch of my back and probably the way my own hips were thrust his way.

"That's more like it," he purred. Shushing him, I sat back down, glanced at the phone, saw it was a text from my brother.

It's official! I don't have Ebola!

I let out an uneven sound of excitement, waved the phone about. Mel glanced over at me, cynicism naked on his face.

"What? Did you win the lottery?"

"My brother! He just had blood tests!"

"I don't think they'll accept that as a replacement for us refusing our own. Here, Dr. Creepazoid," Mel intoned, "Have my wife's brother's blood tests as a replacement for mine and so that she doesn't have to feel guilty for eating a stack of pancakes the size of a baby elephant."

"No," I hissed, though I liked the idea of that many pancakes, especially smothered in syrup. "We can say they're yours!"

"I can't use those. They'll think we're from Arkansas."

"It's not a DNA test, it's, like, cholesterol or something. My brother can get us his files and I'm sure we can fudge them, slap your name on or whatever and fax them over. You've got Photoshop, right?"

"I most certainly do not. What am I, some sort of nerd?"

"You're not smart enough to be a nerd."

"I take great pictures," Mel asserted over my insult. "No doctoring needed. Just look at me."

Ignoring the Disney villain smile he threw my way, I rolled my eyes. I knocked out a quick text to my brother and he got back to me surprisingly quickly. I hit the call button and put the phone to my ear, miming to Mel to shut up.

"Thom!" I cried when he answered.

"Hey, Chipmunk, what's up?"

"Chipmunk?" Mel quipped. I hit him.

"I need copies of your medical records from your appointment. Just the stuff that says you're plague-free."

"Why in the world would you need those?"

"It's for the thing I'm doing. We need medical records but I can't get them … where I am."

"Where are you? I thought you were just helping a friend."

"Okay—I—look. I swear I'll tell you when I get back but I can't right now. I just need medical records and can't really explain why over the phone."

"Are you conning insurance companies again? I thought you'd gone straight and given up your life of crime. Think of the children!" I shook my head, laughing at the reminder that, while Thom is much sweeter and more mature than me, we are definitely related.

"Can you get them, send them to me, or not?"

Thomas chuckled and I heard a door shut in the background. My mother's voice cried out, addressing her baby boy. I felt a little stab of nerves catch me in the chest, speeding up my heart. I must've made a sound because Thomas snorted.

"I'll send you what you need, but I'm bringing mom and dad with me to Seattle if I visit."

"What?" I wheezed. Mel glanced over at me, his brows up as he listened to our conversation. "You can't do that."

"That's the deal." Moving the phone away from his lips, he called out, "I'm in here, Mom! I'm talking to—"

"Okay, okay!" I gave in, knowing that any conversation with my mother was going to end up being much longer than I could handle at that moment. "Fine, bring them. I'll get really stoned and then dad and I'll get along just fine."

"Never mind, mom!" Thomas called, before getting back to me. "Gimme a few hours, I'll email them over. You can get email where you are, right? On the lam? Cheese'in it from the heat? Hiding from the long arm of the law? Hoofing it—"

"Goodbye Thom," I grumbled, hanging up before he started spitting slang at me he'd learned in other countries.

"Chipmunk?" Mel asked. I hit him again as we pulled up in front of the house. I grabbed my bag this time, climbing out of the car and staring at the front door like it was threatening to eat me.

"Is there any way I can get half my payment now?" I asked, thinking of the hectic emotional din inside. The puppies were cute, Julian and Sarah nice enough, but they were still werewolves, still kinda similar to slamming a hearty stein full of club soda and having it bubble up into your nose.

Mel nodded, glanced at me as he made his way toward the door.

"Sure, Sarah's the one who made them."

"What?" I demanded, rushing to catch up. "Here? This Sarah? The cupcakes are here?"

"Inside with the puppies, yep. Come on, Chipmunk."

Apparently I was a few days too late to actually eat cupcakes, but Sarah promised me she'd make more before long. I almost cried when I found out there was no spongy, chocolate rescue available but she encouraged me to play with the kids and it was actually pretty fun.

Walter, Clara, Lorelai, and Christian seemed to prefer being puppies to being kids, but Oliver and Jeremy stayed clothed and human for the three hours we hung out. When back in human form for a snack, Christian managed to grow the hair on top of his head just enough that he had eyebrows and a lopsided Mohawk. Lorelai lectured him in her tiny voice, but he mostly stared at the ceiling, making it clear that he was bored as could be.

Once naptime rolled around, their emotions had died down among the blocks, toy trucks, dolls, and stuffed animals and I could barely tell I was surrounded by anything other than human children.

"Come on guys," Sarah urged. Lorelai growled her mother's way and I had to fight the laughter threatening to explode out of my chest. Sarah glared her down and Lorelai relented, lowering her head and slinking after her mom with her tail literally between her legs. Walter nipped at her ear as he stumbled along next to her and she yipped, chomping his snout before shoulder-checking him to the ground.

As Jeremy reached his brother, he helped him to his feet and they all padded down the hallway. Curious, I followed the puppy parade, finding a long hallway with three small rooms on each side. The kids ignored these rooms, moving straight to the end of the hall to a giant master bedroom. There was a bed against the back wall, but most of the floor was taken up with fluffy blankets, pillows, and opened sleeping bags. One by one, the kids dropped onto pillows, yawned, and promptly passed out.

Lorelai was the only one who found a pillow, circled it once, and then dropped down, spreading her back legs out behind her and tucking her front legs under her breast.

"Nap time, Lor," Sarah said. Lorelai let out a sharp, quick bark and Sarah smiled. I felt a burst of affection bubble out of her before she dropped to her knees and crawled over to her daughter, kissing her on the top of her head. Lorelai let out a small, happy yip, before giving in to a yawn and dropping her head onto the floor. Sarah sat up and surveyed her kids.

I had to admit, it was an adorable sight, despite the underlying strangeness of knowing I was staring at a wee pack of werewolves.

Sarah and I spent a few minutes watching twitchy legs and wiggling noses before she got to her feet and motioned for me to follow. We reached the kitchen and I slammed to an uncomfortable halt when I found Julian had pulled his shirt off and was unbuttoning his pants.

"Ah! Sorry," I said, turning around. Sarah took a step back so she was facing me and smiled encouragingly.

"You're fine."

"I'm … is he getting naked?"

"We're going for a run," I heard Mel say from behind me as if that should allay all my embarrassment. He stepped into my field of view and yanked his shirt over his head, doing a little dance with his hips. Immediately I felt my cheeks go red. Sarah's gaze darted between us and then she glanced over at her husband with a look I couldn't decipher. Her emotions said she found the situation funny but the married look was in a language I'd not managed to pick up in my year of being a wife. Mel's hand went to his pants and the idea of him stripping bare made me panic even more so than usual.

"Are you taking the necklace off?" I demanded, pointing. He froze, hand stalled on his jeans, before he dropped his gaze to the floor.

"I hadn't even thought about it."

"You can't take it off around me."

"But—"

"I will die. Then I will kill you."

Sidestepping our beef, Sarah slipped out of view. I heard denim shuffling, a few grunts and the sounds of joints popping and creaking before I turned to find Sarah standing next to a jet-black wolf nearly as tall as she was. He was skinny, with big ears, brown eyes gone slightly golden, and one white paw.

Julian shook himself out, gave his wife's hip a nudge and then loped across the room toward the wall of windows spanning the back of the living room. Sarah, still holding Julian's clothes, looked between Mel and me.

"What's going on?"

"That necklace he's wearing, it dams up his emotions. If he takes it off around me, I pass out."

"Oh dear," Sarah said. Moving to the doorway at the top of the basement stairs, she dropped the clothes onto the floor and then stepped closer. "You can't take it off, Mel."

"But I want to run!" Mel whined. He dropped his arms to the side and I found myself noticing that the button on his jeans was open, revealing a hairless belly button. Come to think of it, all of his chest and belly were smooth as Christian's bald head, pre-Mohawk.

"Can you loosen it?"

"It's not a long cord; I don't think it'll fit around my neck."

"Well, then you're grounded, Mister," Sarah said matter-of-factly. Mel looked between us, before his lip pulled up in a snarl. Julian appeared behind him, silent despite his nails and the wooden floor. Mel seemed to sense something only just before his brother tackled him, knocking him to the ground. They wrestled and growled and I jumped back to avoid getting caught by one of Mel's bare feet. Sarah sighed, a grin creeping onto her face.

"Boys," she said once again.

"If you get far enough away before you, um." I paused, unsure what to call it. "Are ... wolf-shaped? It probably won't bother me."

Mel put a hand to the floor and tried to get up, but Julian grabbed his arm between his teeth, worrying it until Mel toppled. More growling ensued before Julian managed to hop out of Mel's reach and bound toward the back doors, not silent at all this time.

"I'll do that." Faster than I could protest, Mel dropped his pants and turned to run naked after his brother. I stared after them in shock before turning to face Sarah.

"That may have been the weirdest thing I've ever experienced." Amending, I shook my head. "Maybe not weirder than being attacked by a vampire."

"Well, get used to it. They turn into big puppies when they're together. You get Colter around and it somehow doubles in intensity."

"Colter?"

"Their younger brother. Don't even ask about Lyla. She's ... well, think Lorelai, but bigger and much meaner. Come on, let's sit." Sarah jerked a thumb toward where the boys had run off. "Mel hasn't told you anything about the family?"

"We don't ... talk."

Sarah lifted a brow and I got the impression she was wondering if we did other things to each other with our lips. I elaborated before she could get any wild pictures in her head.

"We're mostly friendly, but he's hard to have around for all sorts of reasons. I try to stay away from him as much as possible, honestly."

"That's too bad. He seems fond of you." She pushed the door until it was wide open enough that it wouldn't swing closed and we stepped onto the covered deck. I heard a sharp yelp from the forest beyond the wide porch and tried to discern if I could see anything in the trees. Sarah took a seat on a fat, wicker chair and tucked her legs under her. I took a seat on the couch across from her, avoiding the sunny side.

"He's fond of terrorizing me, that's about it."

"Hmm," she said, turning to look out in the forest. I noticed her right ear twitch as she stared. A smile spread over her mouth and she turned back to me. "When he was here the last few weeks, he talked a lot about you."

"That's because I got his fake mate killed. He was here?"

"Yeah, he showed up on our doorstep out of his mind with grief, babbling about losing the one woman he'd ever loved. Once he got out the whole story, we realized what had happened and Julian gave him the appropriate amount of shit for sleeping with a succubus. He recovered, things are good."

"Ah, wow. I just figured he'd flown himself to Hawaii to drown his sorrows in coconut shell covered boobs."

Sarah let out a giggle and shook her head.

"We are the worst before we settle down, aren't we?" she asked. I tipped my head, confused.

"We? It's not just the men?"

"Oh, god no. Oh no." She laughed, shaking her head and waving her arms as if the concept needed to be swatted away heartily. "No, no. Definitely not. You haven't met Lyla, right? No, of course not. Or their mother! She has stories that would make your vagina throw up a white flag and surrender."

"Not his father?"

"Oh, their father is human. That's why they're different ages. Much less chance of multiple births with one human parent." Sarah's lip quirked and I felt something fizz out of her that made me nervous. When she spoke again, I knew I was right to be. "So you don't have to worry about him knocking you up with a dozen babies."

"I don't have to worry because I would never sleep with that the stupid—er—I mean—"

"No, it's okay," Sarah said, laughing. "He can be kind of a dick. *I* love him and he's incredible with the kids, but he loves to tease. It's why I don't mind Julian knocking him around when they roughhouse."

"You don't roughhouse?"

"Oh, I'll get in there with them, occasionally. I've kicked Mel's ass a time or two."

"Do tell!" I demanded gleefully. Sarah threw back her head and laughed before launching into a story about the first time she'd spent the night at Julian's, when he was still living at home.

"So, little did I know that Mel'd woken up early and I'd left the bathroom door cracked open. He was fifteen, he was gonna look, you know?"

"He hadn't seen you, like, go wolf?"

"He had. Modesty isn't the same as with humans—as I'm sure you've noticed. It's just a … different … Well." Sarah squinted, like she'd been confronted with a question with an answer so obvious she'd never thought she'd have to answer. "It's not the same, right? Like how a doctor would look at a patient versus how that same doctor would look at a significant other? Maybe? Man, I don't even know if that makes sense."

"I think I get it. Like lingerie versus a bathing suit? They're both revealing a lot, but one's presented in a specific context."

"Yeah, that's kind of it. So, I was showering, and he was being a teenage pervert. I smelled him of course, as soon as the water was off, and it wasn't that I minded him seeing me naked exactly, because it was all stuff he'd seen before, but I still felt he needed to be smacked around. Mel was still skinny, hadn't grown into his giant head yet."

I started laughing at that image, picturing Mel with a big fat parade-float head, and Sarah paused to let me catch my breath.

"You okay?" she asked with a chuckle. I clapped a hand over my mouth, stifling the laughter that still wanted to come out, and she continued. "Well, I whooped him and he was yowling, crying, begging for mercy. Woke up the whole house, and I was still naked but no one noticed or thought I was in the wrong. I think Lyla set on him after I finished, just because he was weak and she saw a chance to strike. Their mother went and made coffee, their father started breakfast. It was awhile before Mel would even look my way unless I was covered in either clothing or fur. Sometimes I swear he still flinches if I turn the shower on."

This was turning into the best afternoon of my life.

Six

An hour passed, during which I learned many amazing and embarrassing things about teenaged Mel. Sarah promised to show me pictures that would be just as humiliating but wanted to do so while he was around for maximum effect. As Sarah shifted in her seat to untuck her legs and sit up straighter, Oliver appeared at the door, rubbing his knuckles against his eye. Without a word, he moved to his mother, climbed into her lap and hooked a hand into her shirt. She kept talking as if nothing had changed, and Oliver yawned and promptly passed out.

As his hand dragged the neckline of her shirt down, I found myself inappropriately curious about things that were none of my business. Remembering that she'd had no issues with me seeing her husband naked, I decided I might as well ask.

"How did you nurse so many kids?" I asked, when she finished speaking. She shrugged a shoulder.

"Like any mother who has multiples. I don't gain any more teats in wolf form, but they seemed to be hungry on slightly different schedules so it was fine."

"Is it rude for me to ask?"

Sarah just shook her head. "Nah. I'd rather you ask questions than make stupid assumptions."

One of the puppies stumbled through the door, yawning hugely, before moving to her mother and sitting down at her feet. When Sarah didn't immediately address her, Lorelai gave a sleepy bark that trailed into another yawn.

Out of nowhere, Julian came bounding out of the forest, hopped the two stairs onto the deck and barreled toward his wife and kids. Lorelai glanced over, letting out a shocked yelp and dropping backward as her father came to a stop, ears forward, tail wagging. Oliver stayed sound asleep, mouth open against Sarah's chest. Julian stood poised over his daughter as she struggled to right herself, tail and legs flailing wildly. She gave an angry growl and he promptly dropped to his belly, licking along her face and neck. This only made her struggle harder, trying to bark through the onslaught of slimy love. I couldn't help but laugh at the tiny explosions of frustration coming from her wiggly limbs.

More werewolves approached, the kids from the house and Mel from the forest. He strolled by, back in human form, completely naked and almost hairless. I tried my best not to stare, but he was pretty good looking so I wasn't at all successful. Julian stayed on the ground, repeatedly grabbing Lorelai when she'd escape his grip and pulling her back to the ground so he could kiss her more. Walter snuck in, tucking himself timidly between his father and sister, which seemed to appease the bigger wolf.

The commotion died down as Mel appeared on the porch again, wearing cotton pants low on his hips. He stood near me, hands on his hips, and surveyed the situation. Abruptly, as he opened his mouth to speak, Sarah sat up.

"Potty! Let's go! Julian," she said, her voice an order. He pushed to his feet, let out a commanding bark and turned to lope toward the forest. Lorelai, Walter, Christian and Clara followed him, still half-asleep, while Oliver and Jeremy stumbled back into the house after their mother. I frowned as I watched them go, turned to look up at Mel.

"Is it a thing to teach them to … go in the woods?"

"No, but it's kind of strenuous changing back into a person," Mel looked down at me and his forehead creased slightly. "You don't want them straining when they have to poop. It can get messy. So, until they're older, it's the woods for the pups."

"Ah," I said, uncomfortable. To distract myself from talk of baby werewolf poop, I reached up and ran a hand along Mel's arm. It was smooth, hairless. He watched me passively, not saying anything until I dropped my hand away.

"You have to concentrate every time you want hair on your body, or does it grow on its own?"

"Little of both."

"That's so much easier than waxing," I observed. Mel laughed, shrugged a shoulder.

"It is handy. Especially if you find a lady with a preference. I can be Grizzly Adams in two seconds flat, if that's what you're into."

"And you can just make yourself grow hair anywhere?" Immediately, I regretted the question. Mel watched me, a smirk on his face indicating his mind had gone straight to the gutter. Surprising me, he made a joke without working blue.

"I've never been to Denmark, but I assume I could grow hair there, too."

"Ah. Well …" I shook my head but, before I could stop myself, another question popped into my head. "And the hair all just falls out when you're person-shaped? You can't control it?"

"No, that we can't control. But, it biodegrades pretty quickly on its own if left out in the elements."

I snorted, shook my head. I had been picturing mounds of werewolf fur covering the forests of the Pacific Northwest, but apparently I didn't have to worry about such things. It occurred to me that this all explained why Mel had been missing his eyebrows when I'd tricked him into coming to my house to kill a succubus. Glancing up, I considered he'd managed to grow his hair to its normal length and fill in his brows until they were attractively thick. He didn't seem to think anything of my staring, so I said nothing.

Julian was the first to show up, the puppies trailing behind him. They were running in circles, nipping at each other and wagging tails. All the biting reminded me that I hadn't eaten in several hours. I slapped the back of my hand into Mel's leg.

"When do we eat?"

"Soon, I'd assume. Julian makes a mean venison steak—though not as good as mine."

Deliberately, Julian charged his brother, slamming his shoulder into Mel's gut and almost knocking him over. Lorelai attempted to copy the maneuver, but it wasn't nearly as effective; Mel just watched her with a grin as she rammed herself against his shin, whining and compacting with the impact.

Everyone filed back into the house where the kids spread out in the living room and Julian disappeared into the back room. When Sarah appeared, so did he, human and fully clothed.

Mel was true to his word; Julian cooked up a proper meal and everyone sat around the table, yelling, chatting, and eating. By the time it was over, the sun was dipping low and Sarah was bringing out the pictures she'd promised.

"Behold: Fifteen-year-old Mel."

"Gimme," I demanded, grabbing the photo album. Twenty-year-old Julian looked good, but I couldn't say the same for his younger brother. Mel didn't grab the book out of my hands and burn it, but he sat off to the side, rolling his eyes and glaring his sister-in-law down. Skinny with a big head, young Mel stared out of the picture next to his attractive, lean older brother. His hair had been longer, just about shoulder length, but thin and shapeless. His fashion sense had left a lot to be desired, as well.

Unable to resist, I snapped a picture with my phone, vowed to send it off to Chloe. As Mel announced that one picture was enough, I realized I'd somehow missed the sound of my brother's text message.

"Oh, he's already emailed me the results!" I announced. Mel, seeming relieved, nodded, pulled the giant album out of my lap. I grabbed for it, intending to keep it, but Mel was quicker. He set it on a high shelf at the far end of the room and then came back to me, reaching down and grabbing my hands. Without asking, he yanked me to my feet, dragged me toward the guest rooms.

"Well, let's see 'em, come on," Mel insisted, eager to use any excuse to get me away from the album. From behind the bar, Julian looked up from washing dishes as we passed, grinned at his brother.

"You have Wi-Fi?" I asked. Julian nodded, but didn't say anything.

Mel poked me in the ribs when I paused and Julian snorted, went back to cleaning up.

"Come on, come on," Mel chided. "The further you are from those pictures the better."

"I'm coming back for them," I said as he continued to shove gently at me. I pretended to fight, making him twist and block like how I imagine a really good game of basketball would be. Finally, he realized he had the advantage: he wrapped an arm around my thighs, tossing me over his shoulder, and carrying me through the door of the bedroom. The action shocked me enough that I wasn't really sure how to react. Sure it was probably demeaning to be carried around like a sack of potatoes, but I'd never actually had it happen to me before, so I let it go.

The last thing I saw as we crossed the threshold was Julian smirking at me, like he knew something I didn't.

Mel set me down next to my bag, which was open on the floor at the foot of the bed, and stood between the door and me, arms crossed. I sighed, looking up into his blue eyes, considered making a break for it, just to annoy him. The look on his face made me think he kind of wanted me to try it. Rather than risk being trapped in his arms again, I dropped down, yanking my laptop out of the duffle, leaving its padded case on top of the pile of my clothes. I set it on the desk and waited for it to boot up as he came up behind me. I twisted enough to look up and really consider him.

"Are you really that embarrassed at pictures of you with a big head and bad hair?"

"Hey, my hair looked great."

"No, it didn't."

Mel rolled his eyes, gestured when my login screen came up. I typed in the password and then turned back to him.

"So I shouldn't send Chloe the picture? She and I shouldn't call you Big Head for the rest of your life."

"Do whatever you feel you need to do, Chipmunk."

I glowered but figured we were on even footing; it was mutually assured destruction. Mel spoke again as I saved the files from my email to my desktop, opened Photoshop.

"I just didn't get much—well, any—action back then."

"No!" I said sarcastically. "Really?"

"Hey, I get more than enough now to make up for it, now. More than more than enough, even. I mean, there's enough, and then—"

"I get it, you're a big slut."

"Damn straight."

I had to edit out my brother's weight and height and fix them to match Mel's, but I was pretty proud of the results after I was done. Mel sat behind me—giving me personal space, surprisingly—and ruthlessly critiqued when he didn't think something I was editing in looked natural. By the time we were done, we had printed the form out and I personally couldn't tell the difference from what Thomas had emailed me. Leaving the papers on the shelf next to my bag, I turned to face Mel.

"So what's the plan for the rest of this sham?"

"We get in there tomorrow, answer some questions, and hope we can get the guy to give us a tour."

"I don't think the tour will include the dungeon where he's keeping these people."

"No, but I'll be able to smell where they've been."

"How? You don't even know them."

"I have my ways," he said haughtily, nose to the sky. I rolled my eyes, glanced at the time and realized I'd been up for fifteen hours. I felt like I should have been more tired, but the puppy energy was still high and apparently getting to me.

"We should probably talk more about what we're saying in therapy," I said after a moment.

"Meaning?"

"Well, we got away with generalities today, but if he's even halfway decent, he's going to know there's nothing going on between us other than a general sense of disgust from me to you."

"That's why our marriage on the rocks, Muffin."

I rolled my eyes, moved to sit on the bed.

"That's not enough. He's going to want instances of good times, bad times, maybe even stories from our wedding. I was blindsided by the questions earlier—I wouldn't have been if you'd just agreed to discuss everything beforehand."

"So we'll make some up."

"On the spot? Just like that?"

"I'm that good."

"I'm not! Why don't you want to deal with this?"

"I'm really not that worried, Gwen. It'll be fine. We're not actually here to fix a marriage. We're here to find out if Doctor Whoever T. Sleazebag is holding two couples—at least—against their wills. We just need to do some snooping, which is, in case you hadn't noticed, what people pay me for. We'll probably be done in a day or two."

"But in that day or two we're going to be asked a lot of questions about our lives as a couple. I do this for a living, you don't."

"No, I do this for a living. You've never privately investigated anything except a jar of jelly beans. We'll push through our two sessions and just say we can't agree on how to fold the laundry or something. It'll be fine."

"I'm telling you, we're going to be found out."

"Found out? You think they're actively looking to find a pair of people paying them a fortune to pretend to be married? No one's going to be suspicious of us."

He probably had a point. It wasn't like we were going undercover in a foreign government trying to learn their launch codes. We were just a pair of people who were inclined to annoy the shit out of each other heading into an environment filled with couples who didn't get along.

"If in doubt," he said after a few moments, "just call me names and pick a fight. You're pretty good at being an ornery bitch."

I squinted at him over a snarl, but this time he had a point; there were very few things I was better at than insulting Mel.

"Okay, fine."

"Excellent." His gaze rolled to the side and it appeared for a second that he was listening to something. Finally, he looked back to me, giving me bedroom eyes that I did not appreciate, despite the fact that we were in fact in a bedroom. "Now, since you're so concerned he's going to be asking in depth questions, we should probably have sex in case he asks about that."

"I can just insult you, don't worry."

"Like I said, no one who can see what I look like would believe any straight woman would be dissatisfied with—"

"Get out," I interrupted, pointing at the door. Rather than pressing the issue, Mel laughed, getting up to leave. Shortly after he shut the door, he pushed it open again.

"I'm right in the next room in case you change your mind!"

I threw a shoe at him, but it only hit the hastily shut door.

Seven

I woke to the smell of eggs and sizzling meat and my stomach demanded I haul my ass out of bed and attack the food like Lorelai so frequently attacked her brothers. It was only after I stepped back into the bedroom from the attached bathroom that I realized I wasn't allowed to eat. I growled into the empty room but it sounded more pathetic than usual after being in a house full of wolves.

So, I settled on mumbling a string of curse words as I dug through my bags for shower supplies.

I felt marginally better after I'd cleaned and dressed myself and even better after I got out to the living area and surrounded myself with the feelings of glee and satiation floating around. I had never considered hanging out with people who were full as a way to diet before, but it occurred to me then.

Too bad I couldn't bottle my empathy and sell the sensations to overweight housewives who had as much interest in eating right and exercising as I did. As I sidled up to the kitchen bar, Julian handed me a glass of water and smiled.

"Mel's up and ready, I think. He said you couldn't eat, so I tried to feed the kids before you were awake."

"It's fine. I'm feeling okay, actually." I said. Julian just nodded, sidestepped as Christian chased Walter through the open kitchen and back around the wall into the living room. Mel appeared shortly after, watching the kids with a goofy grin on his face. I wondered what his emotions would have said at that moment, but I probably could have guessed on my own.

"Ready?" Mel asked, turning to face me. I shrugged a shoulder, took a giant gulp of water and slid off the barstool. We were in the car and on our way within minutes.

"I am not looking forward to letting Creepy stab me with needles."

"It'll probably be his assistant. I doubt he does the dirty work on his own."

"Maybe. Either way, I'm not digging the idea."

"I can sit in there, hold your hand, whisper words of encouragement in your ear."

"You'll just whisper words about your dick."

"Huge," Mel whispered. "Fantastic, beautiful."

"Disappointing, clumsy, pencil-thin," I whispered back. Mel just laughed, keeping his eyes on the road.

We'd barely even gotten in the door of the facility before Rhonda had me by the arm and was dragging me down the hallway we'd walked for our consultation. Mel stayed on my heels, making it look casual, and Rhonda glanced his way, a small smile hiding the spike of irritation I felt from her. She settled us into a room halfway down the hall, wrapping a blood pressure cuff over my arm. Before she started, Mel got her attention, handing her the pages we'd printed out the night before.

"See? I'm healthy as a horse. If there's any physical dysfunction in the relationship, it's all my dear wife's fault."

"Oh, I'm sure she's fine." Rhonda set the pages on the counter, putting her back to Mel as she squeezed my arm uncomfortably in the name of science.

"She eats terribly. I don't know how she stays so averagely sized," Mel said. I leaned over to glare at him around Rhonda's hip and he winked. After announcing that my blood pressure was on the high end of normal, she looked between us both before her gaze fell on Mel. She watched him for a moment and I felt that annoyance in her again, before it rapidly changed to a small bubble of surprise. A smile fixed itself across her lips.

"Mr. Somerset, will you come with me? We can take care of the insurance paperwork and the payment, and we can unpack your luggage."

"Luggage?" I asked. Rhonda glanced at me, nodded.

"Yes, we have your room all set."

"Oh, we're not staying here," Mel said. Shock shot through her psyche like cracks in an expensive vase and her eyes widened.

"Excuse me? Aren't you here for the retreat?"

"We have a place nearby, with my family. We won't need to trouble you."

"But it's part of the program," she said, her voice a touch high. "We monitor your sleep patterns, see how you interact with each other while unconscious. That's what Doctor Coontz had you down for. I'm afraid it's a whole different set of paperwork if you're only here for counseling."

"That seems like overkill," I said. Rhonda turned to me sharply and I felt it. Rubbing a hand over my cheek, where it stung like she'd slapped me, I tried to give her my least threatening smile. Mel took her hand in his, smiled down at her.

"I spoke with, I believe it was, Doctor Howard before even making the consultation. She said that not all couples go quite as deep as that with the therapy, that it would be perfectly acceptable to stay outside the facility for the program."

She paused, displeased at his answer, but relaxing visibly. There was still a trace of annoyance there, but she calmed enough that I no longer worried she might truss us both up and shove us in a closet. I was getting the feeling Rhonda was a little Type A, especially when it came to her job.

Giving a small nod, she glanced at the clock on the wall of the small examination room and reached for the door, still holding Mel's hand.

"I've let the doctor know you're here, so someone from his team will be right with you, Ms. Arthur. Mr. Somerset, please follow me."

Mel gave me a supportive grin as they left me alone in the small room. I dug my phone out of my pocket, but found I had no signal. I stared impotently at it for about a minute, before I realized I was starting to feel woozy. Swallowing, I lifted my head, looking to the ceiling as if maybe it would be steadier than the suddenly spinning wall ahead of me.

I had no idea what was going on, but it wasn't pleasant. No longer was I just sitting in a waiting room prepping to be tested for Vitamin X deficiency, I was suddenly recovering from getting drunk and strapping myself in upside down on a tilt-o-whirl. I hadn't felt that dizzy in years, but I couldn't control the feeling, no matter what I did.

"Ohhh god," I mumbled, squeezing my eyes shut and trying to steel myself against whatever the hell was making me list to the side. The door opened as my shoulder hit the wall and I turned to find an absolutely gorgeous, woman-shaped creature enter the room. I couldn't have told you what gave it away that she wasn't human, especially in the midst of my brainless, hangover-esque episode of nausea, but something in me could tell she looked human but that was about as far as it went.

She looked about my height, with dark hair pulled back in an elaborate twist. Her body was airbrushed-in-a-nudey-magazine perfect, even under the plain white shirt, jeans and white physician's jacket. I caught sight of her teeth as she smiled at me and I had the strange desire to ask her if she'd like to take a bite of me. When she spoke, her voice was low, flowing out of her full lips like a fine wine.

"Ms. Arthur, I'll be administering your blood tests today." She moved through a hazy wiggle in my field of view to the cabinet, picked up the test results Rhonda had sat down. Making vague sounds of approval, she looked the page over, set it down. I watched her as she turned to look me over, smiled. My eyes went even blurrier and I wondered why she had so damn many eyeballs.

Turning back to the cabinet, the woman pulled out some capped needles, clear, colorfully-topped tubes, and a strip of rubber. I just watched her, still feeling like I'd taken some really bad drugs, and trying to keep myself upright. Her emotions were pleasant, mild, but off. My empathy was so confused by the feeling of drowning in dizziness, I couldn't tell what we were feeling yet, but it didn't really matter. I tried as hard as I could to separate her emotions from mine as she took my arm, tied it off, and then crouched down. Ultimately I failed and was left wondering what it was she'd asked me that left her smiling pleasantly from inches away.

"Okay," I said, as she gently tipped my head up to look at the ceiling. I didn't have it in me to fight whatever was happening, but it was just blood tests, so I probably didn't have to think about it too hard. I needed to focus on not passing out from vertigo and the feeling of my flailing guts.

Time passed and I stayed seated, sick out of my mind, unaware of needles or blood loss or anything other than the way the dots in the ceiling panels danced in front of me. When she took my chin in her hand again and tipped my face down to look at her, I felt a sloppy grin split my lips. Numbness was creeping along my body, taking over like it would when I'd had contact with Mel for too long without the necklace protecting me from his emotions. The relief of no longer feeling like any small movement might spill my innards all over the floor was incredible.

"Are you feeling alright?" she asked. This time, I understood her enough to nod. My head didn't want to come back up out of the down position, but chin to chest was a good position to notice at the wad of cotton taped to my elbow.

"Don't take that off for a few days, okay? We should have your test results before too long. Come now," she said, sliding around to stand next to me. Five or six arms gripped me, pulling me to my feet and holding me steady as we moved toward the door. My whole body felt cradled in the wobbly gelatin of being so close to the inhuman nurse-type not-person.

I glanced over into her lovely face, let her lead me along as I considered that she really only had one set of eyes. What had I been thinking before? Six or eight eyes? Get outta here, Gwen, you're drunk.

"Okay," I said in response to nothing, as she pulled the door open for me and let me go. Surprisingly, I didn't topple without the support as she nudged me out into the hallway.

"Down the hall to the left, you'll find Dr. Coontz. Run along." I turned to catch sight of her again, found the door was shut in my face. I have no idea how long I stood staring at the cream-colored wood, but I felt warm hands on my shoulders before my body was turned around and I was staring into Mel's frowning face.

"What happened?"

"What?" I asked. Mel shook me and the fuzzy stupor about me receded, leaving me feeling solid and aware. "What?" I asked again. Mel let go of my arms, shoved open the door to the exam room and peered inside. The beautiful woman and her confusing emotions were gone, but the fact that I'd been standing in front of the only way into the room didn't occur to me.

"What happened?"

"Just blood tests. Wow. I think not eating really affected me. I feel dizzy and sick."

"Well. They promised to make sure to have juice and cookies in the room."

"Cookies?" I perked up, wiggling my jaw as the feeling in it came back in a rush of needles. Relief at not feeling sick stopped me from complaining, even when Mel grabbed me and practically dragged me down the hall.

The second we were in the room I made a mad dash for the tray of cookies on the coffee table. I didn't even notice that Dr. Coontz was standing along the back wall, fiddling with a gadget that shortly after started emitting a low, comforting style of music usually reserved for massages and acupuncture. My hands full of plain shortbread, I turned to face him, stuffing one into my mouth whole and chewing with my mouth open. Dr. Coontz smiled at me, barely sparing a glance for Mel.

"Good morning, Gordon," Mel said from the door, his tone a bit more forceful than was necessary. Gordon took half a second to watch me shove another cookie in my mouth, before turning to give Mel a small smile

"Mr. Somerset, hello. Are we ready to begin?"

"I was wondering if we could get a tour of the facilities at all, before we do."

"Oh, yes of course." Turning to me, he gave me a small smile. "Are you ready now, Gwen?"

"Sure," I said through a mouthful of cookie. He blinked at me and I felt a thin stab of irritation, but he didn't let it show on his face. I moved to Mel before the doctor could try to come lead me by hand and we moved into the hallway. Gordon stepped out, shut the door, and gestured to show us that we'd be walking back toward the reception area.

He babbled on as we walked, describing the rooms to either side of us; they were a mix of exam rooms like the one I'd been in and counseling rooms like the one in which we'd met with the doctor. Out in the reception area, he showed us to the small kitchen, explained that it was primarily for reception use: coffees, teas, and refreshments. He promised us that the center had state of the art kitchen facilities in one of the other buildings and that it would be where all the meals would be prepared.

The hallway at the other end of the reception area led to another hallway with exam rooms and sitting rooms, and at the end of that hall was a wide door that led out onto a back deck overlooking a beautiful garden. Mel hung back at one of the doors in the hallway, pretending to be fiddling with his sock, but the way he leaned toward the door made me think he'd noticed something.

When we got outside, Coontz explained that many of the group therapy sessions took place out in the garden area. There were two other large buildings past the long gardens and low-hedges.

"These are some of our private quarters, where those couples who choose the *full* experience we offer stay with us," Dr. Coontz said, turning to face us. The smile on his rough face was tight, and he swallowed thickly before giving a nod and gesturing back to the building.

"We do also have sleeping quarters upstairs, where we ask couples to stay for one night each week so that we can monitor sleep patterns and sleep activities. I wish you would allow us at least one night to make sure you are making effective use of your nocturnal time together." I caught Mel's gaze in my peripheral vision but I didn't look over at him; I knew he was giving me some sort of eyebrow wag and possibly a lewd gesture with his tongue and I didn't want to encourage him.

I ate cookies and juice and let Mel do most of the talking during the first session of the day. The doctor asked more questions, many of them questions I'd asked my own patients from time to time. His emotions stayed bland for the most part, but his eyes lingered on the cotton on my elbow. It was preferable to him staring at my boobs or even my face, though, so I didn't make a stink about it. After an hour of Mel showing off his surprisingly convincing improv skills, the doctor checked his watch.

"Looks like it's time for the group trust building exercise." He stood, looked between us, and brushed a hand over the side of his wiry hair. This did nothing to tame it. "I understand you're refusing to stay here with us at night, but I wish you would reconsider. It really is helpful to the process."

"Group trust-building, you said?" Mel asked, a pleasant smile on his face. Gordon looked him over and I felt irritation bubble up. After a moment, he nodded.

"Yes, I'll show you out, if you're ready to go?" I nodded, but grabbed for the last cookie on the tray. I'd drained the lemonade jug twice, but the doctor had been quick on the draw to get it refilled any time it dipped below half-full. The cookies, however, hadn't been addressed, forcing me to do my best to make them last.

Mel watched me with a certain amount of affection on his face as I crammed the crumbly shortbread into my mouth, before getting to his feet and holding out a hand to pull me to my feet. Cookies clutched in my right hand, I gave him my left, let him tug me up. Trust-building exercises sounded interesting and definitely better than sitting in the tiny room listening to Mel drone on about how our sex life had been at the beginning of our marriage compared to now.

I munched on my treats as the doctor led us down the hall, away from the reception area and out to a large, well-maintained garden with three other straight pairs and one gay couple. They all milled about on the grass, near each other, but not making conversation. I recognized one of the pairs as the man and woman Mel had embarrassed the day before, when he'd compared me to a lion. Dr. Coontz joined four other doctors at the top of the steps leading up to the porch, and addressed the crowd.

"Good morning, everyone. This is the first of five group sessions we'll be having this week here at Tough Love. This morning, we will be working on building trust." Dr. Coontz babbled on about the importance of being open and honest, and maybe about Transformers or something. He could have been talking about anything at all and I wouldn't have registered what he'd said.

I honestly tuned out as I scanned the other couples. Two of them looked to be about our age and the women had matching cotton balls tucked into their elbows like I did. The one older couple and the two men looked untouched. I wondered why us young women were the only ones being subjected to needles and starvation. As he finished his speech, Gordon left the deck to come back down to us; his fellow doctors did the same, joining their couples.

"We're going to start with something simple: eye contact. Eye contact is quite intimate, whether you may think it so or not. Now, everyone turn to face your partner." Couples shuffled on the grass, turning to face each other as the doctors began to mill about. Dr. Coontz stayed near us, watching us intently. I noticed that odd excitement come from him again and I felt myself shuffle, shying away from it. Mel reached out, grabbing my hands and holding them tightly. I glanced over just as Dr. Coontz reached toward my face.

I wasn't quick enough to pull away and before I knew it, his dry fingers were on my chin, turning my face so I was facing Mel squarely. Mel, however, was looking at the doctor and he did not look pleased, but I didn't know if he was unhappy with me for looking elsewhere or with Coontz for touching me.

"Now, I want you to look into each other's eyes for sixty seconds. Everyone ready?" A murmur went through the crowd and the doctor shifted so that he could see past us. Pulling a stopwatch out of his pocket, he hit the button.

Mel and I stood in the grass in silence. It started out fine, but quickly became uncomfortable. A ripple of nervous amusement ran through the crowd, pushing a giggle out of my chest. Mel smiled at me as I laughed and I fought the urge to move my gaze to his lips. His eyes, while very pretty, were somewhat intimidating. He seemed unbothered by the supposed intimacy and I found myself pretty jealous of how calm he seemed.

Finally, the doctor announced that sixty seconds was up and we could look away. Mel didn't. I started to but decided that, if he could handle it so could I. We continued to hold hands and stare as everyone around us shuffled and spoke. Gordon noticed us playing chicken and he stepped up next to us and glanced between Mel and me. Jealousy welled up within him, an oily, caustic sensation that made me flinch and break eye contact to glance over.

"Very good," he said, his tone bland and not matching the unpleasantness I could feel within him. "It looks like intimacy isn't your problem. Perhaps this next test will be more of a challenge."

We went through more trust-building exercises that I minded much less than the staring contest. I had no worry that Mel wouldn't catch me as I fell or that he was going to lead me astray in the maze, despite the fact that I was blindfolded. We'd been through enough together that, even though I couldn't stand his presence without the necklace, I'd at least gotten to know him as a decent dude. Before we'd gotten abducted by a demon and whammied by a succubus together, I wouldn't have trusted him to hold a few pennies for me, let alone stand at my back and make sure my ass didn't hit the ground. With his emotions dammed up by magic, though, our usual bickering was fun rather than excruciating.

After nearly an hour, we broke for a ninety-minute lunch and I nearly wept with joy at the idea of free food. Mel had other ideas, though, and smuggled me out of the garden, away from all the couples that were lining up for the buffet.

"But!" I whined, as he pushed me toward the side of the building. "I'm hungry!"

"Oh?" he asked, pausing near the side gate. A grin filled his face and he gave me a wink, moving his hand to the button on his jeans. "You want something in your mouth, do you?"

"I have spontaneously lost my appetite. Forever."

"Then my work here is done," he said, shifting to yank the gate open and shove me through in one smooth motion. We got to his car and he leaned in, fishing around in the backseat. I stared up at the house, smelling the food I wasn't going to be allowed to eat and considered audibly pouting. Mel popped up, his arms tucked in the car, as he glanced around intently. Satisfied with whatever he heard or saw, he pulled back completely, slammed the door and came back around to me.

"Come on, let's go for a walk."

"No food, *and* you're making me exercise? I want a divorce."

"Hush," he said, leading me around the side of the bushes hedging in the parking area. He moved quickly until we were nearly out of line of sight of the center, and then he slowed.

"What are we doing?"

"Sleuthing. Investigating. Poking around." Still moving, he turned to give me a lascivious eyebrow wag. "Unless you want me to do some *poking around*."

"I'd probably be the one sleuthing just to locate your junk."

"That's harsh," he said, pulling away. For a split second, I though I'd actually insulted him, but he'd moved to the edge of the tree line to investigate what looked like a clump of moss, and didn't look at all affected by my dig. Unabashed, he shoved his nose against the tree, took a deep whiff and then pulled back, shaking his head.

"Dammit, I can't tell."

"Can't tell what?"

"If it's the Bishops."

"Are we playing chess all of a sudden?"

Mel glanced over at me before shaking himself out of whatever his thought process was.

"No, the first couple I was hired to find, they're the Bishops. This might be her, but the smell's degraded enough that I need my snout to tell for sure."

"So … you know. Grow it out."

He glared my way and we once again made eye contact. I gave in and giggled, this time, but it was mainly because he looked so irritated with me.

"I'm not going to walk around in broad daylight with wolf-face. We'll have to come back later and check."

"So I can go eat?" Mel let out a dramatic sigh and, because of the necklace, I couldn't tell if it was real or not.

"Yes. You can go eat."

The food was a wash. I was starving, so it satisfied my growling belly, but it was all vegetables and lean, white meat that was baked instead of fried. The brochure Mel had given me that I had pretended to peruse but actually just barely glanced at had mentioned something about catering to dietary restrictions. Perhaps I should've requested a restriction from healthy food to see if they'd serve me cake and fried Oreos from then on.

Mel and I separated at the end of the serving line, each heading to opposite ends of the large, sunny cafeteria. I hunkered down next to a couple who looked about ten years older than me and had all the hallmarks of a pair of people who had passed the point of no return, marriage-wise.

They weren't talking, the wife had aimed her body subtly away from the husband, and he was thrumming with boredom. Everything pumping off of him made me feel like a kid stuck inside being forced to watch the whole neighborhood play in the pool on a sunny summer day.

"Hey," I said, plopping down into one of the empty seats at their table, grinning amiably at each of them in turn. The wife, surprised at my appearance, sat up a little straighter, nervous suspicion popping like an exploding light bulb. I tried not to flinch as I took a bite of my unseasoned chicken breast.

"Afternoon," the man said, unbothered by the fact that I'd just intruded on what could have been a private moment between the two of them.

"You here for the whole shebang?" I asked, keeping my expression mild and pleasant. The husband nodded, holding out his hand, his own boiled, bland meal forgotten.

"Yeah, you? I'm Dustin, this is Alicia."

"Hi," Alicia said, still not feeling welcoming or chatty. She didn't outright tell me to get the hell off her little square of cafeteria property or anything, but she felt like the last thing she wanted to do was make conversation with some stranger who'd invited herself over without any warning whatsoever.

I'd seen this sort of grumpiness in my own clients and I was reasonably certain Dustin should start packing his things.

"Gwen," I said, moving on from Dustin's hand to offer to shake Alicia's. She reluctantly obliged but didn't say anything else. "You're staying here and everything?"

"Yeah, aren't you? I thought everyone had to."

"Nah, my brother-in-law lives close and, well, we don't, so the husband wanted to stay with them instead of here so they could catch up. We just drive over here each morning and do all the fun stuff during the day, and then head out later on. How's it been staying here?"

"It's okay," Dustin said with a shrug. "They try to get us to play games and watch movies and stuff at night, like we're at summer camp. Alicia would kill at Scrabble if she played, but she hasn't felt up to it lately."

"Oh no," I said sympathetically, turning my attention to her. "You think you're getting sick? Maybe you should ask one of the—who's your doctor? We got Coontz."

"Howard," Alicia said, a little scrape of her frustration chafing against me. "We interviewed with Coontz when we first got here, but he referred us to Howard *after* we'd signed up. It's a little ridiculous, since we signed up with him, not her."

"What's wrong with Howard?" I asked.

"Nothing," Dustin assured me, giving his wife a soft look of disapproval. "Don't be mean, hon. All the doctors are fine, we did research before we got here. 'Lish just wanted Coontz 'cuz he's been here the longest. Howard's pretty new."

"Maybe that's for the best. She's probably up on the latest studies and stuff," I encouraged, nudging Alicia's arm lightly with the back of my wrist, before taking another bite of my vegetables. Even the lame food was better than having to sit next to a couple whose marriage had disintegrated so quietly that only one of them could tell.

Dustin didn't seem like a bad guy, I told myself. He'd probably have a fine time on the dating scene once things were all said and done with Alicia. And, if not, he could always get a schnauzer.

"Maybe," Alicia said, before shaking her head. "I don't understand why Coontz decided to pass us along, though. I requested him specifically and he seemed happy enough with us until after the consultation. He told us we were in, to be ready for the retreat, and then when we showed up the first day, that Rhonda woman told us we'd been bumped."

"Aw, man," I said, feeling a little guilty. Had Mel and I been the reason for the bumping? I was gonna have to see if my fake husband had dug up anything specific about Coontz that would indicate why he'd wanted to help me and Mel more than Dustin and Alicia. It could have been as simple as a better vibe, but that didn't feel right. Something about Coontz felt inherently wrong, so my lizard brain was unwilling to believe he'd chosen us based on compatibility alone.

"Things are going well, though," Dustin said, though I could feel he didn't really believe it.

"You can tell so soon?" I asked, smiling encouragingly as a way of compensating for the fact that I kind of wanted to gather him close, pat his head, and mumble, "there, there. You'll find another fish in that vast sea some day."

"Well," Dustin amended, his jaw working for a moment before he shrugged and realized he was at a loss for words.

"Howard seems fine, is all," Alicia said, shifting in such a way that it seemed to close up her posture and pull her away from him.

Oh boy.

"Well, that's good. Coontz is okay, I guess. Kind of … intense," I said, settling on a word that hopefully wouldn't send them running screaming from the center. "He asks a lot of personal questions."

"Isn't that the point?" Dustin asked.

"Yeah, of course. I just mean, like," I floundered for an explanation that wouldn't make me sound stupid. "We're not ready to have kids, but he's brought it up a few times, you know? Just seems like it can't be the problem, so why keep mentioning it?"

"He asked us about that stuff, too. I don't want children, though," Alicia said, an edge to her voice making me think I'd accidentally dug up exactly what had crumbled their relationship. "Maybe he didn't want to help us because of that."

"You think?"

"Some people can be very biased against child-free individuals," Alicia asserted, her emotions burbling up in a rough and stale way that came off like she'd gone many rounds with many people over this same subject.

"Hon, I'm sure that's—"

"You are," Alicia said, rounding on Dustin.

"No, 'Lish, you know—"

"I'm not discussing this with you here. We can talk about it *in session*," Alicia said, grabbing her plate as she rocketed to her feet.

"Nice to meet you!" I called after her, feeling bad for causing so much trouble. Dustin twitched, at a loss for how to react. Realizing he was trying to be polite, I gestured after her.

"Don't worry about me, go chase her down."

"So-sorry," he stammered, taking off, leaving his plate alone at the table with me. I shoveled a few more mouthfuls of veg and chicken into my face, trying to shake off the awkwardness I'd just soaked in. It was empathically rough enough sitting there when I was the actual therapist talking to just one half of a troubled couple. Having to stew in the unpleasant friction thrown off by two unhappy married people was threatening to give me a headache.

"Stupid Mel," I mumbled, knowing he was an easy target. He'd brought me here, after all.

"What'd I do?" Mel asked from behind, making me jump. "Actually, what'd *you* do? That ended poorly."

"I didn't do anything," I insisted as he took a seat. "This place is lousy with people who hate each other and don't want to admit it. It's not my fault."

"What'd you say?"

"I just asked about stuff, like you said."

"What stuff?"

"Just … well, not much. She—Alicia was annoyed that they'd gotten fobbed off on the newest doctor in the place when they'd signed up to work with Coontz. I think maybe he dumped them for us."

"Hunh," Mel said, reaching over with his fork to take a bite of my chicken. I scowled at him, but it was mostly out of habit. The food was bad and I had chocolate back at the house. "I wonder why."

"That's what I was wondering, too."

"We'll have to see if we can find out if Howard requested them or if Coontz didn't want them."

"What's the difference?"

"Howard's new, she can't be involved with whatever's going on. Coontz has been here awhile, so he has more clout and there's more to be suspicious of there."

"I'll say," I said, wrinkling my nose.

"You will?"

"He's just creepy. You see it."

"I do, but creepy doesn't equal cult leader. Plus, he spends all his time here. If he's running a cult somewhere, he's got someone standing in for him when the retreat's going on. That's not really what cult leaders do. They like the attention too much to give it up to someone else."

"So we don't think he's got an acoustic guitar stashed in his trunk under some scratchy linen robes?"

Mel chuckled. "He might, I just doubt it's for cult purposes."

"Well, then it's someone else. Rhonda maybe. She's a bit off. Maybe she's secretly recruiting for her cult leader husband. She's one of his ten wives and is only allowed to leave to bring back more wives. Did you look into her?"

"I looked into everyone and nothing definitive sprang up. That's why we're here."

I grunted, unhappy that we were, in fact, there. I finished my meal, shoved the tray away and then sighed.

"How much longer are we here today, anyway? We've had our session, we've done our trust exercises, what else could they possibly want from us?"

"More talking, sweet-cheeks," Mel said, taking my hand gently between his palms and meeting my gaze with an overtly saccharine look on his pretty face. "Communication is the key to any successful relationship."

"We have a successful relationship?" I asked, looking askance. Mel shrugged, still holding my hand but dropping the act.

"Depends on how you define successful." He thought about it for a second before pointing out, "We haven't killed each other."

"Then what the hell do we need this place for?"

Coontz stopped us as we were heading out, begging us again to stay at the facility, and then reluctantly let us leave. The first thing I did when I tore into the house was head straight for my room. I'd hidden candy in my bag and I wanted it, so bad.

After wolfing down a whole caramel-chocolate bar, I wiped my face and headed back out to the living room. Mel was sitting across from Sarah, but Julian and the kids were nowhere to be found.

"You're gonna go back tonight?" Sarah asked. Mel nodded, ignored me when I sat down at the other end of the couch from him.

"Yeah. I'll have Gwen drive me."

"Gwen will do what, now?" I asked. Mel glanced over at me, squinted disapprovingly as he eyed my mouth.

"You've got chocolate on your face."

"Julian's going to cook when he gets back, you shouldn't spoil your appetite," Sarah said. I shook my head.

"No such thing as a spoiled appetite."

Mel lifted his hips to thrust them into the air, making eye contact with me to make sure I knew what he was offering and I rolled my eyes.

"Except for where Mel's junk is concerned. There is no such thing as an unspoiled appetite for that."

"But you're saying you do have an appetite for it."

"I'm saying …" I trailed off, lacking a comeback. "Shut up."

Sarah chuckled, getting back on topic. "It may just be that your nose is off its game."

"Bite your tongue," Mel said, insult lighting him up. "My nose is fine."

"You're out in the city, sticking mostly to human form. I think you're just getting rusty." Sarah spared me a wink, before shrugging her shoulders and sighing dramatically. "I bet Julian could sniff it out in a heartbeat."

"What needs sniffing out?" Julian said from the deck. He'd wrapped a towel around his waist sometime before coming in and grown back his body hair. Unlike Mel, who'd looked freshly waxed every time I'd seen him shirtless, Julian had gone for the more rugged, mountain man look. Dark hair spread along his arms and chest, trailing from his belly button down under the towel.

I fought my brain as it started to wonder if the trend continued lower. You can't blame me! He's a good-looking man and these are legitimate questions you think of when you first start hanging out with werewolves. I did feel a tinge of guilt ogling him with his wife so close, but luckily distraction came quickly.

Puppies poured in then, barking, nipping. Lorelai led the pack as usual, but before she could reach her mother, Walter grabbed her tail at the base, yanked it back. When she twisted to attack, he danced nimbly out of the way, managed a crazy hop, bounce, and leap straight into Sarah's lap. Lorelai growled from her place on the floor but Walter just watched her, tongue hanging out.

"Everyone hungry?" Julian asked. Puppies turned to bark in his direction, and he clapped his hands together gleefully. Turning to look over at his wife, he jerked his head in the direction of the kitchen and she nodded. When they'd all moved past the kitchen and through a doorway I had yet to venture into, I turned back to Mel.

"What'd you find out today?"

"That you're stubborn and should put out more."

"You only just learned that? You're slow, Somerset."

"I can be fast *or* slow, baby, whatever you please."

"I please you to tell me what you learned at lunch in the cafeteria."

"Well," Mel said, shifting to lean forward as if he was about to give me a run-down of something very important.

"We'll have to talk to more people, but everything seemed above board. I took up with a whole table of couples, just asking them about how things are going so far and how they like their doctors. Everyone seemed okay, though it's still early yet. We'll have to check back in after a few days."

"We'll still be here in a few days?" I whined. "You said it'd be two days tops. You swore we wouldn't have to come up with a backstory or anything."

"Our backstory is that you love me *too* much and our problems spring from you not being able to handle all the feelings of lust I conjure up inside you."

"If we're going with something totally asinine then I'd rather be my own transgender twin brother."

"That's gonna be a hard sell with you not acting at all like a man."

"Uhh," I said, realizing he'd pointed out the main flaw in my brilliant plan. Rather than confront my mistake I changed the subject. "So what are we doing tonight?"

"Making sweet, passionate love."

"Not that."

"Okay, we'll drive back out to the center and snoop for real. Then we'll have gymnastic, satisfying sex."

"You know, gosh. I had definite plans to hurl myself off a bridge and into a rocky ravine tonight. So, we'll snoop, and then I'll hurl, and then maybe after that we can discuss the possibility of sex."

"I'd like to request a change in the order of our plans."

"I'd like a different fake husband, but life just isn't fair."

OLIVIA R .BURTON

Eight

"Why aren't you up?"

I grunted at the voice, still at least eighty-percent asleep; with any luck, the voice would go away and I could reclaim the other twenty and get back to dreamland. After a few seconds I felt the bed sag under me, startling me enough that I growled out a disparaging remark and pulled the blankets over my head.

"Gwen, we have to go. I told you to be up and ready by two, and you're still in bed."

"*You're* still in bed. Go away," I mumbled. Mel grabbed my shoulder and shook. I did my best to wiggle out of his grip but he had me pretty good. Plus, he was completely conscious and had full control of his faculties. After another few seconds of silence, in which I blissfully started to drift off again, Mel spoke.

"Okay, then. If you really want to stay here in bed, we can do that."

I squealed as cold air met my back and I felt the bed shift again. Mel tucked himself under the covers, wrapped himself bodily around me, and rested his head on the side of my face, pressing me hard into the pillow like he might try to suffocate me.

I attempted to throw him off, but he had me completely trapped. Even his leg was draped over my hips, calf tucked down over the fronts of my thighs. He was barefoot and I could feel the cold of his heel even though my pants. Sighing obnoxiously, he squeezed my back against his chest. There was a moment, maybe a full minute, where we lay like that, silent, him holding me.

My body and my brain were in agreement about Mel for once: both felt this was pretty nice, even with the near suffocation of having a pillow puffed around my face. The warmth of his tight grip was enticing me back toward sleep, which I'm sure wasn't what he had meant it to do. The contrary part of me that always wanted Mel to never gets his way liked that quite a bit, but just before I was completely out again, Mel started speaking, much louder this time.

"Isn't this fantastic? So comfortable and warm. We could stay like this, just like this, all tangled together, alllll night. Yes, we'll just lay here, snuggled like lovers, well into the morning." He ignored my elbow weakly digging into his stomach and kept speaking. "Then Julian and Sarah will wonder where we've been and they'll come on and find us here, folded together like taco shells. They'll take pictures, send them to everyone we know, announcing our nuptials." I ignored him and he paused long enough to let me comment, but I remained still, hoping maybe I would get so irritated I would go into a coma out of spite.

"'Come to the wedding of Mel and Gwen,' the invitations will say. 'The pair will be married Thursday morning. In bed. Still huddled together.' I may kiss the bride? Well, splendid, I think I'll do just that!" Mel turned his head slightly to press his lips to my cheek but it wasn't really a kiss. If anything, it reminded me a baby who's watched adults kiss and thinks it's really just a ritual sloppy mashing of faces.

I'll admit that, at that point, I was just being stubborn. He'd torn me away from sleep so effectively that I wasn't sure I'd even recognize it were I to see it again. Eyes squeezed shut, forehead pressed to the blankets I'd managed to keep near my face when he'd slid in, I pretended he wasn't irritating me at all. I considered my position, my options, and what I thought of the situation.

On the one hand, it was Mel I was snuggling with. On the other hand, he was delightfully warm and it had been awhile since I'd been properly spooned. Before I could ponder on the pleasant side of the situation, though, he reminded me that hugging me and keeping me awake were not the worst things he could do to me.

"But, really, to be completely comfortable," he announced, still loud despite his lips wetly brushing my cheek. "I need to take this constricting necklace off."

Anticipating my reaction, he tensed his arms, holding me in place when I screeched out a threat and struggled to get away. After my wiggling proved futile, he lifted his face so my head was no longer pinned to the pillow. The room was too dark to make out his expression as I twisted in an attempt to glare, but I was willing to bet my savings he was looking particularly pompous in that moment.

"Get off."

"Well! I had no idea this was all it took to get you in the mood for—"

"No innuendo, just get off!" I struggled again and I felt his chest vibrate with laughter. This was definitely no longer about getting me out of bed; this was solely about being the most annoying person in the room.

"Your words, they confuse me."

"Your face confuses you, get away."

"Promise you'll get up and drive me out to Tough Love?"

"I promise I'll hit you."

"That's not what I asked," he sang at me, tightening his arms just hard enough that I found it tough to take a full breath.

"Fine!" I croaked. "Let go and I'll drive you to the stupid center."

"You didn't promise. You need to say it," he teased. I paused, snarling for a moment, and then took a deep breath when he let up on the python squeeze.

"It," I said. He laughed and, just like that, I was alone in the bed, the covers bunched at my feet. I blinked, looked over to see the dark shape of him standing nearby. I strongly considered yanking the covers back over me and just going back to sleep, but part of me suspected that he'd follow through and take the necklace off. Or worse, spoon me again *naked*.

"Get dressed, Chipmunk."

"You get dressed."

"You are really bad at banter at two in the morning."

"Your face is," I hissed, pushing into a sitting position and trying to make my heavy body obey my orders. My brain was sizzling with annoyance at being forced to wake up, at being lulled into thinking pleasant thoughts about snuggling with Mel, and about the fact that some tiny corner of my mind hoped it would happen again. My body, on the other hand, was solely responding to being jerked out of sleep and forced to move through air that felt positively frigid compared to the warmth of heavy blankets.

Mel just stood there, waiting silently.

"I'm not getting dressed with you in here," I said after a few moments.

"I'm not leaving. You'll just go back to sleep."

"Then I'm going in my pajamas," I said, as if it was some real threat that would net me any leverage at all.

"You're not wearing a bra so I'm okay with that."

Crossing my arms over my chest, I glared up at him. He just laughed, gesturing to the bathroom.

"Change in there. I'll wait out here."

Fifteen minutes later, after I'd taken my sweet time getting changed, I stepped back out into the bedroom to find Mel gone. He'd left the bedroom door open and the light on in the hall. Figuring I was supposed to follow, I yanked sneakers over my bare feet and padded out to meet him. I found him in the living room, naked.

"Oh jeez," I hissed, rolling my eyes and trying to decide if I was more annoyed with him or with myself for appreciating the view. He just smiled, flexed his pecs one after another and then jerked a thumb toward the front door.

"I've got to wolf out, then we'll drive over and I'll sniff around."

"You can't wear pants to wolf out?"

"Have you ever even *watched* a werewolf movie?"

"Hey, The Hulk manages pants." I sighed, decided it was better to just enjoy the view and not give him the satisfaction of my annoyance. "Where are the keys?"

"Hanging on the hook by the door. Do you need directions, or are you good?"

"I'm fine. Let's just get this over with." At my words, he got a thoughtful look on his face, let out a small chuckle.

"I feel like this is the exact conversation we would share just before having sex," he quipped. I rolled my eyes, but he was probably right. He gave a slow roll of his shoulders and leaned his head forward slightly; it brought my attention to the square of blue resting on his chest.

"Wait!" I yelped, taking half a step forward. He lifted his brows, met my gaze.

"What?"

"I thought you couldn't fit in the necklace with your fat wolf neck."

"My neck is not fat," he snapped, genuine insult crossing his features.

"Not the point, Somerset."

"Sarah got me a longer cord. I replaced it earlier. You didn't notice?"

"It looks the same to me."

Mel rolled his eyes and mumbled a word usually reserved for me to him: "Ugh."

Then, he changed.

Watching a full-grown adult man turn into a werewolf was different than watching a small puppy turn human. Yes, that seems like the most obvious statement in the world, but until you've seen it, you can't judge. Until you've been standing in a beautiful, homey living room with a naked man and watched him morph into a majestic canine, you can't really understand what it's like. You also can't really know the strange leaps your brain makes between awe and moronically obvious thoughts like the one above.

Once before, I'd watched Mel start to transform between human and wolf. It had been slow, fascinating, and he probably hadn't meant for it to happen. The circumstances had been much different; he and I had been under the influence of a succubus that two of my friends had just killed.

Standing naked in his brother's living room, however, the process was much different. Rather than changing in fits and starts, gaining hair here and there, it went quickly and as smoothly as such a thing can. Fur grew along his skin almost instantaneously, making his nudity a non-issue.

One moment, he was hairless, chiseled and naked; the next he was Bigfoot.

Like Christian turning back into a human, Mel grunted a few times as tension ran through his limbs. His face pushed outward, as if something shoved through the back of his skull. His ears grew and shifted positions, his musculature rippled and then he fell forward as the joints in his limbs snapped and bowed.

It probably took a minute, all in all, before Mel Somerset the irritating, oversexed private eye was a wolf. A goddamned wolf!

His eyes were still a brilliant blue and his muzzle had some cute little spots of white high up, near his eyes. His tail, which I hadn't even thought to watch for until he wagged it spastically during his post-change shake out, was a pale gray on the underside. He was still beefier than Julian, wider in the shoulders and hips, with a larger ruff around his neck. As he shook himself out, bent and stretched his limbs, I stared.

I wasn't sure I could move.

It was another minute before he got to the door and, when I didn't follow him, he turned, peered out of the entryway. I just continued to stare, feeling a little—no, a lot crazy. Had that just happened? Had I just witnessed a man become a wolf? Or was this all some elaborate fantasy my mind had cooked up in some bizarre *Shutter Island* scenario.

"Am I Leonardo DiCaprio?" I whispered. Mel cocked his head to the side, lifted one doggy eyebrow. Blinking at me, he chuffed out a breath of air and jogged over, nudging my arm with his nose. A giant wolf that used to be a man was prodding me. A werewolf, currently in wolf shape, was nudging my arm. This was actually happening and I was standing there, staring down at him with my jaw hanging open. Apparently this wasn't what he wanted.

Switching tactics, he darted his head behind me and bit my ass.

"Ow!" I snapped. Mel let out a low, quick, breathy bark and lowered his head toward my butt again. That got me moving.

"Fine! Let's go, jeez." Despite the fact that I was already heading toward the door, Mel gave me one more nip, down around the side of my thigh this time, dancing out of the way when I reached back to smack him.

The drive to the center was interesting. Mel sat in the front seat and didn't demand I roll down the window or buckle him in. Well, perhaps he demanded both those things and I was just unable to tell what he wanted; without his emotions to guide me, I found myself pretty clueless about how to handle him.

I couldn't help glancing at him every few minutes, watching his silhouette in the light of the car's control panel. He stayed silent, adjusting to keep himself upright as I turned or changed speed. It wasn't like driving with an actual dog who had no awareness of what you were doing and therefore got knocked against the window or console with every turn or lane merge. As we pulled up into the long driveway, Mel barked once, put a paw on the emergency brake. I frowned at him, slowed down. When I didn't stop, he let out a low growl, tapped the brake again.

"We're stopping?" he chuffed out a burst of air that could have been agreement or derision. "Okay, bark once if we're stopping here, twice if we're—" He barked once, and I pulled the car over. Mel waited patiently for me to turn the car off, unbuckle my seatbelt, and come around to his side. When I opened the door, he hopped out, gave my thigh another quick bite, and took off in the direction of the facility literally faster than I could see.

I stood there, unsure whether or not I was supposed to be following him. The trees around me offered no help and, in fact, made me feel rather uncomfortable and alone. Stuffing the keys in my pocket, I took off after Mel at a quick jog. I wasn't in the best shape, but I could jog for five or ten minutes without killing myself. Not only did Chloe keep me active but I'd also recently acquired a friend with benefits who made me want to ensure my stamina was up to snuff. I hadn't been benefitting from this friend in almost two months, but that didn't mean I was against being prepared.

Unfortunately, when I got to the end of the drive, slowing to a halt at the edge of the roundabout, I realized I had no idea where Mel had gone. I stood out in the open, in full view of the center, and looked around. The moon was a sliver in the sky, barely any help at all. At least I could be reasonably sure that if it wasn't helping me see it wasn't helping any security guards either. I hadn't asked Mel if I should wear a mask or skulk around low to the ground, so I wasn't sure if I was in danger of being seen. Swearing under my breath, my heart beating faster, I slipped back into the trees. Stuck on the idea that I might be at risk of getting caught and thrown in Tough Love jail, I rounded the side of the property, heading toward where Mel and I had attempted to snoop that afternoon.

Two minutes of making hissing sounds to get Mel's attention passed before I heard a loud snuffling sound behind me.

"Please be Mel," I mouthed. I felt another nip on my leg and, this time, I caught him in the face when I swiped backward. Mel stood there, panting happily when I glowered at him.

"Did you find anything?" I whispered. Mel shook his head, dropped his nose to the ground again, and headed off back toward the center. I followed, keeping up with him easily. We moved through the trees for what felt like an hour and Mel made no indication that he'd found anything useful.

"What are you even looking for?"

Of course, he didn't answer me. I felt somewhat stupid for asking, but I talk to animals all the time and know they won't answer. Mel could at least answer me later, when he was back in human form.

Mel stopped sniffing, turning to face me, and jerked his head to the side. I followed his indication and realized we'd circled the property enough that we'd almost made it back to the car.

"Nothing?" I asked. He shook his head, turned and bolted toward in the direction he'd gestured, a spring in his canine step. Sighing, I followed him at my own pace, unlocking my door and climbing in before I reached out to unlock and shove open his door. He hopped in and then moved to the back seat, shifting around wildly like a pig snorting for truffles.

"So you woke me up and bit my ass for nothing?" I asked as we cleared the Tough Love driveway, turning onto the main road.

"I wouldn't say it was for nothing," Mel said, startling me into a yelp and almost causing me to swerve out of my lane. "Your ass is pretty tasty."

"Why are you human?" I demanded, trying to ignore the way my heart was pounding. Sneaking around had wound me up tighter than I'd realized, and my adrenaline still wasn't entirely settled.

"Because I'm done being a wolf?"

"Don't be a dick," I growled. Mel just snorted, catching my eye in the rearview as he ran a hand through his hair, touched both his eyebrows.

"I didn't want to go wolf any place where there might be surveillance cameras. It's just good sense."

"So why change now?"

"Maybe I missed talking to you."

"Oh jeez," I groaned.

"If you'd rather not talk, that's fine too. I can stay naked for your benefit rather than mine."

"Oh *jeez*," I repeated, shaking my head and defiantly refusing to even look in the rearview mirror for the rest of the drive.

Mel led me into the house and into my room, still naked. I had decided about halfway up the walk (as he'd backed toward the house facing me and doing a shoulder-shaking, full body dance in what he probably thought was an enticing manner) that I really was okay with him being naked. It was a nice view and I didn't exactly have to let him *know* I liked what I was seeing. I could just roll my eyes and cluck disapprovingly but sneak peaks here and there when he wasn't looking.

As I toed off my shoes and moved into the bathroom to change back into my pajamas, Mel continued his dancing walk. He followed me to the foot of the bed, where I left my shoes, to the suitcase on the dresser, and to the bathroom. He followed me right up until I slammed the door in his face and locked it. Standing in the bathroom, I stared at the door as if I could intuit his actions through the solid wood. After a few seconds of hearing nothing, I turned, pulled my shirt off, and then pushed down my pants.

Mel started making porn-music sounds from outside the door and I laughed, despite myself.

"Go away. I'm going back to bed. To *sleep*. Alone. Without you, because I am going to sleep."

The porn sounds didn't stop, so I just got my pajamas on, used the toilet in hopes it would make him uncomfortable enough to leave. He stopped making the sounds, but I couldn't be sure he'd gone. After washing my hands and running a brush through my hair as a procrastination tactic, I pulled open the door, peeked out. Mel was nowhere to be seen. On a sigh of relief, I stepped out of the bathroom, turned off the light.

I got two steps before Mel appeared next to me, having at least put on pants.

"What are you doing?"

"Sleeping with you."

"No. Get out. Go sleep on the floor with the puppies."

He got a sappy look on his face and I got the feeling he'd have been perfectly happy to do so.

"No, we should practice."

"For what?"

"On the drive back, I was thinking."

"If it was about your dick, keep it to yourself."

"Shh," he said absently, as if shutting down my insults had become completely routine, and stepped around me to sit on the edge of the bed. I turned to face him, crossing my arms over my chest.

"We should stay at the facility for a night, snoop around inside the buildings. Maybe I'll find something there. There was a door I wanted to check out; I can probably do it when no one's around to notice."

"They're not just going to let us snoop. They're going to be monitoring us, possibly locking our door so we can't leave. I wouldn't put it past Rhonda to drug us to make sure we get the proper amount of sleep. She seems like a tight-ass."

"You give me so little credit," Mel sniffed, surprising me by skating right by the chance to comment on the state of Rhonda's butt.

"In everything. All the time."

"You forget!" he said, raising his voice as if to combat the laugh that wanted to come through. "That I snoop for a living. I detect. I sleuth. You might even say I investigate."

Abruptly, he grabbed me around my waist, yanked me close. "How about I investigate your privates?"

"That just sounds completely unappealing and not just because it's you."

I could feel the heat of his thighs along the sides of my knees as he dropped his hands back into his lap. I didn't move away as Mel shrugged off his own comment.

"That wasn't one of my best, I admit. So, are you game?"

"No, get out."

"I meant," he said through a chuckle. "About sleeping at the facility. Get your mind out of the gutter."

"It didn't go there willingly. Your mind practically tied it up and dragged it there. You're the bad boy here, not me."

He laughed and being this close reminded me of the one night I'd spent at his house, when he'd fed me, gotten me drunk, and given me every opportunity to jump his bones. His laughter trailed off and we stared at each other, making eye contact in the low light of my room. I'm not sure how long the eye contact lasted and the necklace made it impossible for me to know what he was feeling about the situation. I just knew that he looked surprisingly vulnerable as he stared up into my face. I considered a few scenarios in that moment, and none of them involved making him leave. My heartbeat sped up and I was suddenly very aware of every pleasant cluster of nerves my body possessed.

I think we both realized the implications of our closeness and eye contact at about the same time. Unlike in the garden, where it had been a battle of wills, we both broke at the same time.

As we indulged in equally uncomfortable giggles, Mel grabbed my shoulders, pushed me deliberately back, and got to his feet. He paused in front of me for a moment, his eyes searching my face, before he turned and headed toward the door.

"Get some sleep. We've got a big day of fighting tomorrow."

"Brush your teeth," I said as he left. He glanced back, one brow up. I smirked, did my best to smear whatever intimacy we'd somehow stepped in. "You have dog breath."

OLIVIA R .BURTON

Nine

We stood on the grass, just like we had the day before, surrounded by the same couples. Doctor Howard was leading the group therapy session, giving a short speech about the importance of honesty. Mel grabbed my hand and dragged me to the corner of the yard, as far away from the action as we could get without raising suspicion. We followed the doctor's orders and sat facing each other, legs crossed, knees touching. Mel spent more time looking intently around the yard at the other couples than he did looking at me, but I didn't mind.

The awkward moment beside my bed was still fresh in my mind.

"Now, hold hands and look into each other's eyes," Doctor Howard said. A ripple of nervous laughter and embarrassment washed through the couples and I couldn't help but smile.

"Today, we're going to be sharing secrets. I know, I know, married people don't have secrets from each other, right? You tell each other everything." More chuckling popped up here and there and I turned to share a private eye-roll with Mel, only to find him concentrating on one of the other doctors. Following his gaze, I poked at her with my empathy, trying to see what had caught her eye. She was wearing a long sleeved shirt, despite the warmth of the sun, and her posture was relaxed. Nothing looked suspicious about her, and I wondered for a moment if Mel was just scoping for tail.

"Have you all thought of a secret to tell? We'll start small; think of something you may have done as a child or young adult that you've never shared. Maybe you were embarrassed or you just thought it wouldn't matter. Bring your partner into your past, let them get to know you as a youth, strengthen that life-long bond you promised each other."

There was another few seconds of quiet, as she looked out across the couples. Coontz finished weaving through the other pairs, before coming to stand near us. For a moment, he was content to stand uncomfortably close, his feet practically bumping my hip. Fixing a sarcastic smile on my face, I held a hand over my eyes to shield myself from the sun as I looked up toward him.

"Hey Gordo?" I asked. Coontz frowned, looking down at me with a spike of irritation. If I had a nickel for every one of those I enticed out of the people around me I'd have been able to buy and sell Bill Gates. I fought the urge to twitch at the feeling, and took my other hand out of Mel's grip, jerking my thumb toward Doctor Howard.

"You wanna back off just a little? According to her, we're about to share our deepest darkest secrets. I'd rather you not be in on them."

Turning his head slightly as if he couldn't quite bear to look at me head-on, he watched me for a moment. I felt something move around his psyche and it made me nervous and a little nauseated. I couldn't be sure, but it didn't really feel quite ... human. Before I could investigate any further, he smiled, nodded.

"Of course. I'll give you your privacy during the exercise, but we will be discussing what was said in our session this afternoon."

"Sure, Doc," I said, looking back to Mel, dismissing Coontz. Mel barely registered when I grabbed his hands again and rested our linked fingers on my knees. He was still watching the doctor whose name I hadn't caught during our few days there. Hell, I only knew Howard because she'd introduced herself when we'd started.

"Now, let's start with the husbands—Jeff, David, you can choose who goes first," Doctor Howard said. The gay couple each shrugged a shoulder, the man facing me nodding and announcing he'd go first. Mel leaned in and I followed his lead, leaning close as well. When Doctor Howard instructed us to start, Mel hissed out a whisper.

"You get anything off Dr. Gomez?"

"Uhh, the one you were creeping on?"

"I wasn't creeping, I was studying her intently."

"That's what serial killers say," I hissed.

"No," Mel said, distracted, and I felt his cheek hit mine as he shook his head slightly. "Something's up."

"I'm not interested in the state of your penis, man," I mumbled, hoping he took it as a joke and not any indication that I'd been thinking about his genitals in any way. "Get back on track."

Mel snorted out an almost silent laugh, dropping his head down to rest on my shoulder, trying to hide it. Doctor Howard started speaking again, moving on to encouraging the other halves of the couples to share.

"What do you think it means?" I asked Mel. He was silent for a moment, but his whisper was even quieter when he spoke again.

"Have you been getting any weird vibes off anyone? Besides Coontz," he said before I could answer predictably. I considered.

"Not really," I admitted. Rhonda had a stick up her butt, but I was reasonably sure it was just a regular stick and not some supernatural preying mantis creature lodged up there puppeteering her into abduction or murder.

"So I'm the only non-human in the center?"

I paused to consider what he was asking. I hadn't noticed any emotions that didn't seem particularly human that I could think of. Other than Coontz giving me the willies and the woozy, hazy memory of having my blood drawn, everything seemed completely normal.

"Yeah, I think so. Even Creepy's human. Not exactly normal, but human."

"How do you mean he's not normal?"

"All right everyone, sit up," Doctor Howard announced. Mel and I separated and I noted that Coontz was watching us from his place near the deck. His gaze was a touch too intense and, when I reached out to read his emotions, curiosity washed over me in a wave, a bit of suspicion hitting me at the crest. I gave him my best harmless smile and then turned to look around at the other couples, as if I was just killing time while Doctor Howard was speaking.

When we ducked closer for another share session, Mel repeated his question. I thought about it before answering.

"I don't know. He just doesn't react … normally. He gets excited about weird things and irritated at stuff that shouldn't bother him. And sometimes there's just this … I don't know, but it's not normal."

"But you're sure he's human?"

"Yeah." I didn't want to bring up Norma, but the truth was sometimes the feel of Coontz sort of reminded me of the succubus that had gotten her hooks in us. I'd felt Mel when she'd gotten done with him and there had been something extra swimming around in his head. It wasn't the only time I'd felt it, though, and even when there'd been something extra in my own head after being captured by a demon, it hadn't felt exactly like Coontz.

His emotions were definitely weird, but not as intently *dissonant* as Mel having Norma in his head or me having a demon in mine. With Coontz it was almost like his own brain didn't get along with itself, sometimes. Before I could explain the extent of what I meant, Mel nudged me.

"You think we should share an actual secret?"

"Oh sure," I mumbled sarcastically. "Tell me something juicy."

"It's been two months since I've had sex."

I snorted, rolling my eyes and chuckling at the idea. Mel could have told me he was a Vegas Showgirl and I'd have sooner believed him. Mel barely went two days without sex. I was even sure he'd spent the last few days bedding someone in secret any time I wasn't actively looking him in the eye. Hell, I was looking over his shoulder at the moment; who knew what was going on beneath my eye-line.

"Well, my big secret is that I'm Batman," I countered. "But without the tacky codpiece."

Doctor Howard announced that we should separate again, take some time to talk about our secrets, how they made each of us feel. I leaned back, found Mel watching me intently. His expression could have represented anything from irritation to interest. When I lifted a brow and pulled my hands out of his, he shook his head like he was waving the moment away.

"I don't buy it. Batman has to keep in much better shape than you."

"The muscles are all in the suit, just another part of the costume. It's a brilliant disguise, don't you think? You certainly didn't suspect a thing."

"So does that mean you and Catwoman?" He waggled his brows. I sniffed delicately, lifting my chin as I rolled my gaze away. On a heavy sigh, like the weight of Gotham rested on my un-muscled shoulders, I spoke.

"A lady never kisses and tells."

The end of the day ended up nearly a twin of the previous afternoon. We ate bland food followed by another counseling session. While Mel spent most of lunch complaining about the state of the food, I mostly ignored him, looking forward to the lemonade and cookies I knew they would bring once we were back in the sitting room. It was probably just that they seemed extra delicious compared to the lame food they were feeding us, but I wouldn't have been surprised if they were putting some sort of controlled substance into it. Other than sugar, of course: my one true addiction.

Mel was surprisingly good at talking without actually saying anything and I was starting to think that, either the doctor didn't know Mel was bullshitting him or he just didn't care. He asked about our secrets, Mel deflected, going on about how maybe I had been just a little too honest, even going so far as to use my honesty as a weapon.

When I felt the doctor start to get irritated or suspicious, I'd poke in, picking a fight about something or other. Mel never does the dishes, he bugs me too often for sex, he refuses to spend any time with my family. It didn't matter what the subject was, I could take issue with it and Mel could engage in battle with the best of them.

Finally, as we trailed off through another screaming match, the doctor cleared his throat. He gestured to the clock on the wall and explained that it was the end of our time for the day. Before I could stand and escape the tiny room, however, he gestured to my arm.

"How's your elbow?" I realized I'd completely forgotten about the blood draw.

"Um, fine I guess." Mel frowned my way as I poked at the two, fat scabs in the fold of my elbow. I showed the wounds off to the doctor and he nodded, greasy glee splashing outward. It caught me a little harder than I expected, causing me to giggle.

Mel noticed, eyeballing me like he disapproved. I just shrugged, though it felt slow and strange, almost like what I'd felt in the exam room. Something was off, but I felt just addled enough that I didn't have the state of mind to parse it.

"Tonight we're having our usual bonding events that we encourage our couples to join. Would you two be willing to come back for board games and movies?"

"We actually have plans with my brother and sister-in-law, but we were discussing it and we think we should take you up on your offer to monitor us while we sleep. Can you fit us in for tonight?"

"Oh!" Happiness surfed through the doctor and I felt myself let out another giggle, dizziness swirling around behind my eyes and making me feel just a little bit sick. Both men ignored me clutching my rolling belly as they got to their feet. "This is wonderful news! Yes, of course we can fit you in. We have a room upstairs ready just for you. Be back here about fifteen minutes before lights-out and we'll get you all set up. Once you spend time in our beds you won't want to leave."

I snorted, shook my head. "I'll bet."

Mel asked a few questions about what we would need to bring, intercepting Coontz when he tried once again to touch me to lead me out of the room. I hadn't even seen the guy coming that time, but it occurred to me as Mel was shuffling me through the front door that being touched wouldn't have been as bad as whatever had gripped my stomach and started shaking it. I was so queasy and confused Mel practically had to buckle me into the car, but he waited until we'd reached the end of the driveway to demand an explanation.

"What is wrong with you? You were fighting okay, but now you're acting weird."

"Nothing, I feel okay. I mean …" I considered. The further away from the center we got, the better I felt. Whatever had come over me, whatever had been in the lunch or reaching out from Coontz' emotions was receding in the fresh air of the ride home. "Better, I feel good now that we're on the way home."

"Are you sure? This is the second time you've seemed stoned. Is there something in the lemonade?"

"I'm fine," I insisted, shaking my head to get rid of the last bit of dizziness. I was starving, though. "I'm hungry, actually. Lunch wasn't filling at all and I ate all the cookies right away. That's about it."

"No, that's not it. And what's up with your arm?"

"What do you mean?"

"You just got blood drawn, right? It looks like you got attacked by another vampire."

I shuddered at the thought. Been there, done that, would not be interested in a repeat.

"It was just some blood tests. This nice, *very* attractive woman came in, tied my arm off, took my blood, and I left. That's it. I'm pretty sure, anyway. She was good, too; I didn't feel a thing."

"Hmm," Mel said, eyeing me suspiciously.

My mood only got better for a few hours while I rolled around with the puppies. I was even invited to go out on an evening run with the family but Mel insisted I stay back and take a nap. When I tried to refuse, he shoved a glass of cold water into my hand, demanded I drink it all. I took a sip, but he shook his head, pointed at it sternly. I rolled my eyes like a teenager, feeling my happiness taper off in the face of his attitude.

"You were acting weird there at the end."

"End of what?"

"Keep drinking," Mel ordered. "At the end of the session. You looked … sick. But not … I don't know. You didn't seem—just—like you'd been drugged. How do you feel?"

"Annoyed," I said, the last of my relaxation deteriorating as he treated me like one of the children. While I drank, I turned to watch the parade of puppies head toward the door on Julian's heels. Abruptly, Sarah yanked off her top and skirt, standing there completely nude for a moment. She was just as impressive naked as Julian and Mel.

I barely noticed the blond hair growth along her tan skin as she shifted into her wolf form. Before long, though, she had the muzzle and the tail and was trotting after her family, a golden, lupine goddess. Finishing off the cup of water, I swiped a hand over my mouth and sighed.

"I'm so jealous of you guys. You all look spectacular naked and you don't ever have to shave."

"We *all* look spectacular naked?" Mel asked. I turned to glare at him and shoved the empty cup against his chest. Smarmy grin fixed in place, he watched me intently for a moment. None of the evening's intimacy caught up to us then, for which I was grateful.

"You know you do, shut up. I'm going to go nap—because I like naps, not because you're the boss of me. Wake me before we leave."

"As opposed to dragging you there unconscious?"

"Hey, I wouldn't put it past you."

"Dream of me!" Mel sang as I moved toward the back room. Knowing the puppies were all well out of sight, I held a hand up and flipped him off.

Ten

"Brilliant idea," I hissed in the dark. Mel shifted, breathed out a laugh.

"I know."

"I was being sarcastic."

"I know," he admitted, scooting closer in the bed. I sighed, turning my face away slightly in case he still had dog breath. When he spoke again, I smelled toothpaste.

"I have a plan."

"Care to explain it to me?"

"Not for another few minutes. Let's just get comfy. Pumpkin."

"Stop with the food nicknames. What's your plan? They've got cameras spying on us, they're going to know if we get up and go for a stroll."

"Don't worry, I've got it handled. What nickname would you prefer? Sugar?"

"Still food." I should know; it's my primary source of calories. "We've been wasting time here for over an hour and you have yet to spring into action. What are we doing?"

"Being an incompatible married couple. Maybe we should have a fight so we can engage in some make up sex."

"I'm not having sex with anyone watching."

"So I'll throw your panties over the camera. You can pretend we're in some political thriller and the sex will save the world," he said, his hand creeping up my thigh above the blanket.

"Bet you always pretend sex with you is world-saving," I accused, wiggling my hips until his hand dropped away. He laughed again, his whole body shaking with the effort to keep quiet, but I noted he didn't deny it.

We'd arrived on time and Dr. Coontz had led us upstairs in the main building, shown us to our room. He'd pointed out that there were four cameras in the room, all with night vision capabilities and microphones to catch if we snored or spoke or, I guess, committed adultery or some other marriage-ruining action in our sleep. He'd been seemingly forthcoming, showing us the room into which the cameras fed. There was a bay of monitors, each split into four quadrants, showing couples sitting, stretched out, chatting quietly about presumably mundane things.

We'd been instructed to change into sleep clothes and go to bed normally. We were to pretend there wasn't a skinny, redheaded twenty-something with big teeth watching our every move. Mel had been willing to strip down and change right in the room but the doctor had shown us the little bathroom in the corner, where he promised we would have complete, unmonitored privacy.

I still did my best to get changed without getting undressed. I didn't trust the doctor one bit.

Mel poked me in my belly and I realized I'd dozed off.

"Wake up. We're not actually here to sleep," he whispered. I grumbled at him, ignoring when he draped a hand over my hip this time.

"I'm not sleeping," I grumbled. Mel spoke and I could feel his breath on my face, feel his other arm shift as he tucked it between his chest and my hands.

"No. You're not," he stated, his voice a good-natured order.

"What are we waiting for?" I asked, eyes still closed.

"There's still too much activity going on downstairs. We can't snoop yet."

"Well, then be quiet and let me pretend I'm somewhere else."

"Somewhere else?" he whispered, managing to infuse the quiet words with disbelief. "What could possibly be better than being here with me?"

"I can think of hundreds of places and most of them involve eating sweets. A bakery on fire, for instance. Everyone else would be running out screaming, no one would notice I'm saving all the imperiled pastries by shoving them in my mouth."

"I'll feed you something sweet," he purred, his voice audible even to the microphones around the room. I laughed, gave in, and opened my eyes. The room was dim but I could see the outline of his face. We were lying on our sides, arms tucked up between us, my hands folded under my chin. All in all, it wasn't really bad. As if sensing my train of thought Mel caught my eye.

"Come on, you've had fun the last few days. Admit it."

"Eh." I made a non-committal sound, shrugged my shoulder.

"Now who's being a dick?" he asked. I chuckled.

"Fine. It's been fun. Other than the constant sexual harassment, it's been pleasant."

"You're not used to that by now?" Mel scoffed, sighing. "It's almost like

I don't do it *enough*."

"Your family's great," I pushed on, ignoring his teasing and focusing instead on the meals Julian had prepared for us over the last few days. I made a yummy sound. "And the food has been worth all that."

"You are shockingly orally fixated," Mel observed. I snorted painfully, laughing loud enough that I was sure the neighboring rooms had heard. When my laughter died down, Mel slid one hand under mine, while the other moved up from my hip to the back of my shoulder. He paused, giving me the chance to shove him away or refuse the action. It was all so pleasant, so innocent and I didn't even think of objecting. Snuggling with Mel, warm and comfortable, full of home-cooked food and with no immediate responsibilities, I was pretty happy.

Mel pushed closer, our faces less than a finger width apart. I heard him breath out, smelled the toothpaste again, as his hand splayed along my spine. My heart started pounding like an angry landlord of the door of a delinquent tenant.

"This is nice," he whispered. I got the feeling he was asking permission and in the moment I wanted to give it.

"It is," I whispered back. When he tipped his head to catch my mouth, I welcomed him.

His lips were soft, the kiss chaste at first. When I didn't change my mind and pull away or attack him, he scooted his hips closer, giving me gentle, closed-lips kisses on my mouth and chin. Realizing he wasn't going to take it further on his own, I closed my eyes, twisted my right hand to gather the fabric of his shirt in my grip. He closed his hand around my left fist gently but kept the kisses sweet and decidedly innocent.

Fully aware there was probably going to be video evidence of what I was doing, I parted my lips, pressing harder against his mouth, slipping my tongue out to meet his. His grip tightened as he hugged me to him, moved his hand away from mine to slip under my shoulder to lift me. I let him pull my body over his and cupped his face, my thumb rubbing over his cheek. He kept his hands on my back, trailing his fingers up and down my spine and sending shivers out in waves.

My lungs worked to catch up with my frantic heart, my breath coming quicker as we touched and caressed. The sensations were dizzying, his fingers slipping into my hair, mine roaming along the muscles of his chest and stomach. I wanted to feel his skin against mine, the smoothness I knew lay beneath the soft fabric of his shirt. As his breath started to come faster, his hands undecided on where to go, I shoved his shirt up, pressing my belly to his. He ignored my urging as I tried to let him know I wanted him shirtless. For once, Mel seemed self-conscious, concerned with dignity. The thought made me smile and I felt him do the same.

I found the warmth of the stone on his chest, tangled my fingers in the leather cord that held his emotions in check. When I'd gotten my fill of just enjoying the feel of his skin, I moved my hand slowly down, over his belly, heading for the waistline of his pants.

My hormones were in control and, despite the fact that my brain was politely saying, "Ahem. The cameras?" I couldn't bother to worry about them.

Sensing where my hand was headed, Mel shifted abruptly, rolling me onto my back, grabbing my hand and bringing it upward to pin my arm to the pillow. He held himself aloft above me for a few seconds, pressing my wrist against the pillow as I struggled to get back to the task of undressing him. When I stopped moving, submitting to him, he brushed his fingers feather-light down my arm, over my ribs to press against my hip as he lowered his body onto mine. I sighed out with the weight of him, moving my hand down his back, slower this time. He stopped me once again, clasping my fingers with his before I'd even reached the bottom of his shirt.

Annoyance flashed through me as he made it clear he intended to keep things tame. How did he know how far I even wanted to go, dammit? Maybe I was going to stop at getting him down to his boxers. Maybe I was just playing along enough to convince the redhead with big teeth that we were indeed a married couple.

I can say for certain my hormones were *not* that tactically-minded, but he didn't know that.

When he moved his mouth away from my lips, I took a deep breath, realizing the heat and the—ahem—situation were making me dizzy. I let my free hand roam his back but before I could make my intentions toward his pants clear once again, a wave of discomfort rolled into the room, crowding my brain.

I felt woozy, sick. This stupid place was killing me.

"I'm going to throw up," I said. Mel laughed against my neck, kissing along my throat, back toward my mouth. I turned my head away from him, pushing at the hand that held mine.

"What?" he asked as he realized I was fighting, not encouraging; his body tensed over mine before he lifted himself off me, freeing me completely. "Oh, shit, I thought you were kidd—"

"Gonna—Oh god," I heaved, shoving at him with both hands. The door to the room opened and I caught a glimpse of a womanly shape framed there. Before I could get a good look at anything other than her attractive curves, I rolled off the bed, crawled into the adjoining bathroom and retched into the toilet.

The nausea doubled, nearly blinding me. I heard the woman's voice from the doorway and it was an echo of itself, slow and fast at the same time. The pitch of it said worry, but that wasn't what I felt in the wobbly emotions slam dancing through my head like a bad hangover.

I tuned out the words as she and Mel discussed my predicament and concentrated on making sure that my internal organs stayed put. By the time the woman left, I was pretty sure I'd accidentally vomited up a kidney along with my half-digested dinner, but this is why we're born with two, right? I stayed folded over the bowl as I recovered, as the sickness washed out of my mind. In the end, I was fully aware of the fact that I'd let the warmth of the bed and the experiences of the last few days almost talk me into having sex with Mel.

On camera.

As if I could ever live such a thing down. Cursing my brainlessness, I considered the consequences of what I'd nearly done. If evidence of my attraction to Mel existed anywhere in the world, Chloe would find it. Hell, she'd probably already sensed what had just happened and was hacking the mainframe of Tough Love so she could get hold of the video of Mel and me making out. She'd print out screenshots and glue them to every surface of my office, with, "I TOLD YOU SO," scrawled in big, giant letters across every one.

"Ugh," I groaned, pushing to my feet. I grabbed the side of the narrow sink, rinsed my mouth out in the glow of the tiny, blue-hued nightlight. I groaned again, standing upright, turning to face the room. Mel was sitting on the edge of the bed, watching me. I swear I wasn't at all disappointed that he still had pants on.

"I really do make you sick to your stomach, don't I?" he asked. His tone was inscrutable and, without light enough to see his face or the guide of his emotions, I wasn't sure if he was joking. Unsure if making a rude comment was the way to go, I shrugged a shoulder, wiped at my mouth.

"I think I found another you," I said, finally, aware there was someone listening to us. "Like we discussed in the garden."

"Who? Where?" Mel sprung to his feet, turning to look around the room rapidly. I shook my head.

"No," I insisted, stepping close. I reached up and pulled him down to my level, standing on my tiptoes to equalize the height difference as well as I could. "The woman who came to check on us. She's definitely not human. As soon as she got here, I—"

"Doctor Taylor? Of course she is," Mel interrupted, speaking quietly into my ear. "I could smell her and she's just a woman."

"I don't think so," I said, dropping to flat feet. Mel stayed hunched over, but didn't try to close the gap or touch me. "I got sick when she came into the room."

"Must've just been what we were doing, then," he insisted. "Because I can guarantee, if she was something else, I would have smelled it."

I took a step back, glared up at him. I couldn't see his expression, but I knew he could see mine. We squared off like that for a bit, watching each other in the dark, considering what had just happened. Abruptly, Mel turned to look at the door.

"Come on, let's … get out of this room."

Mel's brilliant plan turned out to be as simple as paying the kid in the monitor room two hundred bucks to tell anyone who asked that we just slept in our beds quietly all night. I'd had the smarts to ask if there was a recording that could be eighty-sixed, but the kid had shrugged, pointed to a narrow device that looked like a DVD player. Hitting the eject button showed us an empty tray, which seemed to amuse Mel. It worried me, though. Even if it turned out there was no cult and it had actually been Mel making me sick, Tough Love was looking more and more like a sham by the minute.

The kid didn't seem too bothered by the lie, making me wonder how many other couples had paid him to look the other way while they went to make whoopee in the garden or on one of the reception sofas. I thought of Cornelius and Mira sitting on that couch when we'd first met them and felt a little disgusted on their behalf.

Then I considered that maybe they'd been the ones to defile the couch and I snickered.

Before we'd gotten moving, Mel had grabbed his overnight pack, yanked out a plastic bag with a brush in it and taken a big whiff. I hadn't asked any questions because I wasn't sure I wanted to know the answers. None of the other rooms of sleeping couples had interested him, so we'd moved along quickly.

As we headed downstairs, I watched Mel's back as he leaned close to each doorway, paused, moved on. He'd been different this week than I'd ever seen him, and I wondered if it was the comment his brother had made when we'd first arrived. From the look of it, married werewolf life looked pretty spectacular: adorable kids, delicious food, and the fun of running through the woods without a care in the world. But Mel had reacted almost violently to the idea that I could be the mate that would bring him such bliss.

I chose not to take it personally, as Mel made it pretty damn clear how much he enjoyed being a bachelor. I couldn't be sure without taking his necklace off, but I had to concede that he was probably torn between the desire to get laid and the desire to prove his brother wrong.

"Seems legit," I mumbled to myself.

"Hmm?" Mel asked, paused in front of a room at the end of the hall opposite the one leading to our sitting room.

"The … organization," I said, not wanting to explain my thought process.

He glanced back at me, but didn't act overly interested in what I had to say. "What?"

"This place. We haven't found anything weird yet, right? Just the doctor being creepy, but that's not enough to really worry. I mean, the camera thing is weird. Why do you think they don't record anything?"

"Does it matter?" Mel asked, bitterness scalding his tone. "We're not here to defend their billing practices. If they turn out to be on the level and couples are leaving doing better than before, who cares? Not that I think they *are* on the level, mind you. Once we expose them, forgetting to stick a blank DVD in will be the least of their troubles."

"What if it's all digital and the kid was just messing with us?" I said, feeling like challenging him just because he was being such a jerk.

Mel went still, obviously considering my genius observation and regretting ever questioning my vast intelligence.

"We'll double check when we get back to the room. We can steal a fridge magnet and ruin the hard drive if it comes to it."

"Well, aren't you Mister Prepared?" I snarked, still intent on making him feel as dumb as he was making me feel. *"But* you're still the one insisting you're the only non-person here."

"Because I *am*."

"I still think something weird happened back there."

"Yeah," he said, crouching down in front of the doorknob. "I tried to show you a good time and you got sick as a dog."

I rolled my eyes, crossing my arms over my chest as he pulled a slim case out of his pocket and pulled out a tiny pair of tools. I fought the urge to let out a squeal of interest, dropping down next to him in the hopes that I'd be able to better see what he was doing to the knob.

"Are you picking the lock?" I asked, when he pulled a couple of tools out of what looked to be a well-worn case. I'd never seen such a thing done in real life. I'd long suspected only PIs in movies and noir novels did such things. "Why would you even need this skill? Can't you just rip a door off its hinges and throw it through a wall?"

"Of course. But that lacks a certain finesse and I'd probably get arrested for breaking and entering.

"But picking and entering is okay?"

"It is if no one finds out," he growled, elbowing me out of the way when I leaned too close. The action nearly toppled me, but I caught myself on the wall, glowering at him. Time passed in silence and I shifted to sit on the ground, giving my bent knees a rest. Mel tried several other tools but was, in the end, unsuccessful. Abruptly, he pushed to his feet, glaring at the knob. His body tensed, jerked forward minutely, before he shook his head, looked down at me. I think he was considering moving on to breaking, but he resisted.

"I'm not getting through here, but I want to."

"What's back there?"

"I have no idea. I can't smell a thing beyond this door. It's too heavy to break down, even if I could do so without drawing attention. There's something behind here, and I'll bet it's bad news."

Hands on his hips, Mel stared down at me but I got the feeling he wasn't really seeing my face. I pushed to my feet, feeling the strange urge to coddle away his disappointment.

"Maybe we can pull the fire alarm, get everyone out and then you can have at it with an axe."

"Now whose idea is brilliant?"

"Still mine," I argued just to argue. Mel didn't comment, so I pressed on. "You're the detective who can't detect what's beyond a simple door. I'm just a trophy wife."

Mel sighed. After a second, he relaxed his shoulders, tucked the case back into the pocket of his sleep pants.

"We'll have to figure out another way to get in there later."

"What makes you think it's important?"

"I can smell the Bishops all around here. I know they spent a lot of time over here, in that room, and in that exam room. Their scent is all over this place, faded but there. I've found nothing in the woods, nothing on the grounds to indicate they spent nearly as much time out there as they did here. They weren't out in one of the bungalows, they were housed here, in the main building." He knocked a knuckle against the door, harder than necessary. "They may be behind here and I want to know why."

"Why would they be behind there?"

"Why wouldn't they? They have to be somewhere and we haven't found them anywhere else," he snapped, frustration lashing out in his tone strong enough that I worried for a moment it would break through the necklace's magical barrier. I wondered why he was being so difficult and then bit my lip, considering that I was probably to blame. Not only was he unable to get through a door that vexed him, I'd gotten us both all worked up back in the room and then run off without finishing what I'd started.

"Look," I said gently. "It's well past midnight. We'll go back up to bed." I waggled my brows at him, failing to get a laugh. "And see what we find in the morning. Hell, if nothing else, we probably have a very bland breakfast to look forward to. Does that sound good, big guy? You want my unbuttered toast? My low sodium sausage?"

Mel was silent for a moment and I smiled up at him in the dark, hoping he'd make some crack about offering me a sausage of his own. He didn't.

"Let's go," he said quietly, making me think he was still frustrated and irritated. After a pause, I heard the smile in his voice as he said, "Chipmunk." All was forgiven, I thought. Thank god.

Eleven

I woke up with Mel at my back, his arms wrapped around my waist, his lips against the back of my neck. I didn't think much of it at first. It was pleasant, if a little too warm. He wasn't snoring or hogging the covers and his hands were nowhere near my bathing suit areas.

Opening my eyes as I inhaled deeply, fully breathing in consciousness, I felt my body tense. I was in bed, being spooned by Mel. The last time we'd been this close things had gotten heated and then he'd gotten mad at me. I didn't need him throwing any more tantrums. No matter how nice it was to feel warm and small and safe, I knew having Mel turn into a child over a heavy petting session could only hurt our chances of exposing what was really going on at Tough Love.

"Hey," I said, elbowing backward. Mel grunted in response but didn't move. "Hey!"

"What?" he managed through a yawn. I twisted, rolling in the circle of his arms onto my back. After a second of aiming a threatening glare directly at his mostly slack face, I watched his left eye open a slit. Another moment passed as his brain seemed to process my dirty look and he opened both eyes. I could feel tension run through his body.

"What?" he asked again, alert but confused..

"What are you doing?" I asked, shoving at his arms. He let me move his left hand away from my body, but didn't pull his right arm out from under me.

"You sleep like a jackhammer," he fumbled, clearly still trying to grasp at consciousness and make it stick. "It was self defense."

"Self defense?" I scoffed. Mel only huffed, abruptly yanked his arm out from under me, and pressed both hands to his eyes.

"I had to find a way to stop you from moving. You spent most of the night kicking me. It was the only way to get you to stop. I had to cage you in to keep you from assaulting me or I wasn't going to get any sleep at all."

"I don't know what you're talking about," I claimed, though it wasn't the first time I'd slept with someone who'd complained of waking up sore and bruised. When he just continued to rub his face and yawn, I sighed, looked to the ceiling as if it would have answers. "Well. Just don't do it again."

"I don't anticipate us sleeping together any time in the future. Don't worry," he spat. I peered over at him, wondering if he was serious or playing the part of the beleaguered husband. When he dropped his arms onto the bed, eyes still closed, I popped up, grabbing my overnight bag on the way to the bathroom.

Half an hour later, both of us mum on the events of the night before, we stepped out of the room, carefully avoiding each other as we moved toward the stairs. The monitoring room was empty, all of the screens dead. Mel paused to scan for the computer we'd forgotten to search for the night before but didn't hold me up as I headed past to the landing.

At the bottom of the stairs, Mel jerked to a halt, swinging his head around to face the back door near the small kitchen.

"What?" I asked. Mel put a hand to my arm, twisting to tuck me behind him as if danger was going to burst in with cymbals crashing and thundering threats on my life. The back door slammed open and Jeff stopped just inside, his wide eyes searching the room. When he saw Mel, he let out a sound of relief and stumbled closer, reaching up as he approached the staircase.

"Someone's dead. You have to help?" He made it a question, his voice too calm for the words he'd spoken.

"Dead?" I demanded, peeking around Mel's shoulder. Jeff didn't notice me and I realized, standing so close to him, that he was probably in shock. His eyes were glassy and his skin was pale. His emotions were a white noise hum, an uncomfortable vibration against my skin that I really, really didn't like. It was nothing as bad as Mel on his worst, necklace-free day, but it rubbed me the wrong way and made me worry for his state of mind.

"One—one of the others. We—he's just dead. Just dead. Can you help?"

"Jeff, Mel? Gwen? What's the matter?" Doctor Howard said, stepping out of the hallway behind me. I twisted toward her, gestured to Jeff.

"Apparently we're full-on CSI in here," I said before I could control myself.

"Gwen," Mel chastised, turning to glare at me. I frowned, feeling myself shrink back at his reprimand.

"Sorry," I mumbled, guilt swamping in. Jeff wasn't lying so there really could have been a corpse nearby. It didn't seem real, though, not in the tacky, health-conscious Tough Love Center. Mel had said couples were *missing*, not dead. Surely we'd step outside and find Jeff was mistaken. Right?

Reaching over the edge of the staircase, Mel put a hand on Jeff's shoulder, stepped down the last two steps, and led him toward the doctor. I remained standing on the stairs, keeping my empathy open for anything that might be helpful. I didn't have any cop shades or punny one-liners handy, but I would know if anyone was feeling the emotional equivalent of steepling fingers and hissing, "excellent."

Like watching Mel change into a wolf, I was feeling a little too surreal to take the situation completely seriously.

Jeff led everyone back out the door, his psyche still humming. I followed as well, noting that we were gaining curious onlookers as we moved through the gardens. Other couples out on walks or snacking on croissants and toast from the seating area just outside the cafeteria noticed that something was up, and decided to trail behind. I wanted to get lost in the crowd, to pull as far away from Jeff and from Howard's concern as I could manage.

The body lay at the edge of the gardens, pale and whole. The only sign he wasn't alive was the butter knife sticking out of his throat and the flat white hue to his skin. He looked out of place, not just because he was dead in a small mob of the living, but just in general. His face wasn't familiar and his clothes didn't fit, like he'd borrowed someone else's before stretching out in the sun for a dirt nap.

A series of gasps blew through the crowd as we approached the dead man. Doctor Howard pressed forward, shock blooming in her like a mushroom cloud. Two giant steps away from the body, Mel grabbed her arm, pulled her back.

"He's dead. You have to call the police; don't go any closer."

"I should—"

"He's dead," Mel repeated, his voice calm. Jeff let out a shaky breath behind them, turning slightly to face his partner across the body. I felt the shock start to wear off, replaced by despair. I took a half step back as I realized that this was not a place I wanted to be standing. A sea of sadness was exactly the reason I'd skipped every funeral that had come up as I'd grown. I could block some of it out, but with everyone in the facility making his or her way over to check out what had drawn a crowd, I knew I was in trouble. If I stuck around and bathed in the worry, shock, and sadness of those around me I would end up on the floor trying to carve my own throat up with a blade of grass.

Mel turned to catch my eye but, before he could ask anything of me, I pointed to my head, turned, and bolted.

"So you just ran?" Chloe asked.

I sighed into the phone, watched as a sheriff's car and an ambulance drove up the road past me. I stepped away from the tree line, watched them drive into the roundabout. Chloe was patient with me but I heard a humming and thumping on her end.

"Yeah," I said finally, turning back to stroll through the trees. "I wasn't about to just stand there in a depression buffet and let my empathy chow down. I'd be a crying, snotty mess, by now."

"Right," Chloe said, drawing it out as if she'd forgotten for a moment I was an empath. "How are things going, anyway? Other than the dead body."

"They're …" I trailed off, trying to decide what the right answer was. Finally, I settled on, "okay."

"Just okay? Not good, not bad? You and Mel haven't killed each other or given in to your baser instincts, yet?"

"Uh," I said, pausing as I thought of the last two nights. Chloe pounced. "What did you *do?*"

"Nothing!"

"Not nothing! You tell me the truth, young lady."

I gave a breathy laugh, shook my head. Inhaling deeply as if preparing myself for a dive, I forced myself to admit what had happened. "We came out here to snoop the other day and he woke me up by wrapping himself around me like a backpack."

"Aww," Chloe cooed.

"Yeah, yeah, real cute. I was mostly annoyed—"

"Uh huh, sure," Chloe said, knowing me better than I wanted to admit. I spoke over her.

"And then he threatened to take the necklace off, which is *not* cute. That got me up real quick because I would rather risk being awake and cold than have to murder Mel for emotional assault. But you know, before that … there was snuggling for a good five or ten minutes there."

"Awww!" Chloe repeated, her voice going up an octave. I rolled my eyes, almost wishing I hadn't told her. She'd be teasing me about this for ages.

"We went, we snooped—oh, wait, no. I got to see him become a wolf. That was … surreal. Then he bit my ass and *then* we snooped. When we came back, though, he did what he usually does."

"He shamelessly described how satisfying it would be if you two had sex and you could no longer resist the call of his sexy bod?"

"No, no. I mean, he did, but I didn't."

"You kept your pants on, didn't you? Gwen, honey, we've had the birds and bees talk. You can't have sex through a pair of pants." There was a murmur in the background, almost like a voice. Chloe chuckled. "Not a nice pair, anyway."

"No!" I argued through a laugh. "It wasn't that—my pants are perfectly nice." Chloe hummed and I could sense even from so far away that she disagreed. I stopped pacing and leaned against a tree trunk, deciding I'd exercised enough for the day. This was supposed to be a vacation, dammit.

"There was a moment in my room," I said after a second. Chloe let me think about it, not demanding I explain every syllable of what I'd meant by "moment." "We—it was dark and we were giving each other shit and it … It got sort of, you know." I felt my cheeks go red just mentioning it. "I thought something might happen but he was very deliberate in making sure it didn't."

"Oh?" Chloe asked, her voice stuffed chock full of shock and confusion. "*He* made sure it didn't? Not you? He? He as in Mel, not some other guy you'd just met?"

"I didn't try to start anything, but he literally pushed me back and ran away. Just—he just dashed out like I'd threatened to stab him."

"Wow."

"Then, last night, we were in bed—"

"Together?"

"Well. Yes. We came to snoop and Mel suggested we sleep here—at the center—so we would have easier access. So, we're all warm and snuggled together again, and he starts making out with me."

"Bit of a turn around."

"Exactly. While I am somewhat ashamed to say I was into it, he wasn't."

"Did you check?" Chloe asked, her tone indicating her brain had taken up residence in the gutter.

"I tried. I swear to you, I tried. He wouldn't let me."

"Are you drunk?" she asked. "Were you drunk last night? Are you sure this wasn't some puppy-emotion-induced nightmare?"

"Nightmare?"

"Well, I don't want to live in a world where Mel stops a woman from touching his penis. That is a topsy-turvy world in which everything is upside down and the only way my shit isn't breaking is if I nail it to the ceiling."

"Well, get hammering, because that is this world."

"I—I just—it—it … What exactly happened when you couldn't get to his junk?"

"Not just couldn't get to," I argued. "It's not like it was just out of reach on a high shelf. He blocked me. He played defense. I made a mad dash for it and he literally cock-blocked me."

"Okay, but did you explain to him what you were doing? Sweetie, I've seen you flirt and sometimes it's just ..." She went quiet for a second before trying again. "You come off a little ... Maybe he didn't realize you were—"

"He had to realize. I stuffed my tongue in his mouth and pulled him on top of me. That can't be mistaken for me trying to fix his garbage disposal."

"Okay, but did you maybe think to ask *why* he wasn't into it?"

"No, I got violently ill, threw up all over the place."

"Um. That perhaps sends the wrong message about your intentions. Are you sure he didn't stop you from manhandling his man meat *after* you threw up all over the place?"

"I'm damn sure."

"I'm having a hard time digesting this information." I heard another crash from her end, followed by a squeal and an apology.

"Who's there?"

"Just a friend, don't worry."

"Is she okay?"

"It's nothing. I'll kiss it better."

Somewhere in the background I heard an excited, wheezy squeaking that sounded vaguely human.

"What the hell is going on? It sounds like something is about to explode."

"More like some*one*," Chloe purred, and I could tell she had stopped talking to me altogether.

"Oh, jeez," I said. I didn't want to know about Chloe's sex life, at least not while mine was so comically disastrous. I thought about it for a second, lowering my head into my free hand.

"Good god, I can't even get Mel to have sex with me. What is my life? What are my choices?"

"There, there." Chloe said, focused on me once again. "I'm sure it's just some side effect of Norma's death. You were there. Maybe you bring up bad memories and it's just too soon. You'll get him some day."

"I—no!" I shrieked, shaking my head. "I don't want to get him! You're trying to trick me with your witchy words. Cease your speaking, vile temptress."

Chloe snorted out a giggle and I couldn't help but follow suit.

"Hey, don't blame me. You've finally admitted you want to do the nasty with Mel; it's not my fault you can't seal the deal. I've told you, you're terrible at flirting."

"I got into Owen's pants, didn't I?"

"Ah," Chloe said carefully, as if the subject was awkward. I mean, she did watch the guy kill a succubus and then stab Mel in the balls with a drug-filled syringe. Maybe things *were* a little weird. "Well. Then I take full blame. But, in the meantime, I need to go. I have to do some—"

"*Thing*," I finished before she could be too lewd. "As far as I'm concerned you have something very non-sexual and boring to do. I don't want to think it's anything else."

"Keep me updated on the case. When you know more, shoot me a text."

"Will do. It looks like they're bringing the body out now, actually. I'll find Mel, ask what he knows."

"If he doesn't answer, threaten to touch his penis to get him to talk. Apparently he *hates* that."

"I'm hanging up now."

I found Mel just inside the facility, talking to a very tall woman in a sheriff's uniform. I hung back while he spoke to her, noted that he was a little closer than was appropriate, his body speaking a language it shouldn't have been. When he noticed me, he gave a small wave, angled to put himself between her and me, and then turned back to me after a second. Slipping something into his pocket, he wandered over, jerking his chin toward the front door. I turned with him and he slung an arm over my shoulders, leading me out.

"I've got the bags in the car and we're free to go."

"What happened?"

"I'll explain in a bit. Our sessions are cancelled for today."

"Ah, okay. And tomorrow?"

"They'll call us in the morning to let us know."

We were in the car and halfway down the drive when Mel spoke again.

"Tina was quite forthcoming, once I explained what we were doing there."

"You blew our cover?"

"Oh definitely." Abruptly, he twisted just enough to shoot one finger-gun at me, the other hand still holding the wheel. "And, hopefully, that's not the only thing that gets blown today."

Before I could make an assumption about whether or not things had returned to normal between us, Mel settled back, made an announcement.

"I've got a date tonight."

"With Sheriff Amazon?"

"Officer Amazon, and yes."

"But," I asked, dragging the word out. "We're supposed to be married."

"But," he said, copying my tone. "She knows we're not. We'll discuss the case, don't worry. I have some professional dignity. I won't *just* use her for her body."

I couldn't figure out my reaction to his words. Was I angry? Annoyed? Was I disappointed that he'd rejected me and then immediately taken up with the first single woman to cross his path? I couldn't parse my own emotions.

"Okay then," I said with a shrug so intense it lifted my hands and plopped them back down onto my thighs. "As your fake wife, I give you permission to milk this source for all she's worth."

"Well, thanks for the permission," Mel said, and I wondered if I'd caught a trace of bitterness in his voice. When I looked over to try to gain a clue about his mood through his expression, I found that he was turned slightly away, watching the trees out of the driver's side window.

Considering that we might have been in a fight for which I was completely unprepared, I chose silence as my weapon.

Twelve

I'd been holed up in the guest room for several hours, door shut to the rest of the household. Earbuds, blog trolling, and erotic fan fiction had distracted me from the events of the night before and from the tragedy of that morning. Around three in the afternoon, though, my stomach started to rumble like the God of Thunder, demanding I make a sacrifice or pay the price. I procrastinated some but finally gave in, shut the screen on my laptop, and headed out.

I found Julian across the expanse of gleaming wooden floor, standing behind the kitchen bar counter, humming along to some music from the seventies that I recognized but couldn't name. Most music is like that for me, though. He glanced up when I approached, smiled.

"How are you feeling?"

"I'm okay," I said, hopping up onto the barstool. I crossed my arms in front of my chest, leaned against the granite bar. "What'cha makin?"

"Dinner."

"Already?" I asked. He nodded.

"I'm going to make a stew; it takes some time to get right."

"Ooh, sounds tasty," I admitted, despite the fact that my stomach demanded homage immediately. Julian let out a surprised chuckle as the sound of my belly rumbling and stopped chopping, setting down the knife to consider me.

"If you're hungry now, I'm sure we have something."

"I don't want to be a bother," I said. Julian shook his head, turning to open and shut cabinets along the spread of the wall that separated the kitchen from the living room.

"We don't keep a lot of snack foods around but Sarah likes nuts."

I waited for the inevitable finger-guns, eyebrow wag, or, "that's what she said," but Julian just pulled out a tin of mixed nuts and handed it over the counter to me. Fighting the urge to glare in disbelief, I glanced at the tin.

"Thanks," I said finally.

Julian nodded, went back to chopping.

"So you two are brothers?" I asked after awhile, wanting to make sure. It seemed odd that someone who shared genetics with Mel had missed such a prime opportunity to be suggestive. Julian chuckled, dumped the tomatoes he'd just finished chopping into a wooden bowl, set them to the side. Grabbing a squash, he set it on the chopping board, looked up at me and nodded.

"Yes we are."

"But you're so ..." I trailed off, shaking my head. "Nice. You're not depraved in the least."

"This is what being happily married does to a man."

"I guess," I said, still suspicious. Julian laughed again, picked up the knife and went back to chopping.

"So, what were you two up to last night?" This time he gave a single eyebrow wag and I felt myself blush. Wondering if Mel had told him anything about the evening before, I leaned back. Instead of answering immediately, I crammed a handful of nuts into my mouth, crunched on the salty goodness.

"We just checked the place out," I said as I swallowed. "Mel didn't tell you?"

"He didn't say much when you two got home. We assumed you went to take a nap; he went into his room for a bit before taking off. He's been out in the woods for a few hours. All we know from Mel is that there was a body found this morning, that nothing about it seemed normal or natural, and that the center's shut down for today." Julian set the sliced squash aside, looked up at me. "That's all we know from Mel, that is. You smell like you did some rolling around together, though."

"Um." Feeling my cheeks burn just a little hotter, I grabbed more nuts, mashed my hand against my mouth again and managed to drop a brazil nut down my shirt. Julian just went back to his prep work, letting me choose my words as the music played.

"There was some sleeping together but that was it. Just sleeping."

"Mmm hmm," Julian mused and delight ballooned inside him as he moved to put the other chopped veggies in the bowl with the tomatoes. I used the distraction to shove a hand down my shirt and fish inside my bra for the lost nut. I got it in my mouth before he turned back and I wondered if he would have any insight into his stupid brother.

"You and Sarah have been together awhile, eh?" I asked.

"Yes, fifteen years." He nodded and I felt the delight evaporate into a soft, fluffy cloud of love. I felt my mouth pull up into a sloppy smile, unconcerned with the fact that it wasn't an emotion I was genuinely feeling. Perhaps movie aliens are empaths and that's why they're so easily swayed away from destroying earth by love, affection, and all that gushy crap.

"Wow, and the kids are how old?"

"They're five. We waited awhile to start a family."

"Any particular reason?"

Julian shrugged, still slicing and dicing methodically. I got the feeling it was something he did more for himself than for the end product of a delicious meal.

"We just weren't in that place, yet. We knew we were likely to have a whole litter on the first go and we wanted to be sure we were ready."

"Ah, okay." I fished around in the tin for an almond and Julian glanced up at me.

"You're wondering if I was just as bad as Mel fifteen years ago?"

"I …" Trailing off, I popped the nut into my mouth, gave a shrug. "Yeah, I am."

"I was."

"You turned everything into a euphemism and harassed women until they wanted to *kill* you?" I asked cheerfully.

Julian snorted and it turned into a laugh so hard that he had to put down the knife, take a small step away from the counter. When his laughter calmed, he looked at me with a wide grin.

"He certainly …" Laughing some more, Julian shook his head. "I wasn't a clone of my little brother, but I was just as promiscuous in high school." Julian paused and I caught something arc out of him that felt a little closer to what I was used to feeling from werewolves. "He chooses to be a little more obnoxious than I think I was but I was as relentless about sex." Making a non-committal sound as I thought about Mel's rejection of me the night before, I rolled my eyes. Julian caught the action and tipped his head.

"What?"

"Ah," I started, waving a hand. "It's nothing."

"No, tell me. If my brother's done something I should give him shit for, I need to know. It's my duty to make fun of him."

"Yours too? I thought I was the only one."

Instead of pressing the issue, Julian just smiled, tipped his head. I decided it might be worth it to know what he was thinking. Sensing I was about to spill my guts, he looked back down at his work as if that would give me enough privacy to be bold.

"We kind of, sort of, a little bit fooled around last night." Julian made an encouraging sound but didn't look up. "Then, he stopped it and he's been weird since it happened."

"Weird how?"

"Just …" I laughed. "He's been bitchy here and there. Like a teenager who hasn't gotten his way."

"Yeah, he does that."

"Why, though? He's after me all the damn time but, when I finally give in, he runs, pouts, and makes a date with some woman he's just met."

Julian set the knife down, looking up into my eyes with a frown. "He has a date?"

"In a few hours, yeah."

"But aren't you two supposed to be married?"

"I gave him permission."

Julian blinked at me, baffled, not only in expression but full-on. It was sort of like leather butterflies beating at my head and I twitched at the feeling. As I ate some more nuts, staring back at him as innocently as I could muster, Sarah wandered in. Her arms slid around her husband's waist as she poked her head under his arm and pressed it to the side of his ribs. He shifted to accommodate her position and she watched me, realizing something was going on.

"What's wrong?"

"Mel has a date," Julian said. Sarah frowned.

"With Gwen?"

"No. With someone else."

Sarah gave me a cynical smirk, pointing at me while managing to keep herself hugged close to her husband.

"Weren't you two all over each other last night? I smelled it the second you two walked in."

"I—"

Julian interrupted me, assuming I was going to lie about it. "Don't bother. She's got the best nose of any of us. She gets it from her mother and I'm sure our girls will have it, too."

As I laughed quietly at the quivering mix of pride and apprehension swirling around in Julian's psyche, I shrugged.

"It didn't pan out," I said. When she rolled her eyes and sighed heavily, I shook my head. "I don't want to talk about it anymore. Truth is, I don't even know why we kissed at all. He's just a man I find annoying and who owes me a bunch of cupcakes."

Sarah was quiet for a moment and I could tell she wanted to poke at the situation, to break it down and discuss it until we came to some consensus that wasn't just me brushing off what had happened to Mel. I understood the instinct. I break things down and force people to think through their innermost thoughts and fears and urges for a living. I just snacked on mixed nuts and hoped she'd let it go.

"I'd almost forgotten about the cupcakes," she said, pulling away from her husband. "If Julian doesn't mind sharing the kitchen, we can get started?"

"We? Started? *Baking?*" I squeaked. She nodded at me, dropped down to open a cabinet I couldn't see. "No, I don't bake. It's a terrible idea."

"I'm sure you'll do fine."

"It's not that I'll burn the place down but for my own good I don't learn." I thought of the disaster that would be me with an endless supply of fresh pastries from inside my own home. Sarah popped back up with several bowls and something that looked kind of like a wind-up watering can missing its spout.

"Well, then I won't teach you. I'll just give you some tasks that may or may not help out and not tell you why you're doing them. I might make you change the oil in the car and you won't know if that's part of baking cupcakes. Come on, it'll be fun."

I laughed, giving in. She wasn't serious about making me work on her car, though there was a bit of mischief behind her words. Regardless, it was better than sitting around obsessing on why the sluttiest man I'd ever met didn't want to have sex with me.

As if on cue, Mel walked in.

"Ladies," he said, giving a small smile as he watched his brother long enough to let him know he was addressing Julian, too. Julian ignored the dig completely.

Mel paused to look over what we were all doing and I inspected his body. He'd had the decency to pull a towel around his waist, for some reason, but that wasn't what caught my attention. Instead of his usual bare skin, he'd grown in his chest hair. It whirled over each pec, spread in a thick line downward, across his impressive abs, around his belly button and down into the low-slung towel. His arms were dark with hair as well, and the stubble on his face made him look unrefined and manly. It was very PNW and I wasn't sure how I felt about the stark change in his appearance.

He caught me staring and made it a point to catch my eye. Giving me an obnoxious wink, he smirked, then looked back to his family.

"You're looking rugged this afternoon," Sarah mentioned, glancing between us with a look on her face that said she caught the tension.

"He's a regular Jason Statham," I said, keeping my voice light. "Is that what Officer Amazon is into?"

"A gentleman doesn't kiss and tell, Gwen."

"And how does that apply to you?" I asked. Mel scowled lightly and started toward his room.

"I've got to get ready for my date." Throwing a self-satisfied grin over his shoulder, he paused long enough to speak again. "Don't wait up."

The evening was fantastic, despite it starting with Mel's strange behavior and my unexplainable reaction to it. I joined the family on a walk through the woods, ate more than my fill of cupcakes, stuffed myself on stew, and taught two of the puppies how to properly hide the fact that you haven't eaten the vegetables your mother's served you.

I did get scolded for doing so but I was confident that Oliver and Clara would pass my secrets on to their siblings and consider me a hero for my vast and important knowledge. Come some day soon I would be like a saint to werewolf puppies everywhere who hate celery.

Julian and I had discovered a mutual love for all things meme, Clara had spent an hour intricately styling my hair with a cup of water and a comb, and Sarah and I had bonded over our love of trashy television. For her, it was a fascination with the seedier side of what humans are capable; we'd decided that for me it was mainly about getting to see the worst in people without having to take any of it in through my empathy.

By nine that evening, I'd fallen asleep in a pile of children (and one puppy Christian) on the floor as we all watched The Lion King. I didn't even realize I'd fallen asleep until Julian slipped his arms under my back and knees and picked me up to carry me to my room. I awoke piece by piece, finally realizing what was happening as we crossed the threshold. Meeting his gaze in the light from the hall, I felt myself blush.

"You couldn't just woken me. I'd've walked."

"Nonsense."

He laid me on the bed, took a step back. As I shifted to sit up straighter, he leaned over to turn on the desk lamp. Smiling at me, he paused, looking like he had something to say but wasn't sure it was appropriate. Finally, he sighed, pulled the chair out from under the desk and sat in it, leaning his elbows on his knees.

"Mel's an idiot."

I laughed, pulled one knee up to my chest, hugging it.

"Yes," I said. "I know that."

"But he's a good guy, under all the bravado and the objectionable sexual innuendo." Julian lowered his gaze to the ground and I felt a tiny river of worry run through his psyche. "The succubus wasn't his true mate, he knows that. Whatever chemical reaction normally happens when a wolf falls in love, it didn't happen there. But, he still took her death hard. That was partly because of her power and partly because of his deep down—deep, *deep* down—good guy nature."

I resisted the urge to ask about the chemical reaction he'd brought up. It wasn't really the time for questions, I figured.

"I see him with my family and I know he wants this. I've met wolves who don't, who never find a mate and they're fine. They're happy and no one thinks twice about the fact that they continue their promiscuity right up until death. But Mel isn't one of those werewolves."

"Okay," I said, hoping he wasn't going where I thought it was going.

"I'm not saying you're his mate."

"Thank god," I said, making Julian laugh quietly.

"I'm just saying he took the succubus' death really hard. I'm saying that, even though it's been two months, there's still a sadness there. Whatever dance you two are doing, I promise you it's not your fault he doesn't know the steps. If you want to sleep with him, give it time, let him get his confidence back." Julian sat up, gave me a small smile that didn't quite hide the trepidation burbling through his emotions. I nodded.

"I appreciate the speech, but it wasn't necessary. As much as I gripe, I know he's a good guy under all the teasing and the—the—" I paused, unsure how to explain it to someone who didn't live in my head. Finally, lacking the words, I mimed brutally stabbing myself in the neck, which alarmed Julian enough that he went stiff as a board. Shaking my head, I laughed.

"Sorry. His—he's a lot to handle, emotionally. My empathy suffers—I suffer when he's around without the necklace, that's what I mean." I laughed again, putting my hand to my face. "But I'm not actually interested in him as anything other than a cupcake-pusher. I had a lapse in sanity, that's all. We're friends, that's all it is."

Julian watched me, and I could feel that he didn't believe me. Instead of fighting it, I just smiled, shrugged.

"But I'll tell him you gave me a pep talk."

"Oh no," Julian said, getting to his feet. He towered over me, feigning concern. "Don't tell him. We never had this conversation. I never said nice things about him and I certainly never encouraged a woman to let him have sex with her. If anything, I discouraged you from doing so. In fact, if he asks, tell him you find me *much* more attractive."

When I lifted a cynical brow, Julian nodded, winked like we now shared a secret of the utmost importance, and then started heading toward the door.

"It'll give him horrible flashbacks to high school," Julian explained. "Really rock the foundation of his self-confidence. It'll be great." As he grabbed the door to pull it shut, he gave me a fatherly smile. "Sleep well, Gwen. Don't let Mel's idiocy get you down."

After he left, I went through my evening routine, thinking on what he'd said.

Mel and I had both been chemically addicted to Norma for a time. For Mel, that time had been nearly a full week, during which he'd not only been over the moon in love with her, but also unable to seek comfort in the arms of any other women. We'd both watched her die and reacted similarly, but

I'd been so new to the succubus' power (not to mention I hadn't slept with her, as Mel had) that my rage was brief, easily dissipated by little more than a long nap and a few days of downtime.

Mel had needed six weeks to recover, surrounded by family and the distraction of werewolf life.

Maybe I was being too hard on him for the mixed signals and the general bitchiness. Maybe it wasn't a matter of him rejecting *me*, it was a matter of him rejecting *intimacy*. I had very little experience with being rejected so my knowledge about how to react to it was pretty limited.

Toothbrush in my mouth, I met my own eyes in the mirror, paused as I realized something I simply had not considered before. It wasn't that I had very little experience being rejected; I had absolutely no experience being rejected. Thanks to my empathy, I'd never had the embarrassing moment of asking someone out, or making a move that wasn't accepted. Because I knew before even speaking to someone if they found me attractive, I had never bothered wasting my time with someone who wasn't interested in me.

"Holy shit," I mumbled around the toothbrush. Spitting out foamy saliva, I rinsed my mouth, looked back up at myself in the mirror. Realizing how emotionally coddled I'd been up until the night before made me feel a bit ashamed of my reaction.

Mel was still going through something pretty shitty and I was feeling butthurt because a man—just one man—had stopped me from putting my hand down his pants.

As I dried my hands and flipped off the light, padded back to the bed and climbed in, I considered the last few days. Mel had seemed normal, but I hadn't had the benefit of his emotions to truly know. I'd become spoiled pretty early on, always knowing more about people than they realized I knew. I could judge liars from those who were honest, creeps from those who were simply just a little socially ignorant. I couldn't even account for the number of times in my life I'd avoided someone just because I'd known they were unhappy and I hadn't wanted to be pulled in. Instead of letting them tell me they were sad, I'd feigned busyness or faked a phone call to get away so that I could remain blissful and selfish.

For the last week, Mel had been acting okay, making the same jokes as usual and I had taken it at face value. I had no idea if he was really hurting inside because the necklace made it impossible for me to read him. I was flying blind and Mel was my unfortunate copilot, strapped in next to me while I made jokes at his expense and rebuffed his attempts at closeness.

"I may be the biggest asshole on the entire planet," I said to the dark room.

Thirteen

I woke up once again to the smell of delicious food and thought that I could get used to this. Rolling over into an ungainly stretch, I yawned, opened my eyes to look around the room, I heard the sound of snuffling, a snort, and then the clickety-clack of tiny nails on a wooden floor.

Pushing into a sitting position, I looked around the room, trying to figure out if there were ROUSes afoot or if I was still dreaming.

Nothing showed itself but I heard another round of snuffling, followed by the sound of pawing on heavy linen. My eyes went to the foot of the bed and I leaned forward, crawled along the covers to peer over the footboard. A mostly black puppy was chest deep in my bag, paws working at something I couldn't see. Lifting a brow, I tried to figure out which kid it was; I hadn't really spent a lot of time studying the butt fur patterns of Mel's nieces and nephews, so I was out of luck.

Cocking my head as the pup let out a frustrated whine, I realized what the kid was trying to get.

"No!" I shrieked, launching myself forward. The puppy yelped, pulled back and made a break for the door. Unfortunately, it slipped on the wooden floor, landing chin first, before pushing back to its feet. Lorelai glanced back at me and I recognized the spots of gray on her left front leg, before her eyes went even wider and she tore out of the room. I was left huddled on the floor next to my bag, glad as hell that I'd kept my last stash of chocolate zipped securely in one of the outer pockets. I wasn't really sure what the deal was with werewolves and chocolate, but I knew dogs couldn't have it and that was enough for me to be cautious.

By the time I'd gotten out to the living area, dressed and cleaned up,

Julian was setting out plates for everyone. He gestured to one heaping plate and then moved to the fridge.

"Did you want something to drink? We can make coffee."

"No, I'm good." Glancing over, I saw Lorelai two chairs down, head tilted downward so the curtain of her hair hid her face from me. I gave her a little glare, and Oliver looked between us as he stuffed a chunk of scrambled egg into his mouth. Sarah caught my look too and reached across two of her kids to put her hand on Lorelai's hand.

"What did you do?" Sarah asked softly, no accusation in her tone. Lorelai mumbled, refusing to look up at her mother. I moved to sit down at the seat Julian had set for me and watched all eyes land on Lorelai. Immediately, there was a fizzing to her emotions; it started as embarrassment, but as her brothers and sister started to wonder what she had done, it turned to anger.

"Lorelai?" Julian asked, his voice calm. Sarah glanced at him as he brought his own plate to the table, sat down. Lorelai let out a tiny, human growl and Sarah looked over at me.

"What did she do?"

I felt my own cheeks go red; if it turned out chocolate as deadly to werewolf puppies and I'd smuggled some in, I was probably going to be in trouble.

"It's nothing."

"What happened?" Julian asked conversationally, stuffing a hunk of sausage into his mouth. It smelled divine and I wondered if I could get away with just stuffing food in my mouth and making the situation go away. I was sure Lorelai would have appreciated that, too.

"It's fine," I said. "She was just in my bag, poking around."

"Oh, she found your candy?" Sarah asked. I gave a brief nod, feeling myself prepare for the worst. Sarah turned back to Lorelai, gave her the patented Mom Glare. "Lorelai, what have we told you about other people's stuff?"

"That it's not mine," Lorelai mumbled. Sarah made a small sound of encouragement and Lorelai took a deep breath, let it out in a pouty sigh. "And I don't touch without asking."

"Very good. Now, what do you say to Gwen?"

"Sorry," Lorelai said, still staring at her plate.

"Very good," Julian echoed his wife's words, glee burbling out of him. The rest of the kids kept eating, wiggling and jiggling as they did. About halfway through the meal, the front door slammed and Mel came around the corner, gave us all a little salute and moved into his room without a word. I caught the looks I got from Julian and Sarah, fought the urge to roll my eyes. I was already setting enough of a poor example for the pups; I didn't need to be making it worse with attitude.

After breakfast, I helped clear the table and did my best not to stare holes into Mel's bedroom door. My emotions weren't great; I was still feeling guilty about my personal revelation the night before, as well as shitty that I'd been turned down for sex. I wanted to just convince myself to walk it off, but I couldn't. I was irrationally bothered by it.

Mel finally came out of the room, dressed casually, mostly hairless once again, from the looks of his arms. He padded on bare feet to the kitchen, yanked open the fridge and pulled out a plate Julian had made up for him.

He hunkered down over it at the bar without warming the food, noticed I was staring at him and jerked his chin at me.

"Curious how my night went?"

"Um," I retorted cleverly. Julian glanced between us as he finished loading the dishwasher, closed it. Emotions sitting between amusement and embarrassment, he twisted and wandered out of the kitchen. Mel kept shoveling food into his mouth, watching me.

"I just wanted to know about what happened yesterday. With the dead guy," I clarified, before he could launch into some crude description of his night. Mel took a few more bites before he shrugged his shoulders.

"Let me finish eating and then we'll go. I'll tell you on the way."

"Class is back in session?" I asked, leaning a hip against the counter. Mel nodded, took a bite of toast, chewed with his mouth open. I frowned at him, wishing for once that I could feel what he was feeling. He could be crude and inappropriate, but this seemed different, like he was trying too hard. After a second, I gave a small nod and stepped out from behind the counter, moving past him to my room.

Mel started talking the second I shut the car door. I looked over, unsure if the speed of his speech was a way to get all the information out in a timely fashion, or to keep me quiet.

"The deceased was one Bart Heath, half of a couple who came to the center about seven, eight months ago. Officer Amazon was very grateful to get my tip—"

"Mel," I warned, figuring he was going somewhere untoward. He let the statment hang for a moment before continuing without any indication of whether or not he'd intended it as a pun.

"—about how Bart and his wife Liesel had been guests of the center at the beginning of the year. I didn't tell her Betty came across the information illegally, but I figure she's not going to use me as an official source either way, so why burden her pretty little brain with such unpleasant facts?"

"Betty your assistant?" I asked, picturing the older women I'd only seen in passing and from far away. "She's, like, a hundred. What illicit methods is *she* using to gather intel?"

"She has her ways," Mel sniffed, and I realized he probably wouldn't tell me just because I wanted to know. "Anyway, the Heaths were in the program, they were with a doctor who's since left the center, Dr. Driscoll, and they had their papers signed and stamped 'PAID' so I don't know what Bart was doing sprawled bloodless on the lawn yesterday morning."

"You sure they're paid? You don't think maybe they murdered him and left him there as a warning to anyone else who's behind on their monthly installments?"

"I'm having Betty check into what's been going on with them since they left," Mel said, in lieu of addressing my joke. "I'll bet you a hundred bucks he didn't drive out here just for the scenery and happen to fall on a knife outside one of the cabins."

I was quiet, thinking about the scene, about poor Bart's lonely fate. Mel left me alone, not prodding me or expanding on what he'd learned. After a bit, I spoke, partly just to fill the long silence.

"He wasn't bleeding, either."

"Nope, not a drop on him. And I don't think the clothes were his. They smelled—well, not new, but new on him. They hadn't really soaked up his scent."

"You sniffed his clothes?"

"I did it secretly, don't worry. No one's gonna know."

"So, what're you thinking? If it's about Officer Amazon's nice ass, keep it to yourself."

"I certainly did keep it to myself, all up against—"

"Mel!"

"What?" he demanded, a vicious smirk on his face. "Are you bothered? Does it *annoy* you that I found someone else who *wanted* to sleep with me?"

"Of course not," I snapped, getting caught up in his snit even while trying to remind myself of everything Julian and I had said about him the night before. He wasn't even acknowledging that I *had* actually wanted to sleep with him. It wasn't my fault he hadn't let me. It wasn't my fault some … thing had shown up and made me violently ill. "You do whatever you want with whomever you want. I just don't want to hear the details because I ate a big breakfast and I don't want to throw up all over your stupid car."

"We haven't been making out, I'm sure you don't have to worry about vomiting."

"Don't be an infant."

"Would that be intruding on your turf? After all we can't both be childish and—"

"Oh? We can't *both* be childish? So does that mean I should stop? Because you're the one acting like—"

"Like we were having a nice time and you ran off to hurl in disgust?"

"Would you *let that go*? I wasn't sick because you stuck your tongue down my throat, I explained what—"

"You lied!"

"Screw you, Mel!"

We were so busy screaming at each other in the confined space of the car that I hadn't even noticed until Mel slammed on the breaks that we'd made it all the way to Tough Love. I grunted as the seat belt dug into my chest, but before I could pick up the fight where we'd left it, Mel darted out of the car with some crazy burst of werewolf speed. I was so enraged at his immaturity and my own frustration that I nearly forgot how to open a car door for a few seconds. By the time I caught up with him, I was fuming and probably red as a tomato.

He was just inside, talking to Rhonda, acting as if he was concerned and sympathetic. Too furious to bother with any sort of decorum or tact, I grabbed his arm, aiming to drag him out to the car so I could put him in his place. I forgot, however, that Mel has strength much greater than mine and wasn't going anywhere unless he damn well wanted to. Rhonda frowned at me as I yanked, rubber-banded back, and smacked against his elbow.

Mel looked mildly down at me and I snarled up at him as I regained my footing. Rudely, I pointed to the front door.

"We weren't done. I need to talk to you."

"You're—"

"Ordering you to get your pretty ass outside. Now. *Honey*," I added as if I still cared a hoot about the ridiculous farce we were there to uphold. I stomped my foot for emphasis, let go of his arm, and pointed at the door again.

Rhonda was surprisingly nonplussed by our behavior and I had to remind myself that she likely witnessed marital spats on a daily—if not hourly—basis. Mel sighed, apologized to her, and turned to face the door, moving toward it without waiting for me. He paused just outside on the porch and I shoved his shoulder, griping at him to keep walking. The push did nothing, of course, except tweak my wrist a bit, but I felt I'd made my point clear. Without looking back at me, Mel kept walking to the edge of the driveway, stopping and crossing his arms over his chest without turning to face me. Fists clenched in rage, I whirled on him, punching him in the chest, and hurting myself in the process.

"Can we please be adults?"

"I certainly can, I'm not sure—"

"For fuck's sake, Mel. This is your deal, not mine. You asked me to be here, I didn't beg you to let me come."

"I had to bribe you to come."

"Yes, fine, I'm a shitty person who does nothing unless I get something in return. *Fine*. But that was then and now someone is dead. Someone is *dead*, Mel, and you're acting like an asshole because you think I won't have sex with you. What sort of behavior is that? Just fucking grow up and let's work on making sure no one else ends up dead."

Mel watched me stone-faced for a few moments, but even without the benefit of being able to read him, I could tell I'd made an impact and put him back on course. This wasn't about us, after all. We'd both seemed to forget that in all the moments where we'd been alone in the dark with our hormones, but it wasn't something we could afford to ignore. Someone had died and, for all we knew, more people could be in danger. We couldn't be sure Mrs. Heath wasn't also around, waiting to be stabbed and dumped somewhere conspicuous. If that was the case, us concentrating on our yearning genitals and infantile feelings wouldn't help her one bit.

"You're right," he said after a few moments, and everything inside me unclenched. "You're right. We have bigger things to worry about. We'll go in there and see what we can learn. I've got my phone, so if Betty gets back to me we'll know what direction to head in."

"Okay, good. Okay." I sighed, glad we could set aside his hissy fit for awhile and get back to work. "So. Tell me what our plan is."

"Our plan?"

"Yes, our *plan*. The one you've refused to let me in on so far. Which, fine, okay. I'm not a private *dick*," (I admit, I could've avoided the emphasis on that particular word, but I'm only human,) "and so I don't know what you need to get done or how to pick a lock. I don't have bugs or binoculars or huge … rippling muscles." I trailed off, unsure what my point was or how I'd gotten to where I was. Mel just watched me patiently, his brow furrowed like he wasn't sure either.

Get to the point, Gwen.

"I just … mean … you're the professional here and you're not even doing much, as far as I can tell. You observe the other couples in the gardens, at meal times, but otherwise you just make up a lot of stories and fight with me." I glanced past Mel, found Rhonda watching us through the front window. When she saw me notice her, she jerked back, out of sight. I stepped slightly to the side so his body was between the center and me just in case she had binoculars of her own and could read lips. Crossing my arms, I glared up at him, lacking any further point and hoping he'd apologize for starting this fight and explain what the hell we'd be doing from then on out.

Mel watched me for a moment, his face unreadable, before his lip quirked slightly. I honestly didn't know if he was amused by me or mocking me and I wanted to get mad at that alone. The powerless feeling of never knowing what was going on in his head was horrible. I don't know how normal humans get along with each other at all.

"I haven't been doing nothing in therapy," he said quietly. "I mostly listen."

"The hell you do. I can barely get a word out before you're—"

"Not to you," he explained, gentler than my tone had warranted. "To everyone else. I've been, you know," he tapped his ear, "*listening*. To other therapists, other couples, the staff. No one's been at all suspect except Coontz, and that could be nothing. He's not even the doctor who worked with the Bishops or the Heaths."

"Wow," I said, relaxing as I realized the implications of what he was saying. "You can listen to what's going on in the center *and* have a big, old, immature fight with me about what chores you're not doing?"

"Yeah," he said, as if it was no big deal.

"Wow," I said again. "I can barely listen to the TV and talk on the phone at the same time."

"Well, you're—" He cut himself off and I frowned up at him. Swallowing, he switched tactics, making it clear he was changing his mind about whatever he'd been about to say. "You're not a werewolf."

We stared at each other for a while longer, me wondering what he'd been about to say, him giving me no hint as to what he was feeling or thinking. I felt my stance shift even further away from the outrage I'd started with.

"So," I stated, shrugging a shoulder. "What's the plan today?"

"Today I keep listening. I'm hoping more people will be talking now that someone's dead. We may get lucky," (He didn't even bother with an eyebrow wag or a single finger-gun; we had a long way to go to get back to where we'd been just forty-eight hours prior) "and someone will admit to something, or talk about who they suspect of something."

"Who do you suspect?"

"Coontz, if I had to choose. Howard seems on the level, Kirby's ancient, barely has the upper body strength to crush a paper cup, and Case just doesn't give me the vibe."

"None of the other staff? Rhonda's got something up her butt, maybe it's a cult leader's hand." Mel lifted a brow and I flailed my hand as if that alone should be enough elaboration. "You know, like a puppet thing."

"No, not Rhonda. She's … a handful, but she doesn't ring any bells."

I considered the staff I'd met, the ones I'd been able to read and get a sense of and he was right, no one seemed especially murdery. I thought of the bombshell who'd taken my blood and shown up to interrupt Mel and I getting carnal.

"Taylor doesn't do it for you?" I asked, hoping I had her name right.

"Oh, she does it for me," Mel said with a trace of his usual chauvinism. "But she's not bad news. She's the newest doctor, only started here six months ago—replacing Driscoll, far as I can tell. If the Heaths are involved—and I'd bet my canines they are—she can't be at fault."

"Well that makes no sense," I mumbled, looking down at the ground.

"Why?" Mel asked. I shifted my footing as I looked up and noticed Coontz step outside onto the porch. I leaned slightly to the side to get a better look at him around Mel's beefy arms.

"Because—"

"Excuse me?" Coontz called from the bottom of the porch steps. "Are you two okay? Should we be discussing this in session?"

Mel caught my intent as I sucked my bottom lip under my upper teeth and took a breath. Stopping me from screaming an expletive, he clapped a hand over my mouth, catching my eye and smiling in such a way that I was reasonably certain he was amused rather than annoyed at my immaturity. I scowled at him but didn't chew through his hand to force the issue.

When he was certain I wasn't going to launch into tirade, he dropped his hand and slid his arm behind my back, twisting to face Coontz while simultaneously pulling me up next to him. Throwing a wave to the doctor, he leaned in close as we walked.

"Just play along for one more session and then I promise I'll let you take over the investigation."

"That's not—"

"No, no, I promise," Mel offered, as if sure he knew exactly what to say to keep me from throwing a tantrum. "I'll get you a catsuit and some night goggles and you and your fabulous cleavage can get all up in this place."

"Shut up," I sulked, though I liked that we'd moved back to being friendly enough that he was willing to compliment my cleavage.

"I'm serious. I'll leave the real detective work to you, especially if I can watch you squeeze into the suit."

I socked him in the kidney as we stepped up onto the porch.

I found myself watching Mel intently during the session and apparently Gordon noticed. Mel had no idea, or at least convincingly pretended he had no idea. The idea of Mel multi-tasking the way he claimed to be able to do was far too fascinating.

Around the halfway mark, as Mel was describing all the feelings he had over discovering a dead body and talking about how he had just wanted to get home afterward and cuddle me, Coontz turned to me.

"Gwen?"

"Yeah," I said, still staring at Mel's face. He didn't even look slightly distracted. Maybe no one else in the facility was talking and he wasn't currently eavesdropping? Mel smiled knowingly at me and I realized I had been spoken to.

"What?" I asked, glancing over. Coontz was staring at me, his expression blank, even though I could feel a thread of nerves thrumming through his body. It had been there since I'd gotten near enough to read him, but my empathy, like the rest of me, didn't like being that close to him. I'd distracted myself by thinking solely about Mel and what he was supposedly doing while lamenting the state of things.

"You look like you disagree with what your husband is saying, but you're not voicing your concerns. It's important for the two of you to communicate. Is there anything you feel you need to say?"

"Uh," I grunted. Biting my lip, I shrugged, shook my head. "Nah. He has it about right."

"Are you sure? I'm going to be honest, Gwen." Though something wiggled through his psyche that told me he wasn't really. "You've been less than cooperative during these sessions and I'm starting to wonder if maybe you're just not as willing to work on your relationship as Mel is."

I looked back at Mel and he made an, "ooh, he got you!" face, but blanked it before Coontz could catch him. I fought the urge to snipe and took a deep breath. Turning to face Coontz head-on, I considered my options, considered where we stood, and decided being less than cooperative was exactly the right response.

"What about you?" I asked. Coontz lifted a brow and formed his mouth around the start of a sentence, but I pushed on before he could get it out. "You had a corpse show up on your property here less than twenty-four hours ago and you're just sitting here, talking to us like it's nothing. You don't seem bothered in the least."

"Gwen," Mel said gently. I ignored him, shifting in my seat to lean closer to Coontz.

"No, I want to know why we should give any more time—or money—to a guy who may not even be emotionally stable. You don't have any thoughts on what happened, here? You're not bothered that your center may have managed to get a man killed?"

"Tough Love is not at fault for Mr. Heath's untimely passing," Coontz said. I didn't even need to parse his emotions to make sure: he was lying through his crooked teeth.

"Then what would you blame for his death, hmm? You claim you're here to help people and now someone's dead!"

Coontz stared at me, his expression tight. I poked at his psyche shamelessly, trying to get out anything that might be helpful. It was a gross, unpleasant experience rooting around in his feelings but I was desperate

Mel was considering that this guy was the problem and, while I could be sure he was *a* problem, I wasn't seeing quite enough from him to be sure he was *the* problem. He smelled weird, he made me quaveringly uncomfortable, and I was reasonably sure he was a shit therapist, but there wasn't any guilt in him at the mention of Bart Heath's death. Maybe he was a sociopath, but my money was on Taylor as being at fault for the missing couples and bloodless corpse.

Coontz was a waste of time, as far as I was concerned. A creepy waste of time.

We stared each other down for what felt like an eternity and, thanks to the formless music he had piping out of the tiny player across the room, I couldn't even discern time through song. Finally, Coontz swallowed, dropped his gaze to the table and tipped his head slightly. He was playing it cool and a little disappointed, but inside he was frustrated with my behavior. There was something malevolent in there, too, but it didn't feel like him. It didn't even feel human, but I couldn't get enough of a handle on it to reconcile it as anything but. Irritation and impotence gripped my internal organs with sharp, determined claws and for a second I felt like I was going to get ripped apart from within if I didn't do something.

"What you're doing right now Gwen," Coontz said quietly, sympathy ringing through his tone, "is called deflection."

"Oh, bullshit," I spat, pushing to my feet. Coontz jerked like he would stand with me, maybe shove me back into my seat, but in the end he stayed sitting.

"Honey," Mel mumbled, as if trying to placate a screaming toddler. Coontz held a hand out, palm up.

"I understand you're distressed by the events of yesterday. Why don't I give you two a moment? You can have some snacks, take a second to calm—"

"No, I don't want to be in this tiny, *windowless* room, anymore. I need to take a walk. You two—" I paused, jabbed a finger at Mel. "You go ahead and say whatever you want about me. I'm getting the hell out of here."

Unsure what my plan was in that moment, or even whether or not I had one, I stormed toward the door, swerving wildly when Coontz bolted up and reached for my arm. Without looking back to see if Mel's expression held any clues as to what he thought of my fit, I tore out into the hallway and slammed the door.

No orderlies ran out to restrain me, no alarms went off, and no one jammed down the hall aiming a butter knife right at my throat. I took a deep breath, considered it my victory, and then headed down the hall, peering in to any open room I could find to see if something jumped out at me. Unfortunately, I found nothing labeled CLUE (not even the board game, how about that?) so I just kept moving. Halfway down, I noticed a familiar swoop of red hair stepping into view in the reception area. Rhonda stopped to speak to someone, giving me time to jiggle the handle of the nearest door and rush in. I shut it quietly behind me, cursing to myself.

Pressing my ear against the door, I listened to see where Rhonda might be going. When I heard her strike up a conversation with someone else, closer this time, I swore again, hoped she knew how to keep discussions short and to the point. When a minute or two had passed, I felt along the wall for a light switch, flicked it on, and then rested my head on the wall. I sat that way for a bit, feeling lost.

Turning to face the room, I sighed, still wondering how the hell I'd gotten stuck in such a stupid situation. I'd let my pity for Mel and weakness for sweets drag me all the way out to some island to be jabbed with needles, fed bland chicken, and tempted into wanting to sleep with Mel. Now I was hiding in a room from an uptight admin, unsure if I'd ever escape.

Time passed with my brain running in circles before I focused enough to realize that I recognized the exam room I'd chosen at random. It looked the same as it had a few days ago, right down to Mel's test results being exactly where they'd been abandoned after I'd handed them to the brunette bombshell.

Nothing had been moved since then. Even the needles and tubes were where they'd been left after she'd shuffled about, pulling them all out. They were empty of my blood, thank god, which made things even worse. If she hadn't used those to pierce my skin and drain me, what the hell had she used?

Lifting my arm to inspect my inner elbow I grimaced as I started to realize that I'd been had.

I could only hope it hadn't been had as in, for dinner. Something was up. The bombshell—Taylor, I'd assumed later—who'd shown up and made me feel greasy and sick had been in this room with me, doing something that involved piercing my skin, but not with needles.

The situation had just gone from bad to gross.

"Oh god," I mumbled. "What the hell did Mel get me into?"

I folded his test results up until they were small enough to fit in my pocket and then started poking around the room. I opened cabinets, rolled stools, attempted to find something that might explain what had happened. Heart racing, I tried to come up with a reasonable explanation. Could it be a vampire?

I considered that, feeling myself go a little light-headed at the very idea. The woman hadn't felt like a bloodsucker, but I'd also only met one. He hadn't made me sick, he'd felt sort of good, in a strange way. His emotions had been liquid, burbling against my skin like a hot tub or oozing like honey. This wasn't that, but who was I to say other vampires were the same? The one I'd met had been under the influence of a demon most of the time I'd been around him; maybe that had confused my empathy enough that it just didn't know what it was sensing?

Mel hadn't been able to smell that vampire either; what if that was exactly what we'd run across?

My palms were sweaty enough so that rubbing them on my clothes didn't help even a little. Swearing quietly, I moved to the sink, twisted the knob for cold water.

When nothing happened, I grumbled, twisted the hot water knob. Again, nothing happened. Like an idiot, I tried both once more before crouching down to pull the cabinets open again. The pipes looked fine to me. I'm not a plumber and, in fact, I don't think I've ever even met a plumber, but they looked like pipes, so that meant they should work, right? Leaning in, I grabbed and prodded at them as if maybe they just needed the proper encouragement to work.

I noticed a crack in the back wall of the cabinets, realizing something smelled earthy. Frowning at the smell—not because it was bad, but just because it was out of place—I leaned closer, put my sweaty palm to the edge. Before I'd even gotten a chance to fuss with it too, I could feel the slight temperature change between the rest of the room and the corner of the cabinet.

"Well. This isn't suspicious, even a little." I dug my fingers into the crack, pushing in hopes of dislodging or widening it and figuring out what I was looking at. The cabinet slid easily to the side in a track I hadn't noticed. Beyond it was darkness, the edges of which were dirt for as far as I could see. Considering the lack of proper lighting in the low cabinet, that actually wasn't very far. I dug my phone out of my pocket, flicked it on, and used it to light the short distance beyond.

"Shit," I hissed. "This looks like it could be exactly what we've been searching for."

This had been an entirely accidental find. I hadn't really had a plan when I'd bolted out of Gordon's office and then darted in here to get away from Rhonda. Now I was faced with a choice. Did I try to get Mel in here with me to explore, or did I go on my own? It was unlikely Mel, even if he was listening to me whimper and shuffle around from down the hall, would be able to get away from the doctor and make it in here without anyone noticing. It was even less likely that I'd be able to get back out, grab him, and drag him here without Coontz questioning us both.

We could probably come back tonight, break in, snoop around, and see what was tucked in this musty tunnel but I was there already. It could have been nothing, I told myself, biting my lip. Maybe it was just bad construction, an accidental dirt-filled tunnel behind the exam room. Maybe I'd go tell Mel what I'd found, we'd come back that night, pick the locks, and get caught by some screaming alarm and go to jail and it would turn out nothing was here at all except a steep drop into a shallow hole.

I didn't believe my own excuses, though the part about going to jail did seem pretty plausible.

The light on my phone died down and I glared at it. No signal at all, thanks to whatever the Tough Love center had set up. I didn't know if it was a legitimate marriage therapy technique they'd developed, or if they were just jerks who abhorred texting.

Did I have a choice to make? Yes.

Would I make the right one? No.

Tucking my phone back into my pocket to keep my hands free, I took a breath to steel myself and pushed my shoulders into the cabinet. I crawled in, accidentally slamming my upper arm against the useless pipes and swore under my breath. Twisting to get my wide hips and pudgy legs completely into the tunnel, I stared at the open cabinets I was leaving behind. Biting my lip in consideration, I reached out and yanked them both shut, just in case anyone peered into the room.

For all I knew, they had frequent patrols specifically aimed at making sure there were no sneaky empaths discovering their secrets.

OLIVIA R .BURTON

Fourteen

The mud beneath the heels of my hands was cold, the tunnel still and pitch black. Once I was sure I had my footing, I wiped my hands on my jeans, considered that I was possibly dooming them to a life of being painting pants, and slid my phone out of my pocket. Need your path lit through an uncertain, possibly dangerous, lightless tunnel? I had an app for that!

Using my phone as a flashlight, I looked around the enclosed space, keeping my empathic feelers out to make sure nothing and no one was sneaking up on me. I felt a few rodents in the soil around me but that was it. I had no intention of bothering any gophers or moles, and I was pretty sure they had no intention of bothering me. I took a few steps, realized the tunnel had gotten marginally bigger; I could stand up tall, if I didn't mind my hair brushing the dirt above me.

Crouched slightly, I started making my way through, watching my step, keeping my mind alert. The light from my phone showed me about what you'd expect from a hidden, underground tunnel: dirt.

"Good job, Gwen. You've discovered the underside of the ground. It's like the backside of water at Disneyland, only messier."

My voice sounded strange in the tunnel and it made me pause, turn around, and just double check that I was, in fact, alone. There were no other emotions nearby, but I hadn't come across everything in the universe. Some things had no emotions and if one of them was sneaky, I could have been in danger.

Scolding myself for my ridiculous thinking, I pressed on.

Eight more steps and I spotted something. My phone illuminated a spark of metal in the distance, sticking out of the ground. The little kid in me went, "ooh, treasure!" while the rational adult in me told the kid to shut up and not draw any attention to herself. As I got closer I realized the adult was right; this wasn't treasure. The corner of a pair of glasses was poking out of a mound of soil. It was only as I got closer that I realized they were still attached to their wearer.

Immediately, my heart sounded the alarm through the rest of my organs. I felt cold and light and a little bit dizzy as I froze in place, staring at the body peeking out of the loose earth. My brain, just as eager to be helpful as my heart, came up with endless horrifying images of zombies and their victims. It also happily reminded me that, as the undead, zombies have no use for emotions, so the fact that I could still feel nothing didn't necessarily mean I wasn't about to get my tasty brains scooped right out of my head through my eye sockets.

I felt my knees shaking, saw the light from my phone waver as my arms followed suit. Still, nothing moved except me. The dead guy in the ground remained dead. Even the aforementioned gopher didn't move from its place in its den in the tunnel walls. Afraid to move in case I drew something's attention, I reminded myself that I had gotten myself into this mess. I was down here in the dark with a dead guy because I'd been feeling cranky and superfluous. If I'd just left the room and gone back to Mel, he could have wolfed out, ripped the cabinets from the walls in a manly fashion, and escorted me to the dead guy like a seeing-eye werewolf.

"But you're alone with a corpse," I said, barely above a whisper. My voice didn't wake the dead and somehow that gave my legs the courage to move. Taking two slow steps back, I pressed myself to the walls of the tunnel, asked myself what the plan was now. I'd gotten dirt all over me; reversing course didn't seem like the brightest idea. How would I explain how I'd come out of a sterile exam room so dirty? Going forward didn't seem like much fun, either.

Still, I'd come down here to snoop and slinking back to Coontz with my tail between my legs was not snooping.

"Okay, then," I said to the dead guy. I managed to make actual sounds this time, which made me feel courageously cowardly. Sure, I could speak, but if my voice had done something to alert the dead guy that he was a zombie, my immediate reaction would have been to curl up in a ball and cry. Zombies were like bears, right? That would work.

Keeping my gaze on the corpse, I pressed on.

It was several minutes before I could persuade my brain I couldn't see it anymore. Logically I knew that my tiny phone screen could not illuminate that far, but my eyeballs believed differently. Like rebellious teenagers, they'd gone and tattooed the gory image onto themselves without my permission. By the time I convinced them to cover it up, I'd found another problem: the cave split off in several directions.

Right, left, forward, or back? I had another decision to make, this one just as unappealing as the last. I stood at the crossroads, still pressed to the wall of the cave for a while, before stepping out and turning in circles, trying to decide which way to go. Somewhere around my fifth revolution, I realized I had no idea which tunnel I'd come through.

"Shit! Shit, dammit, fuck!" I said out loud. When that didn't help, I twisted, kicked the edge between two of the tunnels and asked myself what the hell I'd been thinking coming down here. The gopher must've heard me; I felt a tiny, harried explosion of shock from my left. Unless I was mistaken, it was the same gopher that had been to my right when I'd come into the tunnel. He hadn't moved, had been a constant buzz off the side of my empathy since I'd started my skulking walk of shame. There was a blurry part of my memory that wasn't really sure if I'd kept tabs on the little guy while I'd been huddled against the wall staring in terror at the corpse, but I convinced myself I knew what I was doing and decided to press on.

Feeling like the sailors of old, I used the gopher to orientate myself, facing the tunnel I thought would take me back in the direction I'd come. I was done being a detective; Mel could keep it. I was going back to the exam room, even if I had to make up a ridiculous story to explain myself.

You guys have mud baths, right? You're that kind of place? Well I fell in one.

As I headed in what I thought was the right direction, I kept my eyes peeled for my dead friend whose name I didn't know. Glasses was as good a name as any, I thought. It was like a nickname between friends. Maybe if I considered him an old pal he wouldn't rise up with murder on his decaying mind.

Soon, I told myself, I'd see his rotten face, wave a jaunty hello, and push on, promising to bring help for him. Oh sure, I wouldn't be able to bring him back to life, but I could at least get him a proper burial, right? He wasn't a zombie, so that was the sort of thing he'd be into. You know, if corpses could be into stuff.

The light app caught something dull in the distance and I wondered briefly if it was Glasses, or if the gopher had burrowed through the wall to join me and I was seeing a glint off his giant, shiny teeth. Stepping to the side to get a better look, I felt my foot hit something sticky.

"Ugh, really?" I grumbled. Nothing answered me, of course, but not just because I was the only one in the tunnel who spoke English; I'd taken the wrong path. The gopher and my empathy had screwed me. The spot of white wasn't a friendly corpse or a helpful rodent; it was a thick strand of what looked like Halloween webbing. Squinting at it, glad it wasn't feces of some kind, I took another step forward, felt something catch my hair.

Immediately terrified, I yelped, flailed my arm up to bat away whatever had grabbed me. My spasm, unfortunately, only managed to make things infinitely worse. Now, not only was my hair caught, but my arm and left leg had been snared as well. Like the idiot I had become over the last half hour, I reached up with my free hand, trying to pull the dim webbing away from my skin. I might as well have tried to tear a phone book in half. A really sticky phone book that had now captured both of my arms, one leg, and my hair.

"Oh god," I whimpered, trying my best to look around and see what I'd gotten myself into. The light from my phone caught on the strands of webbing that held me, making them sparkle here and there as I continued to struggle.

I'd managed to get myself into beautiful but certain death.

The only saving grace of being stuck in the webbing was that the light from my phone had, mercilessly, not ended up aimed directly at my face. I couldn't move my thumb even enough to close out the application but I could at least see the webbing around me in a way I hadn't noticed before. Somewhere around what may have been the twenty-minute mark, my body had given in and started to sag. The web was light, barely felt along my skin, except when I did exactly this. Then, it would pull at the hairs and my flesh like tugging on a really big Band-Aid.

Despite the sharp pain of having every hair on my body yanked on simultaneously, sagging was a relief. I felt kind of like I'd gotten stuck in some weird, European hammock that, while not comfortable, at least felt very secure and let my tense and stressed muscles have a few moments of relief.

"Gopher?" I called out for the fifth or sixth time, knowing it was useless. "You wanna get Glasses over here? See if he's got a knife or something? Maybe one of you can go get help? Tell them Gwen fell down the well and she needs Lassie to get her hairy ass out here and—" I cut off, as movement teased the edge of my light. "Oh god, oh god, I was kidding! I don't really want the dead guy over here! Don't—"

"What in ludicrous hell did you do to yourself?"

Squealing at the voice, I made the mistake of struggling, trying to see if I was hallucinating or if Mel had really managed to find me. The hairs on my face and neck stung as they were yanked by the webbing and I swore a few more times, making sure that every subterranean mammal who had ignored me in my time of need heard it. As Mel stepped into view, I sighed, whimpering with relief.

"Mel! Oh god, you have to help me! I'm stuck."

"I can see that. What are you doing down here?"

"Not making friends with any gophers, let me tell you!" I whined. Mel lifted a brow, frowning down at me. I realized he had no idea what I'd been doing for the last half hour to keep myself sane; considering the fact that I'd been talking to a rodent about a corpse, I decided I didn't need to explain. None of it would make sense to anyone except me anyway.

Sighing, Mel stepped forward, twitched as a strand of the webbing caught against his arm. He let out an annoyed chuff, ripping at it. It came free painlessly and he paused, looking around the cave more carefully. Shaking his head, he put his hands to his hips, met my eyes again.

"I feel like this is something only you could get yourself into."

"Clearly it isn't. Did you see the dead guy down the hall?"

"Yeah, but I smelled him first. You're lucky you clung to the wall near him for so long; I wouldn't have picked up your scent if you'd bolted. Of course, if you'd never come down here in the first place, this wouldn't be a damn issue."

"Would you please just get me out of this stuff?" Mel shook his head, rolled his eyes.

"Stop wiggling, you idiot. That's only going to make it worse."

"Your face is making it worse; just help me!"

Mel took his time, stepping around me as wide as he could to look me over before making a move. I suspected he may have been checking out my ass instead of the webbing at one point, but I didn't complain. Finally, he ducked under a fat glimmer of a strand, reached across my face toward my left arm. This put me at eye level with his bicep, which flexed attractively as he did his best to tear the webbing and free me.

"Welcome to the gun show," I mused, appreciating the view despite the situation. At least if I died down here, I'd have the memory of Mel's strong arm to send me restfully into the void. He was saving my life, after all. I was allowed to do some admiring. Glancing up, I found him smiling, amused by my reaction.

"What was that?" he asked, knowing very well what my answer would be. I just rolled my eyes.

"Nothing," I mumbled after a moment, making him laugh silently.

Finally, after what felt like an eternity of ripped-out body hair, Mel grabbed me around my waist, pulled my chest against his, and yanked. The webbing around my head took what felt like most of the back of my skull off, but I was free.

"Thank you!" I wrapped my arms around his chest and squeezed. The cave went dark as my phone pressed against his shirt and I felt Mel tense. "What's wrong?" I asked, still hugging him. Mel let out a snort and then sighed.

"Your skin is still sticky. I think you just glued your arms to my shirt."

"I did n—" I froze, as I realized he was right. I could feel the web spreading over my skin, clinging stubbornly. "Ah, shit."

We stood there for a second, wrapped around each other in the dark, and I listened to his heartbeat. It sped up slightly and I smiled with the half of my mouth that wasn't fused with cotton. I could feel the necklace pressed against my temple, and it was warm. Finally, Mel sighed, rolled his shoulders and took a half step back. I whimpered as the fabric pulled against the tiny hairs on my face.

"I've just realized what your plan was all along, Gwen. For shame."

"What?" I asked, knowing full well I'd had no damn plan. Abruptly, Mel shifted, reaching behind him to grab the neckline of his shirt and pull. I stayed put, his shirt glued to my exposed skin as he shredded the already ruined cotton with ease and then stepped back shirtless. In the light of the cell phone through the fabric, I could just see him over the cloth glued along my nose and cheek. Mel grinned at me.

"You could have just asked to see me half-naked. This plan? It's a little convoluted, and way too messy. Now, let's get you out of here."

I did my best to glare at him, but the effect was ruined by the fact that I was so thankful to be free. Probably also by the fact that most of my face was obscured. Mel stepped around me, gestured down the tunnel.

"Aren't you going to get this off my face?"

"Nah," he said.

I glowered at him but lacked a comeback for once.

"Just don't touch me again. I know it'll be hard, considering how fabulous I look, but do your best. And, here, I'll take that." Mel reached out, carefully peeled the phone out of my hand, and lifted it high. "Come on."

"Seriously, will you please help me with this?"

"Walk it off."

"Fuck you," I snapped. Mel turned to leer at me and wag his finger.

"That's a dangerous proposition in your state, but maybe later.".

Fifteen

"I can't believe we haven't reached the exam room, yet," I groused. We'd been walking for a while, keeping our distance so as to not get stuck together again.

"We're not going back the way we came," Mel explained.

"Why?" I asked, trying once more in vain to pull his shirt away from my face. It tore at the hair there, made me whimper. Mel ignored me; I'd been trying the same trick for ten or fifteen minutes and he'd stopped bothering to look at me like I was an idiot.

"Because I'm hoping there's another exit, one we won't have to explain our way out of."

"You hope?"

"Hey, genius, you're the one who wandered down here alone and got stuck in fae webbing. You're just lucky whatever left that isn't still down here. You'd be spider food."

"Spider?" I squeaked, ceasing my tugging. Mel snorted, paused to look down at my phone. Switching it off, he plunged the cave into darkness. I fought the urge to squeak again.

"Your phone's almost dead. I have mine, hold on."

As he shuffled in place, my brain tried its best to be helpful which, thanks to it being a trolling jerk, was not in the least. My jerk brain presented me with images of dozens of giant spiders creeping up on us in the pitch black, making my breath come faster. When the light came on from Mel's phone, I let out a wavering cry of relief. Mel just shook his head, pressing on.

"I think I smell something this way, trees maybe. Could be the roots from above, but I don't think so."

"I just want to go home and shower and eat some cupcakes. This is ridiculous."

"I can't disagree with you," he said, looking me over.

We were silent for another stretch of time except for my futile tugging and grunting and whimpering. I managed to feel like I'd made some headway, at least peeling the fabric away from one nostril so I could breathe easier.

"You said this is a spider? A big spider?"

"I haven't seen it, but I'm assuming so."

"You think it's still here?" I asked. Mel shrugged, and I saw his body language shift, relax a bit.

"If it is, we don't have to worry about it for much longer. We're almost out,"

"Thank god."

"I'm glad you're grateful," he said, turning to smile at me. "But such a nickname isn't necessary. Sir Mel The Awesome will do just fine."

"I'll call you whatever you want if you get this crap off me."

"I'm going to hold you to that."

"Ah, considering how it went the last time we held each other, that may not be the best idea."

Sarah helped me get rid of the shirt and the sticky mess. Following me into the bathroom with a big jug of some cleaner she promised would help, she shut the door, looked me over.

"My, but you're a sight."

"Yeah," I agreed, struggling slightly against the shirt. She laughed, popped the top on the cleaner and dumped some onto her hands over the sink. It smelled like citrus and vinegar and, even despite everything going on, it made my stomach growl. Laughing at my belly, Sarah leaned in, rubbed her hands over my arms, and unceremoniously yanked the shirt away. I cried out, but the pain was much less intense than the emotional turmoil I'd been put through walking into the house with clothing glued to my face. The pups hadn't noticed, but Julian had certainly been trying to stifle laughter of his own.

A few more tips of the jug, a few more rubs, two more good tugs, and I was free. Groaning as I caught a look at my reddened face in the mirror, I sighed. Sarah pointed at my shirt.

"Strip. I'll wash your clothes, get this junk out."

"Ah, thanks," I said, feeling a little embarrassed at the proposition of stripping in front of her. She just stood calmly, watching me like I had all the sexuality of a department store mannequin. I had some trouble getting the shirt over my head without it sticking to the parts of my neck that she hadn't cleaned. Sarah solved it pretty quickly, grabbing my chin and maneuvering my head around so she could rub her citrusy hands along my skin and kill the stickiness there.

I felt like one of her kids, actually, and it wasn't so bad. I realized, after she did the same to my legs as I took my pants off, that this was the reason she'd stayed. She'd known I wouldn't be able to handle this problem myself, which meant she'd gotten to know me as a person pretty well for having only known me a few days.

Once I was down to my undies, she smiled, tapping the jug. "Use what you need; I've got plenty and it'll get all the gunk out."

"Thanks," I said again, giving her a small nod. "How'd you know this would work?"

"Old family recipe. We've lived on this property a long time and before the area started getting developed we had our fair share of strange fae popping up. You're not the first girl to get a face full of some strange goop and need it clean off." As she took my pants off the counter where I'd set them, she frowned down at the denim. Digging through the pockets, she pulled out my wallet and the folded up test results I'd found.

"Oh hey, I had forgotten I'd even found those. Mel's test results," I explained.

"You need them?"

"I don't think so, but you never know."

"I'll leave them out on the desk." She bundled my clothes up, turning the gooey sides against themselves so she was just touching the outside of a cloth ball. Pausing with her hand on the door, she twisted to meet my eyes. "You two okay?"

I looked around, lost. "Are you talking to my tits?"

She let out a quick, sharp laugh and shook her head. "You and Mel. Things seem less awkward than earlier."

"Yeah, we had a big fight and then he rescued me from my own stupidity. I think we're doing a little better."

"Good," she said with a big smile.

Sure enough, I'd lost a chunk of hair at the back of my head. It wasn't so noticeable that I looked like I was balding and couldn't admit it, but I was willing to bet Chloe would still comment on it first thing when I got back. At least I was clean and no longer covered in shiny gunk, though.

I made my way out to the kitchen, found the tub of cupcakes Sarah had left on the counter and peeled the top off. As I took a bite of the morsel (frosting first, of course), it occurred to me that Sarah probably wouldn't have kept chocolate in the house if it were bad for her children. I moved around into the living room as I munched, noting the lack of activity. Finding Mel sitting alone on the couch, laptop open on his knees, I leaned over the back, looked at his screen. He smelled like citrus and soap and I found the scents comforting.

"What'cha doing?"

"Getting chocolate saliva on my shirt from the sound of it," he commented. I looked down, saw a crumb on his shoulder, picked it up, and ate it.

"Is that Wikipedia?"

"Yep," he said.

"You're looking up our spider thing on Wikipedia?"

"Yeah," he said, twisting to look up at me. I stuffed the rest of the cake into my mouth, did my best to chew without getting any other bits of spittle on him. Mel watched me, unfazed by my rudeness.

"Why?" he asked finally. I shrugged.

"It's barely correct about real life things, why would it know about this?"

"No, you'd be surprised what people put there labeled as myth that's actually true."

"Hunh," I grunted, standing to move around the couch. I plopped down next to him, turned the computer so could see it easier, and knocked his hand out of the way to scroll.

"You think the web was from one of these unktomi things?"

"Makes sense," Mel said, handing me the laptop. He pushed to his feet, moved across the room to fiddle with the stereo, but didn't say anything else. I watched him, waiting for him to explain, but giving up after a minute. I scanned the article, picking out paragraphs and sentences that seemed important here and there, and came away with a picture of a creature that seemed like it might be just what we were looking for.

"Spider thing, occasionally human shaped, eats babies, poops webbing—well, that makes me feel *loads* better about getting myself caught up in that tunnel—tricks people into believing stuff that isn't true? Sounds like a winner."

"It's the eats babies part that I'm most worried about."

"Why?" I asked, setting the laptop aside. "It's just grown-ups missing so far."

"Yes, but grown-up pairs, couples. People who could make babies."

I thought about what he'd said for a second, feeling like my brain couldn't get a handle on what he was saying, before I grimaced, before I grimaced when it all punched me right in the frontal lobe.

"Oh, ugh. You think this thing is taking people and forcing them to make … it dinner? Gross."

"I think it's no coincidence we've found two dead men but no women. I think it's not interested in the men past a means to an end."

"But we only found one man out at the center, the other was buried—poorly, but buried—in the tunnels. Why would it hide one, but not the other?"

"I have no idea. Those tunnels are endless, I doubt it ran out of places to put a body." His words reminded me of what I'd found before I'd gone spelunking.

"Hey, I found your—well, Thom's test results."

"What?" Mel asked, still positioned across the room, arms crossed tightly across his chest. I wondered why he was acting so squirrelly. The family seemed to be gone, out for another walk through the forest, and we were alone. The topic of baby-making other-beings couldn't have had him that spooked.

"You found what?" Mel repeated. I frowned at him, waved my hand vaguely back toward my room.

"I found your test results; they'd just left them in that room that led to the cave. I think they'd been sitting there since we handed them over."

"Let me see them."

"Sure, come on," I pushed to my feet, padded toward the bedroom. Mel hesitated, before I heard the lid to the laptop shut and turned to watch him walk quickly to catch up. Once we were in my room, I grabbed the folded up page off the desk, held it out. Mel took it, still just outside arm's reach, and looked it over. I wondered why he wasn't invading my space as I watched him bring it to his face, close his eyes. Taking a sniff, he held his breath, let it out, and then unfolded it and sniffed it again, quicker.

"Something here," he mumbled and I stepped forward as if I could smell it, too. I watched the frustration cross his face before he sighed, tossing the paper in the garbage next to me. "It smells kind of like parts of the cave, but it's really faint. I may just still have the cave scent in my nose. I might be imagining it."

"What do you smell in the cave?"

"Nothing. Well, I mean, *something*, but I can't be sure what. It's faint, barely there. Again, I can't even be sure I'm smelling anything and not imagining it. The cave was musty, the paper doesn't smell like that, but I can't … Dammit."

"Maybe we can get Sarah to sniff it." I grinned toothily.

He glared over at me, but didn't engage my teasing. The room was silent for a bit, before I shifted my weight, jerked my chin at him.

"What's wrong with you?"

"I can't figure this out. This unktomi is the only thing that makes sense, but why haven't I even smelled it? The only scents in the center at all are human. If there's some spider fae wandering the place, kidnapping women, why haven't I smelled it or seen it? Why haven't I heard giant, scrabbling, hairy legs thumping around underneath the floorboards?"

"You think Tough Love has Poe-style floorboards and there's something lurking underneath?" When Mel didn't focus on me enough to address my joke, I pushed it a step further. "The Tell-Tale Thorax. No?"

On a sigh of irritation, Mel looked around fitfully, moved to sit on the edge of the bed. I watched him, figuring he was too distracted and hadn't heard me at all. Just as well; I could tell the joke again with Sarah and Julian around and pretend I'd just thought of it.

Leaning my butt on the desk, I watched him as he hunched forward, elbows on his knees, and stared at the floor. His brow was furrowed, his lips quirked in frustration. A possibility occurred to me and I made a thoughtful sound.

"What if you have seen it *and* smelled it but you don't know it?"

"Meaning?"

"Meaning, it tricks people. What if it caught what you were right off and it's *tricking* you into thinking it's just human? If it knows you're a werewolf, it's going to know what you can do and it's going to work around that for self-preservation. Sarah said her family's been here for ages. I'd bet the rest of the cupcakes that werewolves and unk-whatsits have squared off before." Snapping my fingers, I pointed at him. "That's probably why I keep feeling drunk! You say it's nothing, but I can sense it because it has different emotions. What if it doesn't know, just looking at me, that I'm not just a normal human? Did you know?"

"I knew pretty early on you're weird, yeah."

I ignored the dig. "But I mean, did you know I was fae-style weird? Like, with extra powers? Do I smell or look different?"

"No, you smell human."

"That's it!" I cried, excited at the prospect. I closed in, standing in front of him like I had the other night, just within touching distance. "If it can smell you but not me, it's not going to know to trick me out of sensing it!"

Mel sat back and looked up at me. Brow creased, he searched my face before he groaned, swiping his hand down his face like he had to wipe something irritating away.

"That's so annoying it has to be true."

"How is it annoying?"

"That means I'm useless. If I can't sense it, I can't stop it. It could walk right up to me and kiss me on the mouth and I would just assume it's happy to see me."

"But I wouldn't." I grinned, patting his head. "Stick with me and you'll know when it's around."

"You're sure you'll know?"

"I feel drunk every time it comes by. The first time was in the exam room. I got woozy as hell. There were a few times in session where I got sorta … I don't know, googly-eyed. I just figured I was going blind with rage over something you'd said, honestly, but what if this thing was around? What if it was there when we—" I cut myself off, wondering if I was picking up that can of worms again. Mel lifted a brow, watching me.

"When we what?"

"When we were …" I trailed off, feeling my shoulders rise and my mouth quirk in a nervous smile. "You know. In bed."

Mel's expression remained blank for a few seconds before realization exploded across his face. His eyes went wide, his mouth worked as if he was trying to express something his vocal chords wanted to keep silent. After a second, he let out a strangled laugh, lowered his head into his hands.

"I can't fucking believe this," he said. I frowned down at him.

"What?"

His laughter continued, low and breathy. I glanced around the room, wondering what I was missing. After a few more seconds it died down but he didn't move.

"I really thought you were just disgusted by me," he admitted into his hands. I rolled my eyes.

"Usually I am, but not this week. I've had fun this week. And not just because of the food."

"Good to know," he said, his words muffled by his palms. I hunched over, trying to get look at his face to see if I could tell what he was feeling. Finally, I dropped to the floor in front of him, sitting back on my heels and patting the side of his arm in hopes he'd understand I was trying to make eye contact.

"You've never cared what I think before, what's the problem now?" I asked. Mel lifted his head out of his hands, propping his chin on his folded fists. Sighing, he caught my eye, looking dejected, but didn't explain. After a bit, I reached out, knocking my knuckles against his knee.

"Come on," I encouraged.

"I-I … wasn't lying. In the garden," he said, his gaze sliding to focus on some point beyond my back.

"About what?"

"About …" He swallowed, took a deep breath. "The last time I've had sex. It was with Norma."

"So?"

"So …" He trailed off. His gaze dipped downward, to the floor between us. He bit his lip for a moment, hard, from the looks of it. "After her death, I've had some trouble getting my mojo back."

"But things are good now, right?" I mimed boxing toward his face. "You're back in fighting shape thanks to Officer Amazon?"

"No," Mel whispered, as if he didn't want me to hear it at all "She and I …" He let out another laugh, high and quick. "She wasn't into the Statham look."

"So you screwed up your chance?"

"On purpose. I got nervous."

"Really?" I demanded, a smile splitting my lips. "How'd you even know?"

"Know I'd screw up?"

"Know she wouldn't like you all manly and rugged."

"It's a talent I have."

"It's a wonder I've never see you on Star Search."

"Yeah," he said quietly, shutting his eyes. I watched him, considered his handsome face. While I could admit I was out of my depth without emotions to back up my meager body language literacy, I could tell he was feeling bad about himself. I found myself inching closer, wanting to comfort him. I flashed back to the night at the center, how nice it had felt to kiss him even before the part where we'd been rolling around groping each other. I'd spent most of the time I'd known Mel loathing him, but I'd actually really enjoyed his company since we'd started pretending to be a miserable married couple.

Maybe things could be different and we could get along. Maybe Chloe wasn't just yanking my chain and it would be worth it to sleep with Mel. She wasn't the only one who insisted showing him a good time was indeed a good time. Maybe it could just happen and his confidence would reassert itself and then he and I could be friends. Just two friends who helped each other with work and who didn't suffer because one of us was constantly hitting on each other.

Really, what I was about to propose was for the good of the friendship, I told myself.

"Well, I was lying," I said as I pushed to my knees, my thighs bumping his shins. He opened his eyes as I spoke, his brows lifting when he found me so close. "I'm not really Batman."

He smiled, let out another quiet laugh. I pushed forward, holding his eye until just before I pressed my lips to his. As he had been before, he was hesitant, making it difficult to deepen the kiss. I slid my hands up the backs of his arms, over his shoulders, to cup his face. He let me, dropping his hands away from his chin as I pressed forward, parting my lips. Almost reluctantly, he mirrored me, and I tipped my head, letting out a little sigh as our tongues met.

The memories of the night swirled through my mind a little faster, making me think of the feel of his skin against my hands, the wetness of his mouth along my throat. I let out a small sound of anticipation, shifting to get to my feet, shoving him back as I did. His hands came up to rest tentatively on my waist as I leaned over him, forcing him to lie on the bed under me. Straddling his left thigh, I held my body above his, hands against the unmade bed. I left space between our bodies as I kissed him, pressing my thigh gently against his groin. He moaned a bit into my mouth at the pressure and I lost my mind just a little.

Here I was, an average woman who'd nearly gotten herself stranded in a tunnel and covered in spider poop just hours before, a woman who could barely control herself around candy or pastries, and I had a werewolf pinned beneath me. I knew his strength was much greater than mine, that he probably could have snapped the heavy wooden bed frame with little effort, but here he was, bowing to my whims. I could feel his vulnerability in the way he touched me, in the way he kissed me. I could also feel that I was unequivocally in charge. If I stood up in that moment, backed off, and told him to get the fuck out, he would have done it without even a single breath of argument.

Our relationship had never been quite like this before.

Overwhelmed, I moved one hand away from the bed, our bodies still close but not quite touching. I slid my palm down his body, felt his erection through his jeans. I rubbed my hand over him through the denim. I felt the muscles in his thigh tense, heard his breath catch. I nipped his lip as I moved my hand back across his chest, sliding my fingers into his hair. Giving a little tug as I lowered myself onto his body, I hooked my other arm behind his shoulder to cradle his head in my palm.

One hand at the small of my back, he slid his other to my arm, his grip gentle.

We stayed wrapped together for a bit, kissing, keeping close but almost still. I could feel his heartbeat against my chest and it made me want to touch it, to feel it beneath my hand, to taste it along my tongue. Abruptly, I moved my fingers to his chin, turned his face away from me, kissed a line down his jaw and along his neck. I bit his earlobe, let out a small sound when the pressure made him gasp. Feeling the pound of his pulse against my lips as I kissed his throat, I let out an impatient breath, pulling back.

He blinked up at me, his expression cloudy like he'd just woken up from a really good dream before he'd been ready to leave it. I smiled down at him, still feeling the glee of the power I held over him. Uncertainty touched his features as I paused to admire him. His hand fell away from my arm to drop onto his chest.

In answer to the question in his eyes, I shifted to straddle him. Slowly, I pulled my shirt over my head, tossed it to the side. I watched him watch me as I pressed my palms to his chest, slid them down to his hips under my thighs to grab his shirt. Still silent, still watching as if he expected me to change my mind, he moved to let me pull his shirt off. I dropped it over the side of the bed, pressed my palms against his belly, digging my nails into his skin. Waiting until I'd caught his gaze again, I leaned down, pressed my lips to his.

It was another test of intimacy, the eye contact as we kissed. After a few seconds, I let my eyes draw closed as I moved to lick along the other side of his neck, down to his chest. As my lips found the heartbeat under his breast, my hands found his wrists. I let my thumbs rest along the pulse points there too, before I moved his hands to my back, pressed them against my flesh. His grip was loose and I sighed against his skin as I moved to kiss his mouth again, cupping his jaw gently with both hands.

Frustrated with his lack of ambition, I let out a snarl as I bit his lip. I was gentle at first but, when it didn't make him react, I bit harder, aware that I wouldn't have pushed it quite so far if he was human.

That spurred him to action. I felt his fingers dig against my hips, slide roughly up my back to my shoulder blades. He pressed me against him as far as he could with my elbows between us. The fact that he couldn't pull me flush against his chest made him growl and I felt the rumble of it through his body, against my groin. I smiled into his mouth when he shifted to part my forearms and shove them aside. Before I knew it, he was pressing me to him again, his hands moving along my back.

He rolled, lifting me up off the bed enough with one arm that he could slide us both further away from its edge before he pinned me beneath him. I wrapped my leg around the backs of his thighs, shoving my hands between us to grab for the button on his pants. His body went tense and I felt him pull away slightly.

"No," I said, moving one hand to the back of his head to pull him in. I kissed him once, let it be long and slow before I whispered my plea. "Come back."

I kissed him again, my hand awkwardly working at the button on his jeans. As it came undone, Mel pulled back, the strength of my palm against his head be damned. He met my eyes, his lips parted, and I moved my hand from his hair to press up against his beating heart. My other hand, meanwhile, was still working on getting his fly all the way down. I would indulge his insecurity somewhat but I wasn't about to just give up. I was in this now, dammit. He'd been hounding me for over a year and I wasn't going to let some succubus and her mind games ruin my chance at getting laid.

"You're sure?" he asked, uncharacteristically timid. I smiled, rolled my eyes.

"Would you just fuck me?" I asked, giving the waistline of his jeans a tug to punctuate the order. I couldn't keep the smile off my face. "Otherwise, I'll just kick you out and you'll know you blew your only shot." Ignoring the expression on his face, which was halfway between insult and amusement, I pushed up to kiss him again. I made the kiss rough, moving my hand away from his heart, down to finish the job my other hand had started. His mouth was more intense, this time, as if he just needed a rude bit of snark to convince him he wasn't hallucinating, that I wasn't some trick of the spider fae.

Abruptly, he shoved my hands back, ran his fingers along my ribs until he got to my hips. Our mouths worked at each other, tongues dancing together as he traced his fingers along my skin, sliding them along my belly until he got to my fly. He was much more adept than I, undoing it in seconds before he pulled away completely. Curious where he'd gone, I opened my eyes to find him standing over me. Still, there was a hesitation there that I was beginning to grow weary of. He took his time, his hands gentler than I would have preferred as he slid my pants off. He twisted to toss them on the chair at the desk but, bafflingly, left my underwear on.

I pushed into a sitting position, grabbed his pants and yanked them down, not doing him the same favor. I rolled my gaze upward, lifted a brow when I met his gaze from inches away from his cock. Breath coming quickly, his gaze searched my face, his eyes a touch wide. On a small smile, I leaned forward, hooked my thumb under the base of his penis.

He let out a long sigh as I closed my lips, pressed forward, sucked back. I worked at him, hoping this would finally get the point across that I was, in fact, seducing him. Letting a small moan slip from my throat to hum along my lips, I varied the speed, keeping my mouth sealed around his flesh. As I heard his breath catch, I felt his hand touch my shoulder, still as gently as he'd done almost everything. Slowly, I slid back, moving my hands to the sides of his thighs, running my nails along his skin.

As I did, I felt his hand move up to my cheek, his other hand mirroring the motion. He arched back, pulling his dick all the way past my lips, stepping back to prevent me from darting in and starting again. I looked up to meet his eyes, wondering what he was doing. He watched me with heavy eyelids, still cupping my jaw. I let my hands drop away from his skin and he kneeled down to eye level, slid his hands down my body toward my hips. When I didn't get what he was hinting at, he leaned forward, pressed his mouth to mine hard enough that I was forced back.

I felt his fingers dig into my hips then, before he slid me to the edge of the bed, pulling my panties off as he broke our kiss. Closing my eyes as he leaned in toward my freshly naked flesh, I clenched the sheets into my fists, felt his tongue dart out, teasingly slow. I let out a moan as he moved his hands up my body gently. Unfortunately his tongue didn't change tactics, his touch remaining light. I took a deep breath, fully intent on giving him orders as to what I liked, but I sighed out instead.

I thought about how uncertain he'd been, how uncomfortable he'd acted at the thought of even kissing me. I wondered if insulting his technique would push him farther away instead of helping us both. Still tentative, he slid his hands down my thighs to my knees, dragged his fingers back to my hips, his touch still feathery.

I felt myself getting distracted, thinking more about his unease than my own pleasure. It made me uncomfortable and it definitely killed the mood. Sliding my hand down to the top of his head, I ran my fingers through his hair, gave a tug. I shifted my thighs, arched my back, trying everything I could think of short of verbally chastising him, but he didn't speed up or vary the pressure of his tongue.

If this was what Chloe had been so impressed with, what she enjoyed spending days at a time suggesting I partake of, I was going to have to start seriously questioning her tastes and preferences.

Sick of waiting for him to intuit that his mouth wasn't getting the job done, I sighed, gave his hair a rough tug. Luckily for his fractured ego, he got that message. I watched as he kissed a line up my body, grasping my hips and sliding me further back. He crawled up my body, stopping to give my left breast some sweet attention above the line of my bra before he leaned in to kiss along my neck. Still, he was gentle, slow.

I wanted to fuck like rabbits, to scratch his skin, squeeze his hips with my thighs, bite him, and cry out. Instead, I was one step away from a cuddle and a nap. Sick of waiting, I slid my hand between us, found his cock. I wrapped my hand around him, couldn't quite resist giving a faint squeeze, before I shifted to angle my hips, pressed him against me. As I lifted, tried to encourage him to get on with it, I felt him take a deep breath against my skin, felt the muscles in his back tense.

Then he was in, still slow and steady. I let out a sound of irritation, hoped he took it as pleasure, and wrapped my legs around his hips. I glowered up at the ceiling as I tried to figure out how I'd intended to seduce the hare and had ended up with the tortoise instead.

"Faster," I hissed and he let out a low laugh against my throat. Glad he wasn't crushed by the order, I slid my hands to his face, turned him to kiss me. He obliged, his pace quickening, and I arched my back. Leaning away from his mouth, I raised my arms above my head, tried to find something to grab onto. Gripping the edge of the bed, I lifted my hips to match his pace, letting out a moan as my body crept right up to the edge of pleasure, eyed it gleefully.

Abruptly, Mel stopped thrusting, lowered his mouth to my throat, trying to catch his breath against my skin. He stayed there, body tense, and I realized the tortoise had finished the race without me. Relaxing my arms, I let out a long sigh, disappointment chasing the pleasure away like it was a group of unruly teens and my body was an old man's lawn.

Mel seemed to have no idea anything was wrong and I wasn't sure if I felt good about this or bad. He pulled back, gave me a goofy smile that only comes out after a man has sex, and leaned in to give me a quick kiss. I did my best to smile back, glad at least to see that he seemed to be feeling better about himself.

"You know," he said after a few moments. "I think you just took my re-virginity."

"I what?" I asked, realizing that I really just wanted to get up and out of there. I could claim I needed to clean up, I realized. The thought that we hadn't used a condom followed and I felt myself go pale.

"My re-virginity. That was the longest stretch of time I'd gone since I started having sex. So, clearly breaking a streak like that must net you some sort of acclaim." He leaned into kiss me again and I turned my head. This he understood, pulling back with a frown.

"What?" he asked, one brow up.

"We didn't—you didn't hide a condom somewhere that I didn't see, did you?"

"Ah," he said, pulling back enough to rest his weight on his elbows. "No, but, that's not really an issue."

"I'm not worried about being pregnant, I have an IUD. But you've slept with a lot of women."

"Oh yes I have," he said, a smirk teasing his lips. I rolled my eyes, suddenly remembered why I had refused to have sex with him in the past. "Besides, I can't get you pregnant. I'm not in love with you."

"Well that's a fine thing to say while you're inside a woman," I sniped, hitting him in the shoulder until he pulled back completely. I got to my feet and fled to the bathroom, yelling back, "We'll talk about this after we're cleaned up."

OLIVIA R .BURTON

Sixteen

I didn't want to, but I came back out into the room to find Mel clean, dressed, and sitting on my bed, which he'd made for some reason. As I was naked, I glanced at the door, wondered suddenly how much of our shared activity the rest of the household knew about, and sighed. The door was shut, presumably thanks to Mel, but I still needed clothes. I crouched down to grab clean ones out of my bag, noticed that Mel was watching me with a wolfish grin. I rolled my eyes, but couldn't help my lips tug upward.

"Back to the problem at hand," I said, standing as I pulled panties on. I realized I'd left the bra I'd worn during sex in the bathroom, so I dug around in my bag for another.

"There is no problem, far as I can see. I finally got you into bed and, because we're not mated, there's no need to worry about pregnancy. Plus, as I'm a werewolf, there's no need to worry about diseases. Didn't Chloe tell you any of this?"

"Why would—never mind. You sure about all that? You're not gonna pass some rare form of werewolf herpes on to me?" I asked, reaching back to snap my bra on. Mel took the time to stare at my tits before he answered. I rolled my eyes, folded the bra up to cover them, stuck my arms through the straps.

"That—of course not. There isn't even such a thing."

"Okay. Then, explain the pregnancy thing again? You didn't even make sure I was on birth control. That didn't even come to mind?" I asked, moving to grab my pants from the back of the chair where Mel had so thoughtfully draped them.

"Ah, it's a chemical thing. Werewolves are sterile until we find a mate.

Then, all bets are off."

"Even the women?" My brain picked at a vague memory of having a similar conversation with Chloe, but I wasn't about to let Mel know he'd been right.

"Yep."

"Well, that's odd."

"You mean it's awesome," Mel said, pushing to his feet. He cross the space between us, wrapped his arms around me, and bent in close. I let him kiss me, as that was something we seemed to do well, at least. The rest of it … well, I didn't need to clue him in on that.

If I'd helped him get his mojo back, then so be it. One of Chloe's selling points on sex with Mel had always been that he'd leave me alone after we'd done the nasty. Or the boring, as the case had turned out to be.

Per my calculations in the shower, I wouldn't have to repeat the sub par performance ever again. He would be some other poor woman's problem. Many other poor women would have to put up with what I'd just experienced. I now knew exactly why he didn't have the whole female population of Seattle trying to crush his windshield with a bat, though. I was betting they'd all left his bed with a similar sense of pity.

Oh, no, it's fine that you don't want to sleep together again, I was sure they'd all told him. *We can definitely just be friends. Friends without any sort of benefits at all. Gotta go!*

Pulling away just enough to give my lip a quick nibble, Mel opened his eyes, looked into mine. I gave him a small, blank smile and he pulled back.

"Are you starving? I'm starving. I think we worked up an—" He jerked his head to the side and I caught his left ear twitch. "Ah, the family's home. Just in time, it seems. I should make us lunch." He bent down to kiss me once more and I started to worry he might try to make it a habit. Maybe I could grab a random woman off the street and ask her how she'd dealt with him trying to get friendly after sex. From the way he told it, there was an eighty percent chance that any gal I closed my eyes and pointed at would have been a past partner.

"I may just eat some cupcakes and surf the web," I said as he hit the door. I tried to sound casual rather than hesitant at the idea of spending more time with him. Hand on the knob, he turned to me, gave an overdramatic eye roll.

"Nonsense, you've had enough *web* for the day." He winked like he wasn't sure I'd get the joke without extreme confirmation. "Get decent, come out, and join us." Without waiting for me to agree he slipped out the door, shut it behind him.

"What the hell have I done?" I mouthed. One roll in the hay and he was acting like we were married. Grabbing my shirt from where I'd dropped it, I pulled it over my head, looked around the room for my phone. When I

146

didn't see it, I retraced my steps, tried to figure out where I'd left it.

It was only when I noticed my wallet on the desk that I remembered Mel had commandeered my phone in the tunnels. For all I knew it was dead, sitting in his room next to his sticky jeans. I couldn't even call Chloe for advice.

"Dammit," I grumbled.

The family and I sat around the table, the kids making enough of a ruckus that I got to remain blissfully silent. I sat two seats from the head of the table where Julian kept giving me knowing glances. Sarah was either unaware that I'd had sex with her brother-in-law or just didn't care.

Mel had made a giant meal and then bounced around the dining room, cutting all the kids' meat, offering everyone refills on drinks, and generally acting domestic. I was just thankful he hadn't been overly touchy-feely or called me any cute nicknames as he'd set my plate down. Most of the way through the meal, Julian caught my eye, grinned.

"So. What'd you two get up to, today?"

"Before or after Gwen got us all sticky?" Mel joked. Julian stuffed a forkful of rice into his mouth, watching me intently as I nearly choked on my food. Sarah sighed from her place at the other end of the table and I got the feeling she'd have kicked her husband if he'd been closer.

"Before," she clarified for him. I coughed into my arm, felt my cheeks go hot. Clara shifted in her seat next to me, grabbed my glass of water, and held it out. I did my best to smile at her in thanks without coughing all over her face. She let me drink the water, but grabbed it from me before I could set it down and put it back exactly where she'd found it.

"Say thank you," she demanded, her annoyance at my rudeness snapping against my skin. I coughed, nodded.

"Thanks—" Hack, cough. "Thank you."

"You okay?" Julian asked. "You need Mel to give you mouth-to-mouth?"

Sarah cleared her throat aggressively but, despite the teasing, I wheezed out a laugh; it, too, dissolved into a coughing fit. Jeremy frowned at us, turned to his mother.

"What's mouth-to-mouth?"

"It helps people if they're choking, when they can't breath," Sarah explained. Jeremy nodded, considered her response, and then stuffed a hunk of meat into his mouth, chewed cheerfully. As I stopped coughing, I looked daggers at Julian but he only threw back his head and laughed. Turning back to Mel, I sighed, found him rolling his eyes at his brother and me.

"You're officially family if he's giving you crap," Mel clarified. My face fell and I immediately went back into panic mode over the concept of Mel considering us closer than we were.

"So what happened after I left the room?" I asked, setting my fork down to keep from stabbing myself in the hand as an excuse to jump up and run away. "What'd Coontz say?"

"He seemed to consider chasing after you at first but I convinced him not to." Mel took a bite, chewed, swallowed. "I told him you're prone to tantrums, that I was used to it and to chase after you would just encourage you." He winked at me and I turned to look at my meal, deciding I needed the fork if I expected to shovel food into my face just to avoid looking at him.

"He tried to ask about how long you'd been throwing the tantrums, tried to figure out if it was a new thing. I played along, but after you'd been gone for about a half-hour, we both started to get worried. I sent him out to the garden, said you'd probably gone for a walk, and I followed your scent trail. I hadn't realized when I heard you babbling down the hall that you were intent on getting yourself killed."

"Where was she?" Sarah asked. Next to me, Oliver was getting restless. He'd finished his meal and was starting to kick his legs, making it clear he thought he had better places to be than sitting at the table listening to boring adults.

"She'd managed to find a secret, unlit tunnel with a dead guy in it and decided the best course of action was to wander in alone."

"I didn't wander," I argued. "I investigated."

"Why would you do that without a catsuit?"

"I didn't have one handy at the time and I knew going back to get you wouldn't work. There was no way they'd let us just snoop around if anyone working there knew about that tunnel. Besides, I would have come right back out and told you what I'd found."

"But you didn't," Mel pointed out, his expression a reprimand as he took another giant bite.

"Only because I got lost. The gopher screwed me up."

"Gopher?" Julian asked.

"Ah." I paused, realized how ridiculous I sounded to anyone outside my own head. "I'd found the emotional signature of a gopher in the walls of the tunnel; when I got turned around, I tried to use it to guide me back to the entrance, but it had moved, so I ended up going the wrong way. Thus, spider poop."

"It's probably best she had the guts to check that place out, anyway. She found your bad guy, didn't she?" Sarah asked. Noticing that Jeremy, Walter, and Lorelai had joined Oliver in his impatient wiggling, she stood up, moved to collect their plates. They took this as a sign that they could leave and bolted toward the living room. Sarah let out a loud whistle and they all changed direction as a group, giving me flashbacks to *Jurassic Park*. They flocked straight for the back hallway, leaving me glad for the respite from their burbling impatience.

"We think she found the bad guy. We haven't confirmed it yet. Even if the trickster is the bad guy, we're still behind. We don't know where the other missing couples are, where Mrs. Heath is. We still don't know if anyone else is working with the unktomi or if it's doing this on its own."

"From what you guys have said, I think Coontz is in on it. He sounds like an asshole," Sarah growled. Clara clapped her hand over her mouth and pointed at her mother, who winced. "Sorry, sweetie."

"What do you say?" Julian asked. Sarah threw him a look and then rolled her gaze back to her daughter.

"I'm sorry for the swear," she said. Clara let out a giggle and then leaned to the side.

"Can I go?"

"Wash your hands."

Clara bolted after her siblings, leaving only the grown-ups and Christian. He was watching us intently, as if he understood every word.

"Did you want to go, darling?" Sarah asked. He just shook his head, stabbed his fork into an asparagus stalk and held it up to his mouth to gnaw on it.

"What are your theories, what do you think's going on?" Sarah asked Mel. He nodded in acknowledgement, but didn't answer at first. He finished off his food, pushed to his feet, and went to take his plate to the kitchen. Julian set his plate on Mel's as he passed and then looked to me with a wide grin.

"I think I know what's going on," he murmured at me with a wink. I rolled my eyes, fighting the urge to grouse over how hilarious he seemed to find it that Mel and I had slept together.

"If he's the one who's in on it," Mel called from the sink. "The unktomi is working with Coontz to select viable couples. I'd guess Coontz is drugging them, making them susceptible to whatever suggestions he and the unktomi are putting into their heads, and then having them cut all ties to their families. Betty got back to me, and the Heaths pulled the same vanishing act as the others after they finished their time at Tough Love. With any luck we can still find Liesel alive if we can get back into the tunnels."

"You think she's down there?"

"I don't know where else she'd be. It's the only area I haven't been able to fully explore."

Julian glanced over, made a clucking sound with his cheek.

"Looks like you've been exploring lots of new areas today, Mel," he said. Sarah snorted at his bad joke but had the decency to give him a chastising look afterHe winked at her, turned back to me. Mel was still unbothered by all the teasing and innuendo.

"I'm thinking of that door I couldn't get through; what if it leads to the tunnels, too? There could be dozens of catacombs under there. All the missing people could be down there. I think I'll go back tonight and check it out."

"Alone?" I asked. Mel shrugged.

"Why not?"

"Because you won't know anything's coming if you get attacked. You said so yourself, you're useless."

"Oh, I'd say he's got a use. Wouldn't you, Gwen?" Julian teased. This time, Sarah stalked over, grabbed his chin, and forced him to look up at her.

"Enough," she ordered. They watched each other for a second before she softened, smiled, and leaned in for a kiss. I looked to Christian to see what he thought about this PDA and found that he'd fallen asleep. Asparagus hanging out of his mouth, hand in his lap, he was out like a light.

"Aww," I cooed and Sarah turned to face her son. Julian wrapped an arm around her waist, hugged her against him, before pushing to his feet.

"I've got him," he mumbled, reaching to set the fork and food on the table. Cradling Christian to his chest, he headed down the hall. I found myself smiling as he went, reminded of my brother-in-law and my sister and their adorable children. I'd screwed up my only marriage but I hoped to god to get another shot at this sort of life. The thought of my sweet ex-husband and what he'd be like as a father made my insides melt slightly.

To combat the distracting feeling, I took my plate to the sink. Mel gave me an affectionate grin as I stepped up next to him and noted he was washing the dishes by hand. When I turned back to Sarah, I found she was watching us with a similarly saccharin look on her face. I rolled my eyes, shook my head.

"Would everyone please stop looking at me like I'm with child? It was just sex, we're not getting married and starting a family."

"Just sex?" Mel demanded and I rounded on him. He'd frozen, elbow deep in dishwater, his expression full of insult. That can of worms, it turned out, had found its way into my gut and it chose that moment to start wriggling madly.

"I mean—" I began, not sure what my explanation would be. Mel saved me from myself.

"Sex with me is never *just* sex. It's an experience, an adventure. It's a ride! Nobody just has sex with Mel Somerset, Gwen! You strap yourself in and feel the G's! "

To make his point he turned, dripping soapy water all over the floor as he thrust his pelvis wildly forward. I stared at him, at a loss for the correct response. I couldn't decide if I was more irritated at myself for assuming

Mel had any capacity for marital-type feelings, or at him for being so very *Mel* about the situation. Even recognizing he was making a Simpsons reference didn't surprise me.

"Fine, fine," I said, waving a hand. "You're the best. My mind was blown. I'm surprised I'm standing here, right now. I should be falling at your feet and demanding more."

"Keep your clothes on, you two," Sarah said wryly. "There are children present."

OLIVIA R .BURTON

Seventeen

With the kids playing, the adults were free to form a plan.

"We'll head into the cave tonight, right through where we left before," Mel said.

"We as in you and me?"

"Yeah, hero. You're the one who pointed out I can't hack it on my own."

"I mean, just the two of us? Shouldn't you two get in on this?" I asked, looking between Julian and Sarah.

"Unktomi aren't that hard to kill once you've got one in your sights," Sarah explained. "Once you find it, just point the way and Mel can tear it apart. He may be a city wolf, but he's still a wolf."

"You're sure? You couldn't come with us? Even just one of you?"

"Gwen, I know what I'm doing, don't worry."

"Yeah, okay." I thought about the first time I'd spent any real length of time with Mel. We'd been at his place and he'd casually joked about killing a deer. The unktomi couldn't be that big, he'd probably be able to take it down.

The more I thought about what he was proposed, though, the more I realized that I'd rather have awkward, unsatisfying sex with Mel again than head into that dark cave.

"We'll need flashlights or something."

"Have you never seen a movie?" Julian asked, sarcasm dripping. "Flashlights don't last long in dark caves full of monsters. Monster love knocking flashlights over and flashlights love breaking at all the wrong moments. You need flares or—"

Sarah yelped, jumped to her feet and held up a finger.

"I have just the thing!" she announced, tearing toward the kitchen and down the basement steps. Julian shrugged when we looked to him for answers. After a few minutes, Sarah came back, boxes of glow sticks and bracelets in hand. She tossed three of them at Mel, handed me two.

"You can wrap these around your wrists, ankles, whatever, and they won't fall off or go dead. I got the bracelets for the kids for Halloween, but I can buy more before then."

"They're not super bright," I pointed out.

"They'll be enough, and we won't lose track of each other."

"Enough for you isn't really enough. I'm just a human, remember?"

"Use the whole case, as many as you need," Sarah said. "I can get more."

"I don't know if they'll stay on if I have to wolf out."

"Oh, that won't be a problem." Sarah leaned in, pulled some of the bracelets out of the box and wrapped them around the cord of Mel's necklace. "See? The sticks are for emergency situations, like little glow-stick flares, so if you'd rather thread your necklace through those, they'll work too."

"That's a good idea, actually," Mel agreed. I nodded, pulled two of the sticks out and snapped them, making them glow dimly in the late afternoon light. The kid in me squealed, demanded I scamper down to the dark basement and run around in circles to make myself dizzy on light patterns.

I restrained my inner child and nodded to Mel. "So, when are we looking at going?"

He glanced at his watch. "Eight-thirty? It'll be getting dark out by then and we can drive out, park out in the woods where they won't see us, and head in."

"Your car isn't going to make it through those woods for long."

Mel bared his teeth in a wicked grin. I felt Julian's amusement from the other side of the room and wondered what I'd gotten myself into and whether or not I'd regret it.

Mel drove the rumbling, cacophonous dirt bike much like he'd driven the car: way too fast and with abandon. It managed to be both twice as terrifying and three times as fun. A few times, when I'd laughed explosively out of nervousness, I'd felt Mel's chest vibrate as he chuckled.

Somehow, he weaved through the forest easily, anticipating the trees or demonstrating an incredible memory for their locations, I wasn't sure. As he slowed, I tightened my thighs against his hips, my eyes squeezed shut behind his back. Even through the massive helmet, the sound of the machine was intense and I hadn't dared try to peer over his shoulder to see where we were headed. Finally we stopped and I felt Mel shift his weight to keep us from toppling.

The motorcycle shut off and Mel patted my hand through the gloves Sarah had lent me.

"Come on, we should walk the rest of the way."

I considered the machine's vibration that had been rumbling through my body—starting at my groin—for the last twenty minutes and cleared my throat.

"Would be it too much to ask for you drive us around for just a little while longer? For um," I said, still hugging around his waist. "You know, cautionary purposes." Mel let out a long laugh, peeled my hands away from his body, and climbed off the bike, letting it go to lean on the kickstand. I sighed, hummed the opening guitar riff to The Rolling Stones' *Satisfaction*, and climbed off the bike as best I could without toppling onto the forest floor. Mel pulled my helmet off, wagged his brows at me.

"I promise, though, if you need a little more stimulation, I can provide that just as soon as we take this baby-eating asshole out."

"Ah," I said, feeling even my slight arousal ebb away at the idea. "Yeah, maybe."

Mel leaned forward, ruffling my undoubtedly messy hair, and then set the helmet on the bike. I did my best to smooth my brunette bird's nest down, frowning when I felt the thin patch at the back.

"All right, let's go get this done."

Mel nodded and pointed deeper into the woods.

"This way. We'll pop the glow sticks just inside the cave. I doubt anyone's monitoring this area, but we don't need them seeing the floating lights and thinking there are some forest nymphs running around the place."

"You mean dryads?" I asked. Mel threw me a glance that made me feel pompous.

"I didn't use the proper word only because I figured you wouldn't know."

"How do *you* know?" I asked, before gasping as if in disbelief. "Are you telling me you're literate? Mel, have you learned to read books?"

"I have, but don't tell the ladies. I have a reputation to maintain." He was angled just so I didn't catch his expression in the low light. "Besides, when you've nailed the real thing, you don't need to read about it in books."

"Whoa," I droned, weaving to the side as his words sunk in. "I was fucking around. You've actually slept with a—Dryads exist?"

"There's very little that humans have written tale of that doesn't exist. You guys aren't always correct in what you write, but you generally get the gist."

"Wow," I mumbled, looking around the darkened woods, wondering what might be out there watching us at the moment. Mel let me peer around in silence for a while before realizing what I was doing.

"If it's an unktomi—and I'm pretty sure it is—I doubt there's anything else hanging out here. It's probably run other creatures out of its territory."

"Well, here's hoping. The last thing I need is to piss off a spider monster *and* a wood nymph."

Mel chuckled and I looked him over. He'd gone with baggy clothes and bare feet, just in case he needed to wolf out at any moment. His cotton pants were loose, but the cloth was thin enough that I'd noticed he was wearing nothing underneath. The shirt looked old and worn, and I wondered how long he'd had it and how many times he'd use it as a just-in-case-I-need-to-go-furry shirt.

Finally, we came to the entrance of the tunnels, which dipped steeply into the ground and, to the casual observer, just looked like any other hole in the earth. Mel dropped down, sat on the edge, and then dropped in, turning to hold his hands out toward me.

"Come on," he said. I looked around one last time for any pretty tree fairies to help us and copied his action. As I slid into the hole, I felt Mel's hands on my waist as he lowered me gently to the ground. He didn't let go immediately and I reached out to look for the many lines of plastic against his chest. It was already pitch dark in the cave, even directly under the entrance and I had to feel around to find them. Hooking my fingers around two, I squeezed them, heard them snap, squinted as they lit to life. As soon as they did, Mel let go of me, stepped back and reached up to grab at the rest.

We took a few seconds to illuminate ourselves before Mel took a deep breath and turned to face the cave.

"Here goes nothing."

"Aww," I said, stepping up next to him. "Don't sell yourself short. You're something. Not something good, but something."

Mel rolled his eyes and started walking. I smiled after his back, following him when I was sure I wasn't going to burst into a fit of nervous giggles. The glow sticks were brighter than I'd figured they'd be, but didn't illuminate much of the cave around us. Mel had better eyesight than me though, and I'd put several around my ankles so I could at least see the ground. As we had the last time we'd been down there, we walked down one long tunnel alone for quite awhile. When the cave split, Mel pointed to the right.

"That's the way we came before. I can still smell you. Come on." Jerking his thumb to the left, he started walking again. I glanced down the other hall and then followed him, still silent. Every so often I'd hear Mel take a sniff, pause, and then keep moving. I kept my mouth shut, let him do his preternatural creature thing.

I wasn't really of any help unless the spider showed up, so I just did my best to keep my empathy open to make sure nothing snuck up on us and started diddling around in our brains.

"Well, this isn't good," Mel commented. I stepped up next to him as he crouched down, ran his fingers over something in the dirt. I peered down at what he'd uncovered for a second, before I let out a low, wordless sound of disgust. He'd discovered another body.

"This guy smells even older than the other guy we found. He's been here awhile."

"No wife?" I peered around, managing to keep half an eye on the partially uncovered hand sticking out of the dirt. Mel looked up at me and I noted the sadness in his eyes.

"No, she's not around. Hopefully that means she's alive. Although, if what we suspect is true, it might be more merciful if she's already dead."

Mel stayed hunched over the dead guy for another minute and I wondered if he was investigating or silently saying a prayer of some sort. When he stood, he sighed, stepped wide around the dead guy, and kept walking. I remained silent, glancing back several times, just as I'd done with the first corpse I'd found that day.

After what felt like an eternity, we discovered our path split off into three other directions, the worst Choose Your Own Adventure I could think of. Mel stopped, leaned close to the dirt and inspected it. I took a step past him, peering down one of the halls. I still felt no other emotions but if this passageway was anything like the one I'd discovered on my own before, I didn't want to go down it. I'd lost enough body hair that day, thank you very much.

"You think there's webbing down there?" I asked, turning back to Mel.

I was met with darkness. Immediately, I spun back around, wondering if he'd passed me and I just hadn't noticed. Despite being able to see a short distance in each direction, I found no other sign of light. I was alone and the realization made me sick to my stomach.

"Mel?" I whimpered, feeling my lip tense and tremble. "Mel, you forgot about me." I heard nothing except the sound of my own shaky breathing. My nerves were getting the better of me, creeping into my throat, threatening to strangle me. If I didn't control my lungs, I was probably going to hyperventilate and make myself so dizzy I'd throw up.

Putting hands to my belly, I closed my eyes, forcing my breathing under control. The nausea receded slightly but when I opened my eyes everything looked like I was watching a 3D movie with my glasses askew. Despite the confusion between my eyes and my brain, though, I knew I was alone.

If Mel had left me I hadn't heard it; even barefoot, he'd made some noise walking in the dirt. If he'd run off, I'd managed to miss it.

"Mel?" I asked again, taking a half step in what I thought was the direction we'd come. Still, I heard nothing. After a second, in which my heart started pounding and hammering and thudding and all the things hearts do in horrible situations, I swallowed thickly, tried my voice again. It was tough to speak over the strangling anxiety that had taken hold, but I managed.

"Judas Gopher? Is that you? If you're playing a joke on me, it's not very funny."

Still nothing. Knowing it was fruitless, I slipped my phone out of my pocket; Mel had so thoughtfully charged it for me during our several hours of downtime at the house. It had full battery and the flashlight was raring to go but there was still no signal. I aimed it down each hall, trying to catch a glimpse of glow bracelets or a pile of clothes or something.

I turned, checking each of the four walkways several times, hoping something would jump out at me—ah, bad choice of words. Hoping something would appear to me, harmless and ready to help. Nothing did, at first.

Then, something moved at the edge of my light just as I heard a high, flat sound.

"Mel?" I asked, swiveling my light to catch whatever had moved. The cry came again, longer this time, sounding somewhere between an excited cat and an angry baby. There went my heart again, trying its best to tear my ribs apart like Superman and fly away. I stepped toward the sound, caught the movement again. Something occurred to my brain but my eyes cried, *Objection!* and refused my brain's input. Even as I approached the tiny form on the ground, I couldn't seem to translate what I was seeing into something I understood.

The baby below me wagged a tiny fist, cried out again, and my eyeballs finally stopped fighting the truth.

"Oh god," I moaned, dropping to my knees in front of the infant. He cried as I touched him, as I felt along his wriggling limbs to check for injuries. When I found none, I stuffed my phone in my pocket so the light poked over the top, slid my hands under the baby's naked armpits, and pulled him to my breast. His chubby little legs kicked once more, his arms beating against my shoulder and chest as I pushed to my feet. I murmured comforting sounds, turning back in the direction I'd come.

Another cry came from behind me, freezing me in place. The baby in my arms started whimpering and I felt my throat sting in preparation for doing the same. In an effort to stop the baby in my arms from going full on tantrum, I hugged him close, whispered soothing nonsense. Twisting back, I caught sight of another baby, wriggling and crying, just as naked and alone as the first.

"I got you," I said, rushing forward. The baby in my arms cried out again, beat me in the breast with his fist, and I patted his back. As I kneeled to scoop my arm under the second baby, I heard yet another cry. I wanted to tell myself it was just one of the two babies I'd already rescued, that we would be safe as soon as I figured out which way to go to get out of here. The babies in my arms shared a whimper, their tiny hands grasping each other, before they went for twin, full-body spasms. In answer, the third baby outside of my view cried out, demanding my attention.

I wailed, glanced up, considered yelling for Mel again. As I got to my feet, the third cry became a chorus of third, fourth, and fifth cries. All different pitches and intensities, they made me feel like the worst nurse in the worst maternity ward ever. The two infants in my arms leaned forward, knocking their chins against my collarbone, wriggling some more. I glanced down at them helplessly, looked up toward the other children again. How many babies had this fucking spider forced these women to have?

And why the hell wasn't it taking better care of them?

The chorus of tiny, impotent outrage got louder, reminded me that I was alone and babies were coming out of the woodwork. I took another few steps, looked down at the third baby. She was Asian, with chubby cheeks and dark hair. Her little fists were pumping up and down, her legs kicking out spastically. She noticed me standing there, staring at her instead of helping, and started to cry. I didn't blame her; I wanted to start crying too.

I couldn't rescue them all; I just didn't have the arms for it. Judging by the growing sound further down the cave, babies were appearing faster than I would have been able to handle, even if Mel had been there to help.

"This is like the worst *I Love Lucy* parody ever," I whispered, trying to keep the panic out of my voice. "I can't just stuff you all down my shirt, so we need another plan." The second baby started crying, which got the first one started, and then the third. The noise in the cave was immense, overwhelming. The sadness I could hear from their little mouths was going to make me ill. I dropped down to sit in the dirt, staring back down the hall as if it held the answers.

"Mel! Please be there!" I called, lowering one of the babies into my lap. I cradled him there, but he didn't stop crying. "Okay, we can fix this! I know someone who knows how to take care of lots of babies! Just hold on, I'll— just hold on!" I pulled my phone out of my pocket, hoping the sickness in my stomach would go away, hoping my phone would work down in the caves this time.

As I closed the flashlight app, blinking at the brightness I'd unintentionally blasted directly into my eyes, the babies all disappeared. My lap was empty, the cave was silent. Once again, I was completely alone.

"Oh god," I mumbled, feeling saliva rush into my mouth. It wasn't nerves this time, I knew. As I leaned over, vomited into the dirt, and felt my vision blur, I realized I'd been tricked. I'd been fooled into losing my way down a darkened tunnel, something I would never have done if tiny humans had not been in grave danger.

I coughed, spat, and pushed up, stumbling back from the smell. There was no way I could tell what direction I'd come from but I wasn't just going to sit in one place and wait to be eaten by something that already had a taste for my blood. The dizziness intensified as I started moving, making me pause and reconsider. If I was getting worse, I was probably getting closer to the unktomi. I stumbled against the wall, twisted, and took three steps back in the direction I'd come.

A low growl echoed through the cave.

"Mel?" I whispered, still using the wall to keep from toppling face first into the dirt. I squinted into the darkness, watched as a speck of light moved toward me. The bigger it got, the blurrier my vision got. I tried closing one eye, turning slightly to the side, but nothing worked; the one patch of light had split into five. I heard the growl again, telling myself it was coming from behind me where I'd established the unktomi waited, and pushed forward.

Mel had mentioned dryads and my brain latched onto that fact, convincing me that I was about to be rescued by beautiful wood nymphs. Any second, now, three lovely, womanly shapes would bounce daintily toward me, take me into their arms, and whisk me away from this terrible place.

"Help," I wheezed as the dizziness grabbed hold again, threw me against the wall. I put a hand to my mouth, doing my best to keep in any further vomit, and squeezed my eyes shut. As I tried my damnedest to breathe slowly and calmly through my nose, I considered that this had been a really bad day for making decisions.

I'd decided to explore a cave all by myself, decided to have sex with Mel, and then decided to join Mel back in that same cave. These were, by far, some of my worst life decisions; being in this dank hole definitely topped my previous biggest regret of cheating on my husband. Clearly, as I was getting older I was getting dumber. I was no longer to be trusted. I promised myself that, if I got out of this place alive and intact, I would never make another decision on my own again.

"Any time now, nymphs," I mumbled against my hand, before pushing against the wall to get myself going. When I opened my eyes, I saw that the lights hovering in the darkness had paused as I did. The closest light shot toward me like a missile and I caught a flash of bright blue eyes.

"Don't!" I yelped.

For some reason, it echoed through the air as, "Get it!"

"What?" I asked aloud, cracking one eye open. The heat of a furry body slammed into me and I felt the dry pads of paws smack against my throat and shoulder. Fur grazed my face before my back hit the ground, my head following suit immediately after. I groaned, seeing stars for an instant. I could feel the softness of fur along my arms as something growled above me. The growl was so close I could smell it.

It smelled like dog breath. Dog breath I *recognized*.

"Mel?" I wheezed, doing my best to roll onto my side. My lungs felt like they wanted to explode and I was reasonably sure I'd been hit by a truck at some point in the last few seconds. Despite the paws pinning me to the ground and the saliva dripping onto my neck, I couldn't stop myself from trying to roll away. I lifted one hand to check my head for blood, but the furry creature above me had other ideas.

Canine jaws grabbed my forearm, worried it. I felt my flesh tear, felt blood smear, before the softness of a tongue pressed briefly against my skin. The teeth yanked away on a whimper that was instantly lost to my own scream of pain. My stomach heaved once again and I fought it, my brain forced to make the hard decision to let me breathe or to force me to vomit. My throat seized up and I was briefly unable to do either one.

Curiously, I could hear my voice, even though I was still gagging against the dirt.

"Did you kill it? Is it dead?"

Gasping in a huge gulp of air, I rolled onto my back, filled my lungs as much as I could muster. After a second, I coughed.

"Not dead. Kind of wish I was," I wheezed into the still air. As I cradled my bloody arm to my chest, feeling the sharp pain of rent skin, I cracked an eye open, searched for a clue as to what was happening. Mel in wolf form was pacing off to my left, glancing between the me on the ground and another, uninjured me further down the hall. Despite the pain, I made a thoughtful sound as I met the eyes of the other me. She glared, rushed forward, and pointed at the wheezing me on the ground.

I heaved, unable to tolerate being so close to the unktomi. Mel whimpered again, paused next to me in his pacing. He'd put his back to me, blocking the unkto-me from getting any closer. She was pointing at me, insisting that he'd been tricked, that she could tell what I really was.

I was starting to really hate myself in that moment.

"Mel," I wheezed, before spitting out vomit and trying to push myself up. My body gave out partway up and I slammed back, my bloody arm sliding across the dirt like it was trying to steal home.

I cried out, swore like a sailor on leave. Mel twisted around to look at me, his head tipped in a little doggy 'baroo?' expression. The other me stomped her foot, pointed at me again, and demanded Mel finish the job. Mel turned back to her and I saw his stance shift, his front legs spreading slightly apart. His head lowered and I heard the growl again.

I reached out, touched his foot, and mumbled, "Atta boy."

The other me disappeared and the abrupt lack of extra emotional input was almost as nauseating as having the unktomi right in my face.

"Oh god," I grumbled, shoving at the dirt, trying to push away from the puddle of sick. The pain in my arm surged up through me, making me swear and whimper again. My chosen string of profanity made very little sense, but can you blame me?

"Shitting cucumber cock-bagged mother goddammit!"

I felt hands grab my shoulders, pick me up like I weighed nothing. My feet flattened against the dirt and I teetered, my legs deciding they'd already, in that single moment, had enough of this standing shit. A warm, bare chest pressed against my face and I felt strong arms slide around my shoulders. My arm continued to bleed at my side, unaware that the rest of me was being sweetly comforted.

"I am so sorry," Mel said into my hair.

"Me too," I said, before shoving at him with my good arm. He let me back up, made a small sound of disgust as I leaned to the side and attempted to throw up yet again. Luckily for both of us, dinner had been just awkward enough that I hadn't eaten much; my stomach tried its damnedest, but couldn't evacuate anything else. Fighting my legs as they demanded to be relieved of duty, I stood, bent at the waste, gagging into the air and still bleeding, still sore from the beating I'd taken.

As my raw throat returned to its regularly scheduled breathing, I felt Mel pull me upward and turn me gently so he could see my face. I blinked at him, let out a long, "whoa." He'd gone human so quickly he hadn't thought to grow any of his hair back. Mel looked positively ridiculous without any eyebrows or eyelashes and his bald head looked misshapen in the low light.

I let out a low giggle and Mel gave me a gentle shake.

"Are you with me? How's your—oh Jesus," Mel hissed, letting go of my shoulders and grabbing for my arm. I screeched when his hand touched my wrist, slapping at him and trying to pull my injured limb back as he inspected it. He ignored my attack, twisted my forearm in the light and glowered down at the rough tears in my flesh, muddied by my own blood and the dirt of the cave. I was surprised I wasn't bleeding more, but maybe the dirt was helping me clot.

"You need to clean that, but we can't really do that down here." He winced, swallowed thickly and I considered that Merrin's necklace was a saving grace in that moment. Pain on top of sickness was bad enough, but if I'd had to also endure his rolling guilt, I may have just considered suicide.

"Until we can clean it, I'm going to wrap it. Give me a second." Mel bent down, grabbed my left pant leg, and ripped it. He managed to pull enough denim off that, before I knew it, he'd fashioned crude strips perfect for wrapping around the arm of an adult woman who won't stop fighting and screeching.

He had to pin me against the wall with his back and hold my arm under his to keep me from ruining the wrap, but he managed to cover up my wounds. I can't explain to you why I fought like a wounded animal, but I just couldn't seem to help it. Every time he'd touch me, the pain was horrific and I reacted like I wasn't a sane, adult capable of understanding that what he was doing was for my own good.

Finally, he let me yank my arm back and turned to face me. I inspected my arm for a moment, feeling my entire body shake with the pain of it. When I looked back up to snarl in his face, I noticed vanity had gotten hold of him and he'd grown in his hair. He looked like Mel again, though his eyelashes didn't look quite as impressive as he seemed to prefer them. His face was sad and it made me bite back the insult I'd been about to hurl at him out of anger.

"I didn't—I thought you were right behind me," he explained.

"Yeah," I mumbled, swallowing my anger. It wasn't his fault he'd bitten me, and the wrapping really was for my own good.

"Me too," I said finally, cradling my arm to my stomach. I was probably going to have some pretty wicked scars, if I got to keep the arm at all. God, just the thought of it made me want to vomit again. I pushed back at the desire to curl up in a ball and sob. "So, what happened?"

Mel sighed, relief opening up his face. He stepped forward enough to wrap an arm around my shoulder and then turned us to walk down the tunnel.

"I stopped to sniff something and when I turned around you were just standing there, staring down the tunnel. I asked what was wrong and you said that you thought you could feel something, that we should head down this way. I think this tunnel rounds back to where we stopped before and the creature wanted us to meet in the middle to attack each other."

"I don't know about this 'each other' business. I think it just wanted you to attack me."

Mel made a noncommittal sound that could have meant he disagreed or that he was unhappy to agree. Free hand pointing at some scuff marks in the dirt, Mel moved his hand from my shoulder to my waist, supporting me a bit better. I let him, partially because I really didn't want to be moving around in that moment. Mostly, it was just comforting to not be alone.

"When I saw you it wasn't you. I mean, the actual you was the spider, and the fake you told me to attack the actual you."

"Well, I swear I'm the real me. If it comes to it, kill the other one, the one that's not me."

"Good god, we're a rooftop and a gun away from a bad 80s movie."

"Is there any other kind of 80s movie?"

"You shut your mouth," Mel said, looking down to force a glare. I could tell he as trying to lighten the mood, so I let him, giving back an equally forced grin.

"What happened to you?" Mel asked after a moment.

"You just disappeared. I was feeling dizzy but I thought it was just nerves," I admitted, looking around. The dirt walls were still unremarkable and unrecognizable. "Then, I heard babies crying and I went after them. It was just one at first, so I picked him up. Then there was a second, and a third, and then a whole bunch of them. I could hear so many babies wailing and I panicked. I almost started crying myself, just because I knew I wouldn't be able to rescue them."

"You just heard them? You didn't feel any emotions? Or did the trickster figure what you can do and fool you that way, too?"

"I—" Cutting myself off, I swore. Mel let me work through my extensive cuss word collection as we approached the split in the tunnels again. "I didn't even try to sense how they were feeling. I saw crying babies and I flipped out. Maternal instinct kicked in."

"You have maternal instinct?" Mel asked wryly.

"I … Is there an aunt's version of maternal instinct? Aunt-ernal instincts? I probably have that."

"Either way, it fooled you."

"Yeah. I didn't even think of trying to feel for anything."

"I'll give you something to feel," Mel said, invitingly. When I looked up at him, he winked, stepped away. Turning to face me, he rudely grabbed his crotch, gave me a wag of his brows. I snorted, shaking my head. He was trying to distract me from the pain in my arm, I was sure of it. Short of full-on knocking me out, I knew he was capable of such a feat, but I let him play.

"I don't see much to feel at all, sorry."

Sighing as if it was some inconvenience to be rebuffed as such a dangerous time, he dropped his hand away.

"It's your loss, Arthur," he insisted. As I snorted, he crouched down to grab his clothes.

"Well, we've been down three of these and we know they don't help." Draping his shirt over his shoulder, he bent slightly to pull his pants back on.

"You getting prudish on me, Somerset?" I asked. Mel caught my eye and winked.

"I need you on top of things. I can't have you getting distracted lusting after me at a time like this." Instead of pulling the shirt on, he held out a hand. "Shall we?"

I eyed his hand suspiciously and wiggled his fingers like he was calling me closer.

"The buddy system, come on. If we're touching, it will be harder for the unktomi to separate us."

"You sure?"

Mel blanked his face, lifted his chin slightly. "Come with me if you want to live."

"That would be a first," I said without thinking.

"Hunh?" he asked. I bit my tongue and lifted my arm, as if the injury could explain what I'd said. Mel nodded gravely and I sighed, glad I hadn't been forced to elaborate.

OLIVIA R .BURTON

Eighteen

The next tunnel seemed to hold no answers but, luckily for my sanity, it also held no screaming babies. Mel's hand was a warm comfort in mine as we went but holding it made me feel useless. I was betting either of the corpses we'd found would have been of more help in that moment should something decide to attacks us. With my wounded arm cradled against my belly and my working hand in Mel's, I could do nothing more than watch him as he walked.

Not a bad way to pass the time, mind you, but considering the way the trickster fae had gotten into our heads before, it wasn't preferable.

"So, the plan continues to be to walk around until we find the thing—or it finds us—and then kill it?"

"Pretty much."

"Somehow I am not confident in your plan-making abilities."

"Well, I'm not confident in your fashion sense, but I still let you dress yourself."

I scowled his way as he crouched to take a whiff of another section of wall. Two of the looped, bracelet-style glow sticks had gotten trapped at the back of his neck sometime during his transformation and I'd been fighting the urge to shove them back toward the front. I hooked my fingers into them and slid them back around to hang across his chest. Mel looked up at me from his place on the ground, lifted a brow, and gave me an expression like he knew something I didn't.

"You'll use any excuse to touch me," he said suggestively. I rolled my eyes, felt the sentiment stick in my craw, and make me slightly nauseated.

This time, though, my brain caught up to the situation almost immediately: it wasn't actually Mel making me sick. The unktomi was back and I felt myself start to tremble. Eyes wide, I gave Mel's hand a hard, panicked squeeze. His expression went dead serious in a split second and he pushed to his feet, twisting to push me between his back and the wall. I kept my eyes peeled but I knew I wasn't going to see anything he couldn't.

After a brainless moment, I took a deep breath, closing my eyes.

I'd learned pretty young how useful my empathy could be. It wasn't just about knowing what others were feeling and reacting accordingly. I could sense emotions, see them in the air like a diagram of where the people around me were standing. One of my favorite uses for this power as a youngster had been to make sure that my parents weren't around to catch me as I raided their change jars (or wallets, as I got older) for cash.

Aware that I could track the spider fae in the same way, I searched for any and all emotions within my range, made a mental map of them.

It didn't take much searching: the only thing there was the unktomi. Mel's feelings were still hidden from me and, despite feeling the heat of his body and the softness of his hand, he was absent from my map. The trickster, though, practically shouted its position at me. Now that I could look for it specifically, now that I knew what to pinpoint, it wasn't so hard to locate.

It felt massive and it felt hungry, a gargantuan ball of confusion. I'd been truly fall-down drunk precious few times in my life but I could recognize that reading the unktomi felt like one of those times. It felt like being drunk and trying to focus on a quickly spinning top.

Worse than all that, though, it felt *close*.

"To the right!" I screeched, throwing my body away from the ravenous monster. Mel's hand left mine and the absence it startled me into opening my eyes. I slammed myself against the wall, the pain in my arm almost forgotten against my fear.

I caught sight of Mel's pants in a pile where he'd been standing before I heard an angry growl and the thud of bodies hitting dirt. I heard scrambling, shuffling, and jolted as a spike of pain swamped over me. Outrage followed and then silence fell. Something moved off to my left, another emotion flashing on shock, and I looked toward it. Almost immediately, it got lost in the sounds of fighting and the surprise I felt from the unktomi.

The course of the fight changed in an instant once again. Pain slammed into me, forcing me against the wall, making me groan. It exploded behind my eyeballs, as if my brain had been the one under attack. Combined with the general nausea, it made me lose track of my own body. For roughly a minute, my consciousness was floating in a soupy mess of queasiness.

When my vision cleared and feeling came back to my limbs, I caught sight of Mel pinned to the ground, the gleaming pincer of a gigantic arachnid shooting toward his throat. I let out a strangled plea for the spider to stop but, just as the tip of the thing would have pierced his flesh, the illusion disappeared. I looked wildly around, trying to figure out where Mel and the unktomi had gone.

I couldn't be sure why, but Mel had managed to rid himself of the glow sticks around the necklace. They lay in a pile further down the tunnel, leaving me blind in terms of where he'd gone. Ignoring the incredible pounding in my ears, I closed my eyes, searched for the creature, tried to listen as hard as I could to find Mel. When I found an emotional signature other than the spider, I felt myself let out a small squeak of panic.

Something else was in the cave with us and it was furious. From my left I heard a chuff of air. Immediately, anger and pain swamped over me from across the wide tunnel. It took me a second but I grasped onto it, did my best to locate it. It was hard to concentrate through the swamp of the unktomi's emotions; I wanted to focus on whatever had joined us in the tunnel, because its outrage was awesome. The tiny, ancient part of my brain that pipes up in horrible situations was screaming, "Danger!" and fighting me on which threat was the most prevalent. The newcomer was creeping closer, slow as a lazy river

Finally, I chided my brain into being focused; I found the unktomi, figured out it was moving, too.

There I stood, knowing I wasn't alone, but unable to verify that fact with my eyes. I could barely see past the glow of my bracelets, anklets and necklaces. I couldn't feel Mel and had no idea if he was even there. Whatever had joined me in the tunnel didn't seem to be interested in attacking me, but I wasn't about to just assume the best in a bad situation. For all I knew, Mel had been taken out and the spider had brought a friend to dinner, aiming to make me the main course.

Doing my best not to hyperventilate or barf up my heart, I squeezed my eyes shut and spoke as calmly as I could muster.

"Mel, are you okay? Please be alive."

He didn't answer. I froze, felt the unktomi shift positions, move minutely toward me. It was on the ceiling and I could feel its anger, sailing along a ribbon of some other emotion I couldn't yet place. I cracked an eye open, trying to see it in the darkness. I realized then that I was the only idiot who'd given away her position. I was lit up like Christmas morning, babbling and whimpering at every damn thing. Mel had been smart enough to ditch the glow sticks and stay silent. He hadn't killed it yet, but maybe only because he couldn't.

Maybe he didn't know where to go. Maybe the unktomi had fooled him into letting it go, and was keeping its position secret. I certainly couldn't see it. The second emotion I was feeling from it snapped into focus, cracking against my ribcage like a baseball bat.

It's afraid!

"I see you," I announced, trying something I was sure wouldn't work, but that had to be tried anyway. Looking up in the direction I knew the spider was hiding, I pointed, doing my best to look tougher than I felt.

"Yeah, asshole. I see you," I said when I felt it move again, the fear in its psyche thumping me a little harder. "I know you think you're smart, making yourself invisible with whatever crazy-ass powers you have, but I can still see your ugly face. That's my power, seeing stupid unktomi faces even when they think they're hidden. Come on, drop the tricks and fight like a man. Or … like a spider, if that's what you're into." When it didn't answer, I took a step forward, jabbed a finger toward it through empty air. My stomach rolled and I felt my body convulse starting at the tip of my finger. Forcing my gag reflex to calm itself, I tried one more time, hoping my words didn't come as bile.

"You're not fooling anyone, you hairy son of a bitch. Not only can I see you, but I can smell your fear. It smells like shit. There's no use hiding anymore, you coward."

The illusion fell away, the spider appearing so close to my face that I realized the only reason I hadn't jabbed it with the tip of my finger was that I just hadn't reached quite far enough. Six brilliant eyeballs the size of grapefruits stared down at me as one hairy leg stretched my way. The spider's bulbous body hung low, away from the ceiling, the hairs along its abdomen shining in the light of my glow, fat as pencils. Pincers like knives danced below its eyes, closing together, pulling apart as if it could already taste my flesh. Whimpering, I felt my very insides tremble under the force of its anger.

Mel appeared along a *whoosh* of air for a fraction of a second in my field of view, jaws grasping at the leg before it could get to my face, taking it with him back into the darkness. The spider fae scrambled back as the sound of cracking carapace filled the tunnel and its blood gushed into the empty space where its limb had been.

My head nearly exploded with a cacophony of pain, shock, and fury. I clapped my hands over my ears, as if blocking out the sounds of fighting would help, and plummeted down onto my butt in the dirt. The spider's emotions grabbed hold of my psyche, dug in, tried to pull me down with it. I pressed my face to my knees, fighting the urge to scream as the pain intensified. Somewhere past the agony in my head, I could hear growling and smell the cloud of dirt that had been kicked up in the scuffle. I lost track of how long the fight lasted. It could have been ten seconds or ten minutes. I was moaning into my knees, the pressure in my head threatening to crack a fissure in my skull.

Then, it was over.

The pain my head was gone, replaced with the oozing of concern along my skin. Silence had fallen, both inside my head and through the tunnels. After one last huff of air, I felt the warmth of someone stepping up next to me.

"Gwen?" I heard a woman's voice ask. I twisted away, still gun shy after everything my poor mind had just been put through.

"Gwen!" Mel demanded, horrified, and I felt his hand on my chin. He tipped my head up, looked into my face. I realized I was staring at his eyes and I didn't even remembering opening mine.

"Are you actually you?" I asked. Mel glanced up and I followed his gaze. Sarah stood next to him, stark naked and watching me; it was her worry I felt like honey on my skin. I blinked up at her, reached out to touch her knee to make sure she was actually there.

"Are you okay?"

"My head hurts," I answered, poking my finger against her leg again. She glanced down at my touch, finding me funny but also sad. "Are you actually here?"

"Yes. Come on." Mel grabbed me under my arms, picked me up like a pile of dirty laundry, ignoring the way my head lolled along my shoulders. Sarah rolled her eyes, exasperated at his lack of compassion, and stepped to the side. Jerking a thumb to her left, she spoke.

"Show her."

Mel adjusted his hold on me, lowering me to my feet, despite the fact that my legs may as well have been overcooked noodles. After a slight adjustment to make sure I would stay upright against him, he pulled me away from the wall, the soles of my shoes skimmed the dirt. Digging a hand into my pocket, he pulled my phone out, clicked it to life, and turned it to face away from us.

There, on the ground in front of us was a massive, hairy, very dead spider. Two of its limbs had been torn off and its belly had been ripped open. The sticky white goo oozing along the dirt was only half as disgusting as the thin, greenish liquid dripping down its pincers from its ruined eyeballs. The spider looked like a giant child with an affinity for popping bubble wrap had gotten to its face.

"I'm going to be sick," I groaned, twisting away from my werewolf bodyguard. Mel tensed, spinning fast enough that I felt myself go lightheaded.

"Is there another one?" he demanded. I shook my head, dry-heaved.

"No," I finally croaked in answer. "That's just disgusting."

Sarah laughed from her place off to my right and then crouched down to retrieve Mel's clothes. She pulled the shirt over her head, stepped forward, and handed him the pants. Gently, he unloaded me onto her and I leaned forward to dry-heave some more.

"Come on, heroes, we should get out of here," Sarah said when my gut got itself under control.

"I'm completely turned around and I've got so much dirt up my nose, I don't know if I can smell my way out. How about you?" Mel asked. Sarah nodded and I felt a mix of pity and amusement burble out of her.

"You give me too little credit," she said, and twisted, taking me with her. As we walked, I started to smell something familiar but decidedly unpleasant. Mel let out a quick laugh and I glanced over as he slapped his palm against his forehead.

"I can't believe I didn't think of marking our path."

"Considering your plumbing versus mine, I can't believe it either."

I wrinkled my nose as I realized what they were talking about.

Nineteen

I hissed, whimpered, cried, and begged for mercy as Sarah peeled away the denim that Mel had wrapped around my arm and unhooked the glow sticks from my wrist. I squeezed my eyes shut before I had to see the damage, but judging from Sarah's hiss, it was bad. Things immediately got worse when she grabbed my arm above the elbow and held it under a stream of cold water.

I shrieked, yanked on my arm trying to get away from the pain. Sarah had that damned preternatural strength, though, and my arm was staying exactly where she wanted it.

"You're going to pull your arm out of socket," Julian said, stepping up behind me and putting a hand to my shoulder. He may as well have been a brick wall; I could barely move.

Mel had, of course, disappeared into his room the second we'd gotten back, explaining that if he didn't brush the eyeball taste of his mouth soon, he was going to take after me and never stop vomiting.

"It's bad, but you're not gonna lose the arm," Sarah said. I cracked an eye open, saw the mottled skin, bloody gashes, and clumps of dirt Sarah hadn't yet managed to clean out and felt my knees go weak. I was bleeding again, despite the fact that my skin looked bloodless.

"Oops," Julian said, wrapping an arm around my waist to hold me upright. I whimpered again as Sarah plucked at some dirt.

"Don't faint," she ordered.

For some stupid reason, my brain obeyed. I wanted to pass out, believe me, but I was hyped up on adrenaline or something, and my mind was not going to give in that easily. Unfortunately, this left me in the position of being completely aware of the pain as she worked.

173

After an eternity of cold agony, Sarah turned the water off, gestured toward the kitchen table. Julian nodded, dragged me over, and sat down, holding me in his lap. When I tried to lower my arm, he grabbed it, used his incredible reach to hold my wrist up in the air, keeping the arm above my head. Sarah disappeared down into the basement.

Feeling nearly sick with pain, I twisted enough that I could see Julian's face.

"Please tell me it's over," I said. Julian shook his head and I felt pity roll out of him. I looked up at my arm, saw that the gashes were still dribbling blood. Sarah appeared with an armful of towels and a giant red box with a white plus sign on the front.

"I have some bad news," Sarah said, setting her haul on the table. "You can't go to a hospital."

"But that's where the drugs are," I whimpered. Julian barked out a laugh.

"Well, we have some of those here, so I guess that's the good news," Sarah said, her voice cheery.

I dropped my head back to Julian's shoulder as Sarah opened her kit and started fiddling with something behind the lid. I whimpered up at him, making him laugh and shift his grip so it was more comfortable for both of us.

"You remind me of Lorelai, sometimes."

"Is that a good thing?"

Julian tipped his head, considering me. After a moment, he nodded.

"I think it will be for her. Assuming she has better taste in men." Julian winked, and I felt a hand on my chin. I rolled my gaze over as Sarah shoved a pill the size of a cockroach to the back of my throat, dumped a glass of water in after it. I swallowed, coughed, sputtered, and felt Julian's grip on me loosen.

"More news—which could be good or bad, depending in how you look at it—is that I have some … well." She paused, looked to her husband behind me as if nervous about explaining. "Let's call it medical training."

"Okay?" I asked, feeling myself start to struggle. That didn't sound good and my subconscious was already certain I was going to be in more pain within moments. Julian's grip tightened and I felt him lower my arm toward his wife. She unhooked the glow sticks from my wrist, laid my arm as gently as she could on the flat surface of the towels and pulled a curved needle out from the first aid kit.

"No, no, no," I moaned. Julian sighed behind me and I felt more pity spurt out of him. He gripped my arm above my elbow and kissed the top of my head.

"It doesn't hurt as much as you'd think."

It didn't take as long as I would've guessed and did in fact hurt less than

I'd expected. Still, I was so emotionally exhausted when it was over I couldn't even think to thank Sarah for sewing me up. She seemed proud of making my arm look like Frankenstein's monster, but when she'd finished bandaging, my eyes were starting to go blurry and I couldn't really tell her emotions from the everyday feelings of breathing. In fact, breathing felt pretty cool and I spent a fair amount of time just inspecting how it felt to let air pass through my nostrils, or over my teeth and tongue.

Noticing my slack-jawed stare, Sarah laughed, shook her head.

"I wish the drugs took a little longer," Sarah sighed.

I did my best to respond logically but it came out as, "Where are air?"

Chuckling, Julian got to his feet, bringing me up with him, and then hunched down as his wife stepped close. Sarah hooked my good arm over her shoulder, leaned in to catch the kiss Julian offered, and then led me toward my room.

"Whassa?" I demanded with all the coherency of a drunk toddler. Sarah smiled and I felt the cloud of concern within her fade toward amusement.

"Let's clean you up."

Thanks to the drugs, showering with Sarah wasn't even a little awkward. She stripped me (which I also found pretty fascinating to feel), shoved me into the shower, and then started dumping soap and shampoo on my skin. Any time my arm would head toward the water, she'd grab it, shove it well out of the spray. I think I started humming at some point and I might have even hit on her. My brain doesn't have all the details, but she didn't treat me like anything other than one of her children, so I couldn't have done anything too horrific.

"I feel fritty pantastic," I announced as I dripped onto the bathroom rug.

Sarah barked out a laugh as she wrapped a towel around me and secured it in some complicated way that I simply could not figure out, no matter how hard I thought about it. She remained naked but tossed a towel over my head before we left the bathroom, leaving me effectively blind. I followed her lead, didn't object when she sat me down on the bed and started drying my hair swiftly. After pulling the towel off my head, she wrapped it around herself, bent down to look into my eyes.

"Yeah. You'll sleep pretty well tonight," she told me. I felt my lips tug up in a smile but it was like they were someone else's lips. I was wearing a mask of my own face and it was hovering above my skin, smiling when I gave it the order to do so.

I reached out to touch her face but found that the action was delayed. By the time I actually lifted my arm, Sarah had bent down to my bag to pull out my clothes. My hand touched empty air but I felt it swept out of the way as Sarah came back into view.

"Arms up," she ordered. When I just turned to stare at my hand and wonder why I found it as completely incomprehensible as lentils, she sighed. "Okay then." Without ceremony, she yanked my arms up, shoved the sleep shirt down over them until my head poked through the neck hole. The action made me snort and giggle. She put a hand to my back, guided me until I was lying down, and then pulled the towel away from my body, smoothing the shirt down over my torso.

"It might lack a certain amount of dignity for both of us to try to get your underwear on, but I think I can manage your pajama bottoms. What do you think?" she asked.

"You're pretty."

"Well, as long as you agree."

Before long, I was bundled up under the covers, high as a kite, unbothered by the fact that I was going commando in my pink, fuzzy sleep pants. She was right, though; I slept really fucking well for awhile.

"How are you feeling?" I felt an arm slip across my waist as the voice crept into my ear. A hand pressed against my belly under the covers, pulled me back against a warm body. The painkiller hadn't quite worn off but I wasn't so high that I didn't recognize the feel of Mel spooning me. I grunted, wondering briefly if I'd been transported back in time. Did I have to deal with that fucking spider all over again?

"Are you awake?" Mel asked. I groaned, shifting my arm. Pain shot through it, making me seize up, yelp, and adjust back into a position that wasn't agonizing.

"Goddammit," I grumbled. Mel pulled away and I cracked open one eye, looking at him in the light of the open curtains. He looked worried.

"Did I hurt you?" he asked.

"What are you doing?" I demanded, suddenly realizing it was not two nights ago; I hadn't been in such pain then.

"I wanted to see how you were doing."

"And you needed to manhandle me for that?"

"No, that I did for your benefit."

"Uh huh, real beneficial. Fuck, I can't believe how much this hurts. Even with the painkiller. I can't believe you did this to me. Keep your mouth away from me."

"That's not what you said yesterday," Mel said with a wink. There was tension along his forehead, though; his joke was forced.

"Well, I should have," I snapped, rolling onto my back. Sensing my ire was ebbing, Mel settled in again, propping his head up on his elbow. "Why aren't you all torn up?" I demanded, cradling my arm against me. Mel shrugged.

"I'm tough."

"You don't even have a scratch," I growled, grabbing his arm with my free hand and holding it close to my face. He let me inspect his skin in the dim moonlight, run my fingers along his wrist. After a few seconds, he spoke quietly.

"Ah, I'm not tough everywhere."

"You're a weakling in Denmark?" I asked, turning to look at him. I let him take his arm back, but he just draped it across my hips.

"Remember the fight over Norma's death?"

"Very well." I grinned toothily. "Prior to seeing pictures of you as a teenager, that was my favorite Mel-related memory."

He sighed, put upon by my constant teasing.

"There's a reason your boyfriend jammed me where he did with the needle. My, ah." He paused, his gaze rolling to the ceiling, as if it was too embarrassing to face me while he explained. "My penis and—um, they're—it isn't—Well."

"Spit it out," I demanded, ignoring the opportunity for innuendo.

"It's not as thick-skinned as the rest of me."

"So if I call it ugly, it'll run into its room and listen to emo rock?"

"Yes, that's exactly what I'm getting at. My penis has an embarrassing taste in music."

"I always suspected that about your penis," I mused. Mel scoffed and I felt his hand move slightly further across my belly, his fingers curling over my hip. I frowned over at him, suspicious of his actions. We watched each other in the dark for a few moments, before I let out a sigh of disbelief.

"I'm not having sex with you," I said.

"How do you know my penis isn't exactly what you need to get better?"

"Because I'm not an idiot." Mel's silence said he didn't believe that one bit and I lifted my good arm, smacking him in the shoulder. He laughed.

"It's pretty terrible of you to assume I came in here just to have sex with you."

"Didn't you?"

Mel was quiet, holding out for awhile, making me guess at what he was going to say. Finally, he spoke. "Okay fine, but can you blame me?"

"Yes!"

"I just mean," he said through another laugh. "That it's been awhile for me, and here you are, willing—"

"Except, I'm not willing."

"Well then, here you are, cute and—"

"And the only woman in the house who wouldn't beat the living hell out of you for trying?"

"I wasn't going to bring that up, but yes."

"You are such an asshole," I accused, shifting to roll back onto my side, hoping he would understand that I was just teasing. He stayed where he was, still warm against my back. It wasn't so bad having company.

"I really was just worried about you," he said quietly.

"I know," I said. "I was just messing with you; it's habit to think you're an asshole and pick a fight with you."

"You need new habits."

"Eh," I mumbled noncommittally.

"I wouldn't actually have sex with Sarah, either," he murmured after a bit.

"Because Julian will kill you?"

"No!" he protested, sounding legitimately insulted. "Because she's not just my brother's wife, she's my sister, now. She's family."

"That's surprisingly sweet of you."

"Well, it's true. You, on the other hand—"

"Are badly injured," I interrupted. "Because of you. You didn't get to see what a mess you made of my arm, but I did. I don't want your mouth anywhere on me ever again."

"I really am sorry about that."

I let his apology hang for a second, before replying.

"I know." We were quiet a little while longer and, as I felt myself start to drift off, I sighed, mumbled into the pillow. "You can stay, but no funny business."

"Yes, ma'am," he said, and I felt the bed shift. Curious, I rolled over just enough to see him. He'd adjusted to lie on his back, tucking one hand behind his head. I watched him for a second, noted that he'd grown his eyelashes out again, that his hair looked soft and shiny in the moonlight. I noticed the necklace resting against his bare chest, and thought about how, once he took that off, we'd probably be back to sniping at each other at every opportunity. I wasn't sure I could resist, considering how painful it was to be around him without magic involved. That would be a problem for Seattle-Gwen, though. Right now I was fake-married Gwen. Harstine Island Gwen. Sleepy and in pain as hell Gwen.

I rolled back over, fell asleep almost immediately.

Twenty

When I woke I wasn't alone, despite the fact that Mel had gone. Four puppies and two kids in purple sleep shirts were spread around the bed with me; two of the puppies were twitching and Walter was snoring quietly. I fought the urge to grab and hug each and every one of them, my insides feeling gooey at the sight of them.

My bladder, however, reminded me that being pinned to the bed by six five-year-olds was seriously going to hamper my ability to pee.

Using my good arm and some slow tugging and shifting that made me feel like a bed ninja, I managed to slide myself out from under the covers, get to my feet, and walk across my pillows, dropping as silently to the ground as I could. I ran for the bathroom, prayed the puppies wouldn't wake up and rush away by the time I got done.

I looked myself over in the mirror, winced at the bruises Mel had managed to leave along my body. I had welts on my chest and shoulder where he had slammed into me as a wolf and my lower back had scrapes running along my spine. I sighed, vowed to make him double my cupcake payment, and slipped back into my room. The pups hadn't stirred even a bit and I crept backward toward the door watching them snooze.

I found Julian and Sarah standing in the kitchen, him leaning over her shoulder as she grinned and worked on something I couldn't see past the bar. The closer I got, though, the more I realized how incredible it smelled.

As I lifted myself onto the chair, resting my arm as gingerly as I could on the counter, Sarah smiled. "You're up!"

"The kids are all in there."

Julian opened his mouth to speak, but only grunted in pain as Sarah jabbed her elbow hard against his gut. As rubbed his belly, Sarah slid a massive cupcake across the bar, smiled at me.

It had pink and purple frosting piped out to resemble a swollen, massive flower. I almost cried with joy, lifted it and curled my tongue against the sugar. After I'd licked the frosting off, Sarah reached forward, snatched it away.

"Hey!" I snapped.

"The kids found Mel in there early this morning, probably after being awakened last night by all your screaming and wailing," she explained with a teasing wink. Before I could pout, she pulled a giant pastry bag out of a bowl next to her, piped on another giant flower, all pink this time.

"Bless you," I said, as she handed back the cupcake. "Where is Mel, anyway?"

I mashed as much of the sugar into my mouth as I could manage. Julian watched me as most people do when they encounter my sugar addiction: with a mix of disgust and fascination.

"He left around two hours ago to deal with the center. He said to bring you out there, if you're up for it."

"What time is it?" I asked around the cupcake.

"It's only seven. I had planned to have all your cupcakes done by the time you woke, but you're up early."

"Other than Mel waking me up for sex, I slept like a rock."

"He did what?" Julian asked.

"I mean, he didn't really."

"Sure," he teased. I pointed at him with chocolate-covered fingers.

"Don't you start. I've seen what your wife can do and I'm betting I could get her to beat you up if I asked nice enough."

"It's true. She could," Sarah admitted. Julian chuckled, nodded.

"Yeah, all right. How's the arm?" Julian asked. Sarah licked some frosting off her finger and set down her piping tube.

"I should check it, actually," she said, going to wash her hands. I felt myself tense at the prospect, but realized it was probably a good idea. When she came around to my side and took my wrist, I glanced between her and her husband.

"It's a good thing this doesn't turn me into one of you. I'd be the worst wolf."

"You think?" Sarah asked as she unwrapped my arm.

"That whole hair thing looks complicated. I'd be like one of the kids, growing Mohawks everywhere but my head."

"When Mel was little, he always had furry hands."

"Oh my *god*," I said, jerking around to face Julian. Sarah squeezed my wrist before I could accidentally yank my arm out of her grip. "Please tell me you have pictures—video—elaborate, painted art depicting tiny Mel with furry palms. I will mount these above my fireplace—I will install a fireplace, just to mount these pictures there. Then I will invite him over for dinner every night, just so that I can point and laugh."

"Wow," Julian said, staring at me askance. "You've really got a hard-on for my brother."

"Just for making him as miserable as he's made me."

"It's not looking so bad, actually," Sarah said. I took one look at my arm and then jerked my gaze to the ceiling.

"I'm going to have to strongly disagree with you," I said. Sarah let my hand go and moved to the dining table. I kept my gaze high, trying not to think about my wounds. The air seemed to agitate them, though, and I found myself shaking slightly. Sarah came back with a giant tube of antibacterial gel and gauze for days. She managed to wrap my arm again and looked up to meet my face.

"You know anyone at home who can help you take care of this?"

"I might," I said, thinking of Chloe. One of her most frequently used skills recently, had been nursing a sick empath back to health.

"Good." As she finished wrapping me, she sighed, dropped her hands into her lap. "I'm sorry we couldn't get you to a hospital. They would have known right away this was a canine bite and it raises a lot of questions."

"Ah," I said, pulling my arm back against my chest. "Yeah, I didn't think about that."

"Thank you for understanding, though," Julian said. I nodded, glanced back at him as something else occurred to me.

"Where did you come from, last night?" I asked Sarah. She gave a small smile, shrugged a shoulder.

"You guys had been gone awhile so I figured I'd go check on you. Julian stayed with the kids because," she pointed to her button nose. "I've got the sniffer. It didn't actually take long to find you, but I would have been there sooner if I hadn't paused to mark our way back, just in case."

"And you're okay?"

"Yeah, we're a pretty tough species. I'm just glad you're safe. I don't know how Mel would have taken it if you died. He may have ended up here for another six weeks."

I rolled my eyes, caught her not-so-subtle insinuation. Julian snorted behind me but when I turned to glare his way, I found he'd decided to play the sugar card. I snatched the cupcake from his hand, gave him a cursory glare as I peeled the wrapper down the side, and took a giant bite.

We arrived at Tough Love half an hour later, after I'd gotten dressed and finished off two more cupcakes. Sarah had bypassed the deputy parked at the end of the line easily and his roaring emotions had explained why before she'd even mentioned it.

"That's my cousin."

"I figured you knew him," I grumbled, realizing a week with mated wolves and a magical necklace had somehow become enough time for my mind to damper how bad it was being around an unattached werewolf.

Sarah patted my leg, found a space at the edge of the lot, behind the many ambulances and sheriff's vehicles. We got out just as Mel had stepped out onto the porch. He waved loosely in greeting and then turned as Officer Amazon stepped out, tapping him on the shoulder.

I watched her intently as Sarah and I approached, wondering if she felt any differently about Mel since their chaste night together. She was less flirty than she'd been the last time I'd seen them together, but she wasn't unhappy or bitter.

"And, this is my fake wife," Mel said, resting his hand gently on my shoulder. "She discovered the tunnel in the first place."

"Ah, Ms Arthur, it's nice to meet you. I'm Tina," Officer Amazon stepped up, held out a hand. I considered her hand for a moment and then gestured to my bandage.

"Rain check?" I asked. She smiled.

"Right, no problem. Mel here's given us all the important information, but I have to say that, if you hadn't discovered that tunnel, we wouldn't have had grounds for a warrant, wouldn't have found everything we did."

"Are they okay?" I asked, remembering that, yes, we had been there to save actual people, not jut imaginary babies and a fake marriage.

"They're going to be, eventually. I'm actually headed to the hospital after this, to see if any of the women are well enough to give statements about what happened here."

"Well," I said lamely. "Good luck."

"Thanks. Mel? Good to see you again." She patted his hand and swept past us toward the group below. I turned back to Mel, raised my eyebrows.

"Recap, please?"

"The official explanation they're going with is that Coontz was drugging couples, imprisoning them in the caves, and breeding babies to sell on the black market."

"Oh, Black Market," I mused. "What can't you explain?" Sarah snorted; Mel continued as if I hadn't said anything.

"That door I couldn't get through did lead down into more tunnels and they found all the missing women—and some of their husbands, including the two couples I'd been hired to find in the first place. There was a surprisingly involved birthing set up."

"So what's the actual story?" Sarah asked.

"Last I heard, they still haven't gotten it out of Coontz."

"So it really was him? He's not just—"

Sarah cut me off with a growl, a fierce rumble that vibrated not just her body but her emotions. I hadn't felt that level of hatred ... well, maybe ever. I groaned as the rancid, steely pain of it thrummed my body and made my wounds ache more.

"What is it?" I breathed, shuffling to the side as if I could hide behind Sarah from whatever it was she was suddenly so angry at.

"Wendigo," she snarled, her teeth bared in threat as she advanced toward the front door. It was hard to tell because of the color of it, but the hair on her arms looked longer and thicker. Mel went stiff, darting between her and the entrance.

"You're sure? Where?"

"You can't smell it?" she asked, growling again when Coontz came into view, his hands cuffed behind his back. Her hands curled into claws and I swear the only thing that stopped her from charging the doctor and tearing him apart was Mel's hand and maybe the fact that we were surrounded by armed cops.

"Coontz?" Mel asked, turning to look the man over in confusion. "He smells bad but—"

"He smells *corrupt*," Sarah said, her nostrils flared. Coontz was escorted by us, glaring my way as if I'd personally been responsible for his arrest. I mean, I guess I kind of was, since the cops wouldn't have been sniffing around and shut down his whole operation if I hadn't found that tunnel. Sarah was positively vibrating as he passed and I wanted desperately to understand her ire.

"What's that mean?" I asked. Sarah watched him get loaded into the back of one of the cars, staying silent and focused until the car started heading down the drive.

"Mel," she said after a moment. "I can't believe you didn't know what Coontz is the second you met him. It's glaringly obvious."

"I—I mean, he just—"

"What's a wendigo?" I interrupted, letting Mel off the hook.

"Not all—" Sarah tugged my arm, pulling me around the side of the house so we were tucked into an area of the porch not crawling with cops and center staff. "Not all fae spawn get powers. Some are just ... *more* than human."

"But not as much more as, say, feeling the emotions of others?" I asked, hoping I was understanding her use of the word, "fae spawn." Sarah nodded, but it was a distracted action and I figured she wasn't focusing on what I'd said.

"They're susceptible to certain fae magic that humans aren't, but can't do anything special. Sometimes that sort of susceptibility will manifest in something like attraction to or devotion to a fae creature if they catch its eye. It doesn't stop with a crush, either, it becomes an obsession. It's uncontrollable and anything the creature asks it to do, even if it asks him to kill himself or someone else, he gleefully does it. Eventually the man—it's always a man—loses himself to the thing and it consumes him. Only, because he's not entirely human he doesn't die, he just … changes."

"I didn't know that," Mel said quietly, shaking his head. "I've only come across them in their … what would you call it, final form?"

"It's as good a phrase as any," Sarah said, before elaborating when she caught my confused look. "They deteriorate, they wither away. It's like the only thing that could sustain them is the creature they fall in love with but fae are fickle where humans are concerned and lose interest quickly. If I had to guess, Coontz is only still human because the unktomi's been using him to fetch it food. Otherwise it probably would have eaten him—"

"Eaten *him*? He's not a baby."

"They'll drink any blood, they just prefer babies," Mel said, giving me a look that said I'd have known that if I'd actually done the research like he had.

"Most likely the damn thing would have guzzled and ghosted the asshole a long time ago, or simply moved on and Coontz would have already gone full wendigo. I don't know how long it's been around—"

"Couples have been going missing for years, almost since the center opened."

"Has Coontz been here the whole time?" Sarah asked.

"Yeah he's the only founder who still works here," Mel said, his jaw tight, his face filled with anger.

"Then, I'd guess the thing was feeding off whatever it could get its pincers on until it found Coontz and got him to cooperate."

"You think Gordo fell in love with that creepy-ass spider you killed in the—actually, do we have to worry? With the cops tromping around, don't you think they'll find the thing?"

"Unlikely." Mel said. When he didn't elaborate, I turned to Sarah.

"They won't find it. And no, I don't think Coontz saw the bulbous, hairy body of that thing and decided it was his one true love. More than likely it fooled him into thinking he was that same hot doctor you thought it was—"

"Or some other hot doctor," Mel said thoughtfully.

"Hmm?"

"Well, if Taylor was the spider and she—it only started working here a few months ago, it can't have been pretending to be the same doctor forever. The Heaths, they were working with a Doctor Driscoll, who left right before Taylor started. Probably not the first time it changed identities."

"Why would it do that?" I asked, at a loss. What the hell did a spider care about what human face it pretended to have? I mean, sure, it could've had to look hot to keep Coontz on a leash, but past that, what was the point?

"To keep suspicions off the center, maybe," Mel suggested. "Coontz stayed because it was his investment, but everyone else who's worked there stayed awhile, moved on. Maybe he suggested it to make sure it didn't look like something was up. Coontz didn't treat any of the missing couples."

"I can't believe you didn't know right off what he was," Sarah said. "You could have saved that poor man's life if you'd just followed your nose."

I snorted before I could help myself, picturing Toucan Sam coming across a cartoon corpse and looking horrified. It wasn't funny, the idea that Mel could have missed a chance to save Bart Heath's life, but we still weren't entirely sure why he was killed so who knew if Sarah was even right.

"He smells human!" Mel argued. "Bad, but human!"

"He does smell pretty bad," I agreed, shaking my head. "Like … old cheese. And dirty socks. And … garbage, maybe."

"How can you smell him?" Sarah asked, surprised.

"What do you mean? He smells terrible."

"Yes, but not on a level that a person should—maybe it's your empathy!"

"You think my empathy could smell him?"

"Well, you experience emotions in a physical way, right? You're one of those?"

"As opposed to …?"

"I mean, you're the type that actually feels the emotions?"

"Yeah. Take Mel here, he's like feeling being stabbed while on fire while occasionally being punched in the stomach."

"Really?" Mel asked, but Sarah pressed on.

"Yeah, that's what I mean. What if you were sensing his changing emotions as a scent?"

"It's possible. I've never smelled emotions before, but I've never met a wendigo before, either." I considered the possibility and shook my head. "That's wild. I wonder what else exists with smelly emotions."

"You said that, without the unktomi, Coontz will deteriorate?" Mel said, his entire demeanor changing. "We have to get him out of that jail. He—"

"It'll be taken care of. Several of the local cops are family. *They'll* know instantly what he is and what to do."

"What is there to do?" I asked, fearing the worst. Not that Coontz deserved a trial and I was sure we didn't want to go finding a jury of wendigos to decide whether or not he should go to jail, but it was coming up way too often that the only way to solve a problem was to kill it.

"He's already started to turn, so he can't he saved. It would be cruel to make him fall apart and die on his own," Sarah said. Mel sighed.

"She's right. Wendigos are like zombies, they crave life and usually try to get it the same way zombies would. If he's allowed to live others will die."

I sighed but didn't argue. I didn't have to be there for the actual death, however it would go down. I could probably use my great powers of delusion to just pretend this all hadn't happened and everything was fine. I didn't have to think about what Sarah had told me about how Mel had said the women were being held or how many shallow graves they'd already sniffed out. I could just pretend Mel and I had spent a nice week getting to know each other as people. I wouldn't have any nightmares about those tunnels or that spider once my supply of cockroach pills ran out.

Sure.

Twenty-One

The drive back so Seattle was relatively painless. Sarah had me take a few pills home with me, made me promise to not take more than half of one at a time. Mel and I had slipped back into a rhythm of talking about nothing, making fun of each other here and there, and generally acting as if nothing had changed on the trip. When we got out of the car at my place and moved around to the back to pull out my bag, I leaned a hip against the taillight, looked up at him.

"How'd you know it was me?" I asked, finally. I'd been wondering since we'd left, but I was afraid I knew the answer.

"You—ah." Mel paused, my duffle in hand, and closed the trunk, his lip quirking. After a second, he turned to face me, smiling. "You tasted familiar."

"You've never bitten me before," I said, reaching out with my good arm to grab the bag. Mel's smile crumbled as he noticed my bandages and he slammed the trunk, taking a step back as if afraid he might do more damage to me just by being close.

"Not your blood, your skin. The trickster got everything else right—the way you looked as an arachnid, the hairy spider legs, the gross smell—but the taste was familiar. I don't know why that was its weak point. Maybe it was just working too hard and missed a step."

"Maybe," I agreed, though we'd never actually know.

"It confused the hell out of me and I jumped back. Then, as I was noticing that the you I'd attacked was just lying there, while the other you was being so aggressive, I realized what had happened."

"Well," I said, feeling my cheeks go pink. I had figured it had to be

187

something related to the fact that he'd had his mouth all over me just hours before. "I guess it's a good thing we'd … you know."

Mel stared at me for a second, before his smile slowly took over his face again. I sighed, rolled my eyes.

"Go on," I sighed, knowing what was coming.

"Do you know what this means?"

"I know what you think it means, but—"

"It means that, if we hadn't had sex, you'd be dead. Having sex with me saved your life." Mel shifted his stance, crossed his arms over his chest, his eyes glittering. We were home and he was definitely still the same Mel he'd been before the trip. "My dick saved your *life*."

"Goodbye, Mel," I said, turning to head back to my front door. Behind me, Mel let out a giddy laugh. I glanced back enough to frown at the sound and he caught my look. His body shifted immediately as he lowered his arms, shot me from the hip with twin finger-guns, and then brought them to his lips to blow away imaginary smoke.

"It'll never happen again!" I yelled over my shoulder as I pressed the key into the lock.

He laughed and I heard his car door shut. I was chuckling too as I stepped into my living room but the second the door shut I stopped, confused at the sight before me.

The skinny, dark-haired girl from The Internets was rushing in from the kitchen, had been moving even as I entered. She looked a little better than she had when Mel had been proposing, cleaned up and wearing nicer clothes. Her delicate features were filled with glee as she wrapped herself around me, hugging like we were old friends. I froze, bag in hand, wondering why she smelled like Twinkies and Chloe.

"Chloe," I called warily, scanning what I could see of my house, hoping this poor homeless youth—I mean, she looked about twenty—hadn't broken into my house to steal my snacks. I had enough of that from the candy thief, I didn't need another wayward creature prowling my home and pilfering my sugar.

The hug ended and the girl pulled back, shaking her head to flip her hair out of her face. I realized her features were a little stronger than I'd been able to make out before, her form a little more muscular than I would have assumed. She was more androgynous than feminine, actually, and I wondered if she'd always been that way or if whatever type of fae she was had a tendency to change genders.

Mel was a were*wolf*, maybe there were were-*girls* out there. I was busy wondering if this creature started menstruating under the light of the full moon when her—its? His? I couldn't tell—gaze plummeted to the bag in my hand and she gasped.

"You forgot the cupcakes!" she accused, her voice deeper than I would have guessed. I looked down, realizing she was right. Briefly, the stranger in my living room was forgotten, no longer an issue in the face of missing sweets.

"Goddammit!" I swore, dropping my bag. I yanked open my front door, looked out desperately, but I'd known even before doing so that Mel had long before driven off with my treats in the back seat. Turning back to my living room, I found Chloe standing just outside the kitchen, smiling.

"Hey! How was the trip? And what's up with the back of your head?"

"She forgot the cupcakes," the girl whined. I turned to her, looked her up and down and frowned. Her oozy emotions were focused on disappointment, but there was a spike of nervousness there, too. Somewhere at the back of her psyche was a vibrating globule of arousal. When she turned back to face me, I frowned.

"Who are you and why are you concerned about *my* cupcakes?"

"Because they're delicious!"

"Gwen," Chloe said with a chuckle, closing in on us both. "This is Izzy, my new boyfriend." As Chloe said the B-word, Izzy started wheezing, making the erratic sounds I'd heard over the phone. Glee rocketed forward through the wobbly gelatin of his psyche and I felt a shiver run through me at the strangely delightful experience.

I took a second to look Izzy over again, to reorganize my brain so that "girl-thing from The Internets" could settle into the same compartment as "Chloe's boyfriend," and then shook my head, sure I wouldn't be able to change the associations that quickly. Chloe hadn't had a steady relationship in the entire time I'd known her. She wasn't as bad as Mel, didn't sleep with everyone who nodded hello on the street, but she liked to have fun and it wasn't unusual for her to have dates most nights of the week. Chloe, who reads body language as well as I read emotions, and who knows me better than I know myself, wrinkled her nose in worry, sensing my confusion.

"Izzy's not human," she said, as if it was personally her fault.

"Yeah," I said, and Izzy grinned, before walking over to Chloe and wrapping himself around her like it was the end of a long, hard day and hugging Chloe was the only think that could bring him comfort. Trembling glee oozed into contented pleasure and I grinned, unable to help myself.

Chloe cooed into his ear, kissed his cheek, and then smiled my way, a little tense, like she was a fourteen-year-old girl presenting her very first boyfriend to a stern father. I wondered why Chloe was so nervous about my reaction and decided I should probably stop making it all worse by glowering and huddling against the door like I thought Izzy might attack.

"I'm … it's nice to meet you, Izzy," I said, forcing a grin. I should be nice, I thought. There was no reason not to be nice.

"Sometimes, yeah," Izzy said, his tone thoughtful. "There was that one time where you fell in that quicksand, though."

"What?" I asked. He didn't answer, his gaze focused on some middle distance, his expression inscrutable.

"Not human, remember?" Chloe said, by way of explanation.

"I don't understand what's happening," I said.

"Now that's an every-time thing," Izzy said, in a tone I usually only hear from people who knew me well.

"Hey," I snapped, deciding in an instant that I didn't care who Izzy was dating; he was no longer welcome in my house. I was supposed to be in pajamas, splayed on my couch eating a hundred cupcakes and two sheetcakes, not standing in my living room trying to detach my empathy from the sticky blobs of affection and titillation floundering around some strange creature who wasn't making any sense.

"Come on," Chloe said, detaching herself from Izzy and closing in on me. "Let's get you settled in. I've no doubt you need to do laundry, and probably did before you even left."

"What's happening, here?" I demanded as she took my bag and started heading toward the laundry room. "That's the girl from the—I mean, the boy from The Internets, the one Mel hit on."

"So it is," she said as she rounded the corner into my hallway. I sighed, exasperated, torn between following her and sticking around to make sure Izzy didn't do anything I didn't want him to. I wasn't even sure what he might get up to, but he was a stranger in my home and my recent experience with strangers in my home had led to missing Twinkies, enigmatic sticky notes, and the occasional smiley face drawn in lipstick on my bathroom mirror.

Deciding Izzy couldn't be any worse than all that, I headed down the hall and found Chloe in my narrow laundry room, filling the washer with water and soap.

"Is he gonna eat my Twinkies? He smelled like Twinkies. You should go back and tell him not to eat my Twinkies."

"What's up with the arm? And why are you balding?" she asked, ignoring my tirade. I reached up with my good arm to touch the back of my head.

"Is it that noticeable?"

"Well, it's bandaged and you've been favoring it since you came in."

"Not my arm, my hair."

"Eh, you can wear a hat. What's up with your arm? Did you get into it with one of the puppies over a half a Skittle?"

"Mel bit me," I said, deciding to ignore her mocking.

"Like, sexy bit you?"

"No," I groaned, making it clear in my tone that what he'd done to me could not have been considered sexy in any sense of the word. Leaning against the wall, I folded my arm against my belly, suddenly very aware of the pain being dampened by the half a pill I'd taken on the drive back. "He attacked me. His sister had to sew me up and I couldn't even go to the hospital because of the questions it would raise. My arm looks like a map of all the railroads in the country if they'd gotten drunk and tried to make out."

"Railroads can't get drunk," Chloe said, sorting my clothes by color with the speed of some magical laundry machine that probably didn't exist but that certainly should be invented and delivered straight to my door.

"Well, then they wasted a lot of vodka."

Chloe snorted, tossed a few dark shirts into the water. I watched her work before clearing my throat and considering my words carefully. I didn't want to tell her what I'd been doing with Mel before he'd unknowingly tried to kill me, but I knew it would come out eventually. It would be like when I'd done something wrong as a kid: just tell mom what you did and take your metaphorical lumps.

"Speaking of not at all sexy, I had sex with Mel," I said, feeling my shoulders creep toward my ears as if the blowback from my revelation would be painful. Chloe turned to me, her face lighting up.

"Oh, do tell!" she said, abandoning the laundry in an instant and focusing all her attention on me.

"It was pretty bad."

"Like …" Confusion burbled out of her. Her jaw flexed twice before she got any more words out. "Good bad? Like, 'baby you look phat in those jeans' good?"

"No one says that, anymore."

"Explain."

"Well, it's an older slang—"

"Gwen!" she snapped over a laugh. I snorted, indulged myself in a giggle.

"I mean it was *bad*. It was unsatisfying and kind of awkward and I have no intention of doing it ever again."

"Well, you had no intention of doing it the first time."

"Yeah, but." I paused, realized I didn't really have an explanation. "I don't know. He wasn't … unbearable this week."

"High praise."

"*Plus*, he owed me cupcakes; you know what I'll do when cake is involved—especially chocolate cakes with pink frosting flowers the size of my whole face."

"You are quite a whore when it comes to cake."

I pouted, thinking about my sweet, delicious payment bouncing around in the back seat of Mel's car. "He'd better not give those cakes to anyone else. I'll kill him."

"So, it was bad? Like … bad? Bad like stale cake bad?" Chloe asked, ignoring my threat on Mel's life and going back to my laundry.

"No, like broccoli bad. Legitimately bad. Stale cake I can dunk in chocolate sauce or smother in caramel. Or eat with ice cream. You can always do all three if the cake's more—"

"I am having a really hard time believing that," Chloe interrupted, knocking me off my sugar overload tangent. "I've been there and it was great."

"It was just ... Ugh, I don't even want to talk about it. He got off, I didn't, and then he got all bouncy and kissy and made dinner and," I quickly rambled out the rest, eager to be off the subject of Mel and I having sex, "then we went and fought a spider fairy, and I got torn up, and I woke up with some puppies."

"Holy shit, you what?"

"Woke up with some puppies?" When Chloe didn't engage my joke that time, I shrugged. "It was a trickster fae. Um ... Ink ... uncle ... shit."

"Unktomi?"

"That's the one. How do you know?"

Chloe just shrugged like it was no big deal, but that little worm of panic I'd been seeing in her the last nine months scrambled through her psyche like a giant, hungry bird was swooping straight for it. I pushed on, not liking that I'd made her worry.

"It made Mel think I was the bad guy, but when he attacked me he figured out what was really going on. I'm just lucky things weren't worse. Sarah showed up, the two werewolves kicked its ass, everyone was rescued, and ta-da! The end."

"That's what was up? The unktomi was killing couples and the center was covering for it?"

"Oh, no, sorry. It had—well, it was working with this guy there, a wendigo."

"A *wendigo?*" Chloe demanded, horror rushing through her.

"Yeah, you've heard of them?"

Horror got doused by fizzy anxiety and Chloe shook her head rapidly for a moment before answering.

"That undead thing that eats people in that episode of *Supernatural?*"

"Uh," I said, knowing what she was referencing but still feeling a little lost. "Maybe. I don't think this is quite the same thing, since I don't think it ate people whole—though, it did live in caves in the woods."

"That's awful, even if a real wendigo is only sort of like the TV one. So, did you see it? Was it gross and bloody?"

"It was the doctor helping Mel and me, Coontz."

"Now I'm really lost. Was Coontz eating people or not?"

"Not. Wait. Maybe? I don't know. They—Coontz and the spider—were drugging women of birthing age, knocking them up, and then holding them hostage so the spider could eat the babies.”

“Oh my *god*,” Chloe said, horror splashing across my chest like she’d thrown a bucket of ice water my way. “Please tell me you found a giant flip-flop and smashed the shit out of that thing.”

“Mel just sorta ate its eyeballs off and Sarah tore open its belly. It was one of the grossest things I’ve ever seen.”

“I bet,” Chloe said, anger still burbling. We stayed silent for a bit, before Chloe flicked her gaze to my face, hesitation pursing her lips. “Did it … did it actually eat all of the babies?”

“Mel said it had been going on awhile, and from the size of it I can assume it was well-fed, but I didn’t ask to see the paperwork on how many. I don’t want to find out. Knowing it existed was bad enough. Remember I told you I got super sick when Mel and I were making out? That was just because the thing was nearby.”

“The wendigo, or the spider?”

“The spider. Coontz just smelled bad.”

“That doesn’t sound like what we saw on TV.”

“You have to get the whole story from Sarah, she was the one who figured out what was going on. I’d given up thinking it was him and wouldn’t have even known he was anything other than human if the unktomi hadn’t been involved. That thing, though, was the real problem. Any time it got near me, I’d get dizzy and nauseated.”

“You sure it wasn’t morning sickness?” Chloe asked, her lip quirked.

“Bite your tongue,” I snapped, knowing what she was inferring. “Owen and I use condoms, and Mel claims he’s sterile. Which is a big boon for the world, quite frankly.”

Chloe rolled her eyes. “I believe the thing about the spider and everything you were texting me about the werewolves—those puppies sound amazing, by the way, I need to meet them—but I’m still having trouble with the part about Mel being bad in bed.” Chloe shut the lid on my washer, waved me out of the narrow room, and then steered me back toward the kitchen once we were in the hall.

“You don’t have to believe it for it to be true. I’m still feeling kind of sick over the whole thing.”

“But—”

“Hey, you and I probably just like different things in bed, okay? You like sex with women and dressing up like Little Bo Peep. I like sex that doesn’t involve Mel.”

“I only donned that costume once, thank you very much.”

“*That* costume, sure.”

OLIVIA R .BURTON

Twenty-Two

Chloe danced into the kitchen ahead of me, going straight to the cup cabinet, pulling down a glass. As she stuck it under the tap, I realized Izzy had settled his skinny butt on the floor in front of my fridge and that every one of my magnetic poetry pieces had migrated from the freezer door and top half of the fridge door down to the floor and the bottom edge.

"What is he doing?" I demanded, outraged. "What are you doing? Don't do that! What are you doing?" Disinterested in my tantrum, Izzy glanced lazily over at me as he picked up a word from the miniature stack next to the sole of his foot and placed it deliberately. "You ruined it!"

Annoyance waded forward to take over his psyche. It was a little disorienting and sort of tasted like Jell-O made out of foil. "I *made* it."

"You *ruined it!*" I repeated, wanting to rush over and slap his hands away from my fridge, though I wasn't sure where my anger came from. The first time I'd found the fridge as it had been before Izzy got his grubby paws on it, I'd been horrified, worried, and a little insulted at the tone taken by the caterpillar-sized magnets. It had been almost a year, though, and I'd sort of started relying on seeing them every morning. I'd never gotten the hang of understanding what they were trying to tell me until after the fact, but they'd still been a constant surprise and an occasional delight.

I thought back to when I'd read the phrase, "werewolf puppies!" spelled out on my fridge door and how confused I'd been. Now, of course, I realized the creature that had left them there had known that I'd meet Mel's family at some point, just like it had known so many other things that would happen in my life. That was how it always went: a phrase made no sense until what it was referring to happened and then I'd read it again while getting juice or ice cream and have an, "Ah ha," moment.

My brain screeched to a halt as Izzy's words echoed faintly through my thoughts.

"You made *what?*" I asked warily, feeling my brain stick on the idea like a fat kid trying to climb a wall in gym class. I'd been that kid and I knew firsthand my brain wasn't making it over without a lot of help.

"The timeline," Izzy said with a sigh, placing another magnet. "It wasn't this one, exactly, but it was still helpful. The stuff still all happened, even if the order was wrong. You'll understand next year. Maybe. If you don't take that early flight home."

"Early … next … what?"

"That's pretty cool," Chloe said, stepping up next to me to rub my shoulder and press a glass of cold water into my hand. I drank it without thinking, still suffering from a sputtering brain and alarmed shock.

I was staring at a very convincing skyline of Seattle formed out of magnetic poetry along the bottom of my fridge. Whatever help the words had been before, they were nonsense now, lost to Izzy's bitterness and boredom.

"You're the—you did this? You put those … and ate my … it was you?" I asked as I finished drinking. Water dribbled down my front and Chloe dabbed at my chin with a towel, setting my mostly empty glass on the counter as if she didn't trust me to hold it anymore.

"I am the, yes, yes, yes, and yes," Izzy answered, as if my questions had been whole and made perfect sense.

"You're the one who's been stealing my Twinkies?" I accused, outrage blooming.

"That's rude," Izzy insisted, sticking magnets to the fridge to express exactly that same thing in crooked sentence form. "I was helping remember? You wouldn't have realized Norma was dangerous if not for this."

"I don't understand what's happening," I said, shaking my head. I did, sort of, but I didn't want to believe it. Nearly a year of waking up disappointed I couldn't eat some thing I'd bought—like last weekend's frozen French toast delight that I'd wanted to stick in the microwave and dip in corn-syrup-laden, maple-impersonating junk food—and now this. Nine months of spending money on crap I wanted but statistically wouldn't enjoy, and now *this*. A human gestational period worth of confusion and sticky notes and *now this*? "You owe me!"

"I paid up!" Izzy argued, popping to his feet and rounding on me as if we'd start taking swings at each other. Instead of putting up his dukes, he tucked a hand into his back pocket, pulled out half a bag of Sour Patch Kids and dumped a bunch into his mouth, chewing angrily.

"Those are mine!" I shouted. Izzy tucked them against his chest, turning away like a spoiled child being asked to share for the first time. Before I could grab the bag and run into my room and eat them hiding in the corner of the closet, Chloe took me by the shoulders, steering me out to the living room. I fought her a bit, but she'd done this sort of thing before and knew how to keep me focused forward. She settled me onto my couch, sat with her back to the front window so I'd have to look away from the kitchen or rudely not face her at all. I sighed, gingerly crossing my arms over my chest.

"Do you know how much money I've spent feeding him over the last year?"

"The same amount you'd have spent on junk food anyway," Chloe pointed out.

"But—"

"It's okay, Gwen," Chloe said, patting my knee. "Look, I ran into Izzy at the Internets and we got to talking."

"About how he's stalking your best friend?"

"Not stalking!" Izzy insisted from the kitchen, before one of my cabinets slammed and I heard the telltale crinkling of a Twinkie wrapper. Chloe grabbed for me, shoving me back into my seat before I could get to my feet and rush in to tackle him to the ground. Fairy creature or not, I was willing to try to take him. He has half my width and I had rage on my side. Plus, even though he was her boyfriend, Chloe had known me first and would probably have my back if things got too heated.

"I wouldn't do that," Chloe said, a little thread of panic wrapping around my throat and tugging. I coughed at the strange feeling, worry eking its way in through my wall of blind offense and making me take a second look at her. She had my back, all right, but just not in the way I'd expected.

"Why?" I asked warily.

"He's not human, remember?"

"So? Mel's not human and you've never stopped me from wailing on him."

"Mel's—it's not the same. Mel can't really be hurt, not by you. Izzy and Mel aren't the same. Mel sleeps his way through Tinder and howls at the moon. Izzy sees the future. Not always linearly, not always *helpfully*, but there's a chance he'd know what you were about to do and instead of shoving him to the floor, you'd swing, miss, and fall on your face and break your nose or something. Just trust me. Let me explain."

"Yes, please explain why you're cavorting with this creature that's eating my food right now," my voice got louder as my annoyance over my impotence grew, "behind me as if I can't hear him going through an entire box—"

"We got to talking," Chloe said, the hard edge of her frustration jabbing me in the chest and cutting me off with a grunt. "And, I don't know, we like each other, we enjoy the same things, and he's fun. Izzy …" She trailed off, her lips tugging up as if she couldn't help but smile. I felt soft and fluffy feelings puff up inside her, a mix of infatuation, lust, giddiness, and all the good stuff that goes into that glittery, wrapped package people call puppy love.

Despite my previous feelings, I could tell I was getting sucked in, enjoying the cotton candy feel of crushing on someone. Chloe let out a tiny, overwhelmed sound that was almost a giggle, shook herself out of it, and then sat up straighter, clearly trying to get back on track.

"Look, he's a good guy. He's a little strange, and I'm sorry about—well, not sorry he saved you from eating thousands of calories worth of tooth-rotting crap, but sorry you're sad that you didn't get to enjoy the treats you bought yourself. He's not here to *hurt* us and he's not gonna show up randomly and steal your food while you're asleep anymore, either. I got him to promise to steer clear of your candy drawer at work, okay? Just be nice, *okay?*"

"Steer clear completely? Not even dip a finger in there and steal an M&M?"

"Yes, he'll keep all ten fingers out of the drawer and off your M&Ms."

"And off my Skittles! And licorice. And chocolate bars. And—"

"Yes, he gets it, Gwen. And, god, I'm going to have to clean out your office soon. You've got more stashed around that place than I realized."

"No," I argued, suddenly worried I'd given away too many of my secrets. Chloe shook her head and I could tell by her expression I was gonna have to beat her to work Monday and eat the incriminating evidence. A subject change was needed before I accidentally revealed I'd lost a few packets of gummy bears in the records room, too. "So … that's it then? He's just here? For good?"

"I don't know about 'for good,' it's not like we're getting married or something. But yes, he'll be around more. Well, maybe not more. Apparently he's been around a lot, we just haven't seen him."

"I don't even want to know what that means."

"You're out of Twinkies!" Izzy announced as if personally offended, stepping up next to the coffee table and shaking the empty carton like it needed to be punished. "You telling her about the office cat? She looks mad."

"Office *cat?*" I demanded. Chloe winced, whining out a low groan.

"I was gonna ease her into that one."

"I can't … I can't," I said, settling on the very general statement of just not being able to. I couldn't handle the idea of Izzy, or Chloe in a relationship, or the fact that I'd slept with Mel, or the idea that I was out of Twinkies, or anything else that had happened that week. I just wanted to curl up under the covers and sleep for a week. "I can't."

Late that evening, as I was settling in with Sonny for some trashy television, a box of cheesy crackers, and way more soda than any one person should have in a sitting, I heard a knock at the door. I sighed, glaring heartily from my place on the couch and trying to reach out to see who or what had come to bother me. My empathy found nothing there, but Nothing knocked again. I wanted to ignore it, to leave whatever nutty night-solicitor was there to bother me be, but usually there isn't a knock at my door from something without any emotions, so I figured I should probably check before it got angry and hulked through the wall or wiggled its nose and turned me into a newt.

Only non-humans have no emotions and I was spending a lot of time, lately, getting schooled in the fact that it was a bad idea to anger them.

"One sec," I yelled toward Nothing, considering that maybe I should invest in a baseball bat or something to keep handy just for safe-keeping. "Come on Sonny, back in your cage for a bit." Sonny didn't complain as I tucked him in, for which I was glad. I didn't know if the bars of his cage would keep him safe if whatever was the door wanted to hurt us rather than sell us on some preternatural form of the Watchtower, but hopefully it'd be the latter.

Mel stood outside, three of Sarah's pastry containers in his arms. Despite the fact that he was holding chocolate, my mood took a deep dive south. Sure, he was bringing the cupcakes back, but he'd taken them in the first place, thoughtlessly leaving them in the backseat and driving off as if I wasn't owed payment for the emotional turmoil of learning I'd spent a week with some cannibal creature that might have been planning to feed me to its spider girlfriend.

The expression on his face matched the one on mine and we squared off for a bit before I realized that my taste buds had not gotten the frustrated-with-Mel memo. My mouth was already watering at the idea of fluffy chocolate orgasms touching my tongue. Mel spoke before I could demand he hand them over.

"Did you tell Chloe I'm bad in bed?" he asked, pushing past me.

"Um?" I responded, still staring outside at empty air. When had they talked? Why had she told him? *Were the cupcakes in peril?* I shut the door, whirling around and rushing into the kitchen after him. This could be a delicate situation, I told myself. Say the wrong thing and the chocolate could pay for it.

"I ... don't really remember what I said." I tried for a grin, easing forward and reaching out toward the cakes. Mel glared me down, leaned slightly away to keep me outside taking distance.

"Well, what *do* you remember?"

"I ... remember you saved my life! And how I'm super grateful!

Grateful enough to take those heavy treats off your hands. Buddy? Pal? Here, let me just—"

Mel let out a sigh, shaking his head at my one-track mind, and moved to the far end of the kitchen, sliding the stack of containers on the counter and pushing them up against the wall as if worried they might jump to the floor if left too close to the edge.

I watched him go, noticed that he'd grown out the hair on his arms again. Most of the trip with his family he'd been pretty hairless, maybe not wanting to go through the effort of growing body hair—other than to ruin his chances with Officer Tina, of course—if he was just going to lose it again when he changed. I tried to remember if Julian had done the same while I was there, and realized I hadn't really noticed him, except for the one time I'd spent way too much time noticing him and had then felt guilty about it.

"What's with the Grizzly Adams arm hair?" I asked, intent on getting my mind off the mental image of Mel's married brother's happy trail.

Mel glanced down, turning hid arms over as if he hadn't seen them before. When he looked back up at me, his gaze stuck to my arm, lingering on my bandages again before he met my eyes. A beat passed, before he gave me a sleazy grin, his face just a little too tense for it to be entirely legitimate.

"Had a date. A few of 'em actually. Nothing like being back in the game after a long hiatus."

I wrinkled my nose, hoping he didn't try to elaborate. Instead, he kept our eye content intently, lifting both arms to flex unsubtly in front of his chest like a pro-wrestler trying to intimidate his opponent by ripping open his shirt with just the force of his pecs. Unable to take him seriously, I laughed, snorting at how ridiculous he looked. Mel chuckled, dropping his arms to his side and relaxing. We watched each other for a moment and it actually kind of felt like a legitimate friendship. I'd worried maybe it would have been like Vegas and what happened on Harstine would stay on Harstine, but he and I were still joking, still teasing, and still friends. Sex with Mel had been a dismal affair, but at least it had its perks.

"Did you seriously just show up to bitch about the fact that I didn't enjoy having sex with you?" I asked after a moment. He rolled his eyes.

"I came to set the record straight. I am not bad at sex."

"You were with me."

"Lies. Lies and treachery. You want me to call Karen, Candace, and Rina? They have the experience fresh in their minds. *Fresh*," Mel said, and I got the feeling that he meant it so literally that I probably didn't want to get too close. "They'll explain you're just confused."

I took a deliberate step back, holding my hands up like I was warding him off. "I'm not confused. You seemed to enjoy yourself, so good for you.

But I was underwhelmed."

"No one is underwhelmed when they're under Mel. Did you consider that maybe it's your fault?"

"Nope."

Mel's eyes went to slits and he stepped forward, pressing into my personal space. It only occurred to me as he stepped close—and didn't smell of some other woman's perfume or musk, thank god—that he had to have been wearing Merrin's necklace. I'd gotten so used to *not* feeling him that I hadn't even noticed when he'd shown up and it hadn't been pure torture.

"At least give me a chance to prove how wrong you are."

I shook my head, pressing my hand firmly against his chest, barely noticing that he took my mild push as an order and stepped back.

"I'm not having sex with you," I said. Mel looked me over disapprovingly, shaking his head.

"Well, no, I didn't mean now. You look terrible. And from the smell of it, you haven't showered since last night. You still smell like every one of the puppies."

Ignoring his assessment of my scent, I looked down at my stained pants and comfortable shirt that had seen its share of disastrous hair dye experiments. I wasn't wearing makeup and my hair was obviously still thin in the back. I hadn't brushed it after my nap in the car, so it was probably either flat or excessively frizzy. I ran a tongue along my gums, found a chunk of cracker tucked between two of my teeth.

"I look fine," I insisted, though my tone couldn't quite match the confidence of my words. Mel clucked his tongue, shook his head.

"And you thought I was the one who couldn't tell reality from fantasy." Abruptly, he stepped around me, brushing his bare arm against mine. I turned, watched him hit the door at a stride. As he grabbed the handle and pulled it open, he turned to face me.

"I'm telling you, though. One day, you'll come to me, begging me give you another shot."

"Won't happen."

"No, no, hear me out. I know these things. I'm an expert on women."

I barked out a laugh.

"One day, you'll be hard up, and I'll be there—also hard up." He shot me a single finger-gun and then reached up to his neck. "In the meantime, take this back."

I yelped as the necklace slid over his head, as the magic holding his emotions in check fell away. Terror filled my chest as I expected to feel a week's worth of feelings bowl me over. Lust, annoyance, hunger and amusement rushed through me, swirled around my organs, scalded my skin, but didn't fry my brain or outright kill me.

It took me a moment to really come to grips with, but I didn't faint or drop into a coma. Cracking open an eye that I hadn't realized I closed, I caught his eye, gleeful even in the face of his thorny emotions groping at me from the door.

"I didn't pass out!" I announced, excited. Mel draped the necklace over the back of my chair, smarmy grin plastered across his sculpted face.

"Yeah, I only put it on as I pulled up to the curb. I was just messing with you." On a wink, he yanked the door shut, leaving me to curse his name.

About the Author

Olivia is a vegan thirty-something living in New Mexico with a clowder of cats and a stink of litter boxes. She enjoys vexing her kitties, cooking, watching action movies, and making up collective nouns for things that don't already have them (like a "stink of litter boxes"). You can find her and all information about her different series at OliviaRBurton.com.

Gwen Arthur Novels

Visit OliviaRBurton.com for more information

www.ingramcontent.com/pod-product-compliance
Lightning Source LLC
Chambersburg PA
CBHW072057170626
46813CB00004B/1389

* 9 7 8 0 9 9 7 6 3 3 3 5 1 *